STOLEN PIECES

Also by S.K. Golden

The Pinnacle Hotel mysteries

THE SOCIALITE'S GUIDE TO MURDER
THE SOCIALITE'S GUIDE TO DEATH AND DATING

STOLEN PIECES

S.K. Golden

SEVERN
HOUSE

Content Warning
While Stolen Pieces is a light-hearted story overall, there is a mention of miscarriage/stillbirth, as well as depictions of violence throughout.

First world edition published in Great Britain and the USA in 2024
by Severn House, an imprint of Canongate Books Ltd,
14 High Street, Edinburgh EH1 1TE.

severnhouse.com

British Library Cataloguing-in-Publication Data
A CIP catalogue record for this title is available from the British Library.

ISBN-13: 978-1-4483-1314-3 (cased)
ISBN-13: 978-1-4483-1315-0 (e-book)

All Severn House titles are printed on acid-free paper.

Typeset by Palimpsest Book Production Ltd.,
Falkirk, Stirlingshire, Scotland.
Printed and bound in Great Britain by
TJ Books, Padstow, Cornwall.

Praise for the Pinnacle Hotel series

"A sprightly series launch!"
Publishers Weekly on *The Socialite's Guide to Murder*

"The heroine's serenely coy sensibility vividly evokes the 1950s"
Kirkus Reviews on *The Socialite's Guide to Death and Dating*

"With her creation of an intriguing upstairs/downstairs world, Golden channels the spirit of the late Hugh Pentecost's Beaumont Hotel. Readers will be eager to check into Evelyn's next adventure"
Publishers Weekly on *The Socialite's Guide to Murder*

"A catty yet decorous whodunit festooned with period trappings"
Kirkus Reviews on *The Socialite's Guide to Murder*

"This first novel – and likely the first in a series – effectively evokes the social milieu of the late 1950s, hiding Evelyn's intellect behind a fluffy indulged façade"
Booklist on *The Socialite's Guide to Murder*

"*The Socialite's Guide to Murder* is nonstop entertainment – at turns witty, charming, touching, and spellbinding"
Kelly Oliver, award-winning author of the Fiona Figg Mysteries, on *The Socialite's Guide to Murder*

"This book has all the things I love in a mystery novel – a unique sleuth, a quirky cast of suspects, and a twisty whodunnit"
C. J. Archer, *USA Today* bestselling author of the Cleopatra Fox Mysteries, on *The Socialite's Guide to Murder*

About the author

S.K. Golden is the author of the Pinnacle Hotel cozy mystery series. Born and raised in the Florida Keys, she married a commercial fisherman. The two of them still live on the islands with their five kids (one boy, four girls – including identical twins!), two cats, and a corgi named Goku. Sarah graduated from Saint Leo University with a bachelor's degree in Human Services and Administration and has put it to good use approximately zero times. She's worked as a bank teller, a pharmacy technician, and an executive assistant at her father's church. Sarah is delighted to be doing none of those things now.

www.skgoldenwrites.com

For Paul
Again

Acknowledgments

This was the first book I ever wrote. Bee popped into my imagination when I was on bedrest while pregnant with my twins. I would've been so incredibly bored without her for those seven long weeks. Massive thanks to my agent, Madelyn Burt, for never giving up on this story. Victoria Britton and the entire team at Severn House for bringing Stolen Pieces to life. Ayesha, Leira, Barbara, Jamie, and Samantha for being with me through the early drafts. Jordan, for being my ideal reader every time. My parents, Steve and Alice, for their unwavering belief. My children, Samuel, Avery, Eloise, Madeline, and Margaret for being the best part of my life. My husband, Paul, for his unending support.

ONE

Bee was retired. Comfortably retired, more or less, and had been for quite some time. But there were days like today that made her question whether hanging up the wigs and fake IDs had been a smart decision.

She couldn't go back.

Well, she could. Quite easily. She still had most of the wigs in a hidden panel in her master closet. Like Batman, except dumber.

But she wouldn't. She wouldn't come out of retirement. She was going to do things the right way, the legal way, even if that made it the hard way.

After all, her son was watching. And since she could no longer control his father, it was up to her to set an example for Oliver.

'This has to be the ugliest outfit ever created,' Liliana said. She stood behind Bee, and in the full-length mirror, her brown-haired reflection bobbed around Bee's shoulder. Liliana, Havana born and Miami raised, never left her house without a knife somewhere on her person and bright red lipstick on her full lips. 'And I'm including that monstrosity Anastasia wore to the PTA meeting last week.'

Anastasia huffed from Bee's vanity. Even several feet away, her reflection towered over both of theirs. She flicked her butt-length bleached-blonde hair out of her face and narrowed her cloud-grey eyes. 'Feathers are fabulous.' She'd moved from Russia a decade ago, but the accent had yet to soften. 'You are just jealous because when you wear them, the children squawk at you.'

'Your child!' Liliana snapped. She tugged Bee's blonde hair too hard when she spun around to yell at the other woman. '*Your* son was squawking and encouraging the others! Yours!'

Anastasia smiled. 'He is an exceedingly clever boy, my son. A natural leader.'

Liliana yanked Bee's hair again. 'Now, listen—'

Bee grabbed Liliana's wrist and worked her hair free. 'All of our sons are clever, OK? That's why they're friends.'

Oliver was best friends with Liliana and Anastasia's boys. They all attended the same private school in Miami, and the Anas – as she referred to them exclusively in her own head – became Bee's best mom friends. Technically, Bee's only mom friends. Technically, Bee's only friends. But who's counting?

'Can we get back to dressing me down please?' Bee ran her palms over her red pantsuit, critical blue eyes trailing the movement in the mirror. Tailored nicely, it highlighted her slim figure without being revealing, buttoning all the way to her collarbone. 'Maybe pearls?'

Liliana plucked the strand of saltwater pearls from the jewelry box and secured it around Bee's neck. 'Perfect! You look ready to win the popular vote but lose the electoral college!'

Anastasia plopped on to the four-poster king-sized bed with a laborious huff. 'Why are you doing this to yourself? Why must you make yourself so plain? It makes me sad in my heart to see you like this.'

'I need an investor, Anastasia,' Bee said. She slipped on a pair of black closed-toe heels. 'I don't have enough capital to start a bookstore on my own, and banks don't give loans to single mothers whose only source of income is child support, as the rude bank manager explained between peals of laughter. Rosalie Waters loves this kind of stuff. She owns all those art galleries in up-and-coming neighborhoods. And she donates to rec centers all the time. I just . . . I need her to see me. To talk to me. And she'll partner with me; I'm sure of it. She'll love me.'

'Because you'll make her,' Liliana said. 'Right?'

Bee grimaced. 'No. No, I'm going to be myself. I'm going to be honest. No smoke and mirrors, no creative lies. Just me.'

'But this is not you,' Anastasia said. 'This is . . . I do not know what this is.'

Bee pulled on the hem of her suit jacket. 'This is dressing for the job you want. This is a totally normal thing that normal people do on a normal, everyday, business-related basis.'

Hogarth, her overweight brown-and-white English bulldog, tried to jump on the bed next to Anastasia. His large body proved too much weight for his stubby legs to propel, however, so he sneezed and trotted out of the room with his nubby tail wagging.

'My husband has friends,' Anastasia said, her attention on the dog. 'Let me have you meet them. They will invest in your pathetic dreams.'

'My dad too,' said Liliana. 'Have you met my dad? Martin?

Anyway, he could invest, or he could get his boss in on it. Then at least you wouldn't have to go to Rich People Church.' She patted Bee's cheek with her small palm. 'Well, I don't know if the people are rich, but the pastor sure is.'

'Thanks, guys,' Bee said with a sincere smile. 'But that would be exactly like dealing with Russian Charlie or Cuban Charlie, and I don't want to do business with Charlies of any nationality. I want my own thing. And I want it the right way. The legal way.'

'Just because something is legal doesn't make it right.' Liliana sat next to Anastasia on Bee's bed. 'But we love you no matter what scheme you've got going on.'

She shook her head. 'Not a scheme.'

'Eh,' said Anastasia. 'It's a bit of a scheme.'

The nanny, Malika, ushered a suit-and-tie-wearing Oliver into the master bedroom. Scrawny for his ten years, Oliver was her ex's mini-me, with a round, boyish, handsome face, dark eyes that shone like he had a joke he couldn't wait to tell, and a mop of curly black hair on the top of his head. The suit jacket sleeves hung loose past his fingertips, his slacks rolled up above his brown oxfords.

'Mom,' he said. 'I feel foolish.'

'What?' Bee pulled him into a hug and planted a kiss on his forehead. 'You look perfect!' She took his hand and turned to face Malika. 'Well, what do you think?'

A nineteen-year-old daughter of Pakistani immigrants, Malika had half a foot on Bee and weighed at least twenty pounds less. She was tech-savvy and detail oriented, a perfect foil to Bee. Her elbows and knees were sharp, and her tongue even sharper. Malika had long brown hair, umber skin, dark brown eyes and was never without an opinion.

Typically of the negative variety.

'He looks ready to give a press conference about unsolicited text messages to minors while you stand silently at his side.'

'Nailed it!' Bee held out a fist and waited.

Malika rolled her eyes and tapped her knuckles against Bee's. 'You don't pay me enough for this.'

Bee followed the parking lot attendant's direction and pulled her silver Mercedes S-Class into an empty spot.

Oliver gaped at the massive building from the backseat. 'What is this place? This is – this is a mall? Or an airport?'

Bee released her seatbelt. 'This is church.'

'Whose?'

'Rosalie Waters.' She caught her son's eye in the rearview mirror. 'And you are going to be on your best behavior – understood?'

Oliver held out a hand. 'Money please.'

'Money?' Bee huffed. 'Excuse me?'

'Fifty bucks.'

She glared at his reflection and rifled through her Gucci clutch. 'Twenty.'

He snatched the crisp bill and shoved it into his suit pocket. 'Let's go wow this old lady!'

Bee followed her son out of the car and through the parking lot. He looked like his father, but he thought like her, and she had enough self-awareness to know that would be a combination she'd struggle with once he hit puberty.

The megachurch did resemble a mall, she supposed, or an enclosed sports stadium. An ugly, brown, solid-concrete building with tropical landscaping and a large, Vegas-style fountain outside the front doors. People wearing black T-shirts with white letters proclaiming the church's name across their chests opened the doors and greeted them with blinding, straight-teethed smiles, like every single one of them had the same dentist apply the same veneers to all their teeth.

Her phone rang. Bee dug it out of her clutch and frowned when the caller ID read UNKNOWN. She silenced it before tucking it away.

Oliver headed towards the free café, and she trailed behind, looking for Rosalie but doing her best to look like she wasn't looking for anyone.

Her spy – the nanny – had staked the church out last week and said that the older woman had a special table at the church's café where she drank her coffee before service. And then Malika had puckered her lips and furrowed her brow and said, 'So grifting and stealing are out, but spying is forever, huh?'

Bee slid into the empty seat across from Rosalie. She crossed her legs at the ankles, clasped her hands on the tabletop and smiled. 'Good morning. Is this seat taken? All the other tables are full, and my son and I are new here.'

The older woman wore a bright pink, modest dress, a wide-brimmed hat with fake flowers pinned to the gray hair she'd styled in a tight updo and a long frown. 'I suppose you may join me.'

'Thank you so much.' She waved at Oliver, who stood in the line for pastries, licking frosting off his too-long sleeve. 'My son will be a minute. Have you been attending here long? I hear the pastor is remarkable.'

Bee knew almost nothing about the pastor, save for what Malika had told her. He had incredibly tall, well-oiled black hair, spoke in a southern accent and wasn't shy about asking for donations. Malika had also mentioned the man who led the worship service wore skinny jeans that left little to the imagination, but as that was neither here nor there, Bee decided not to mention it.

Rosalie sipped her coffee. 'He's fine. A little young for me, I suppose, but so many other churches in Miami cater to individuals that I don't want to spend my free time associating with.'

Bee kept the smile on her face. 'I'm Beatrice Cardello, by the way.' She offered the other woman her hand. 'I don't believe I caught your name.'

Rosalie literally and figuratively turned her nose up at Bee's proffered hand. 'Cardello, you say? Of Cardello Industries? The same company that bought out that factory, fired all of our local people and staffed it with their out of towners?'

Bee's hand didn't shake when she lowered it back to the table, a fact she was perhaps too proud of. 'My ex-husband's company. We're divorced.' She winced at herself. Calling him her ex-husband made the statement of divorce unnecessary.

Bee forced her face to relax, her lips to turn up into a pleasant smile. 'I'm actually trying to start up my own business. I've been looking at opening a bookstore near my son's school. Someplace the kids could go after school or on the weekends to read, or do homework, or play card games. I found a storefront, you know, but it's currently a little out of my price range. Just looking for like-minded investors really.'

Rosalie Waters shook her head and rose from the table. 'I should have known. You Cardellos – slimy gutter rats, the lot of you. Your husband is a snake. A serpent. The *devil.*'

The smile fell, and Bee didn't try to stop it. This woman had managed to call her ex a rat and a snake. Both of which were true, of course, but the least she could do was pick a single metaphor and stick with it. Two different animals were excessive and unnecessary. Plus, she'd called him a snake and a serpent. Pick one, lady. *One*.

Oliver stood at the front of the pastry line, cinnamon rolls and muffins piled high in his arms. He waved and a Danish fell to the floor.

Bee blinked away the itchy feeling in her eyes. 'Charlie is a good father,' she said. 'He's not the devil.'

Rosalie clasped her weathered hand on Bee's shoulder and squeezed. 'I'll say a prayer for you today. Seems like you need all the prayers you can get.'

She left her coffee behind and hobbled into the sanctuary.

'Aw, did I miss it?' Oliver dumped his baked goods on the table. 'She left before I got to wow her. So did she say yes? Are we gonna get to open the bookstore?'

Bee shoved a cinnamon roll in her mouth so she wouldn't have to tell her son the truth.

TWO

Bee pulled the cork out of a bottle of rosé with her teeth and filled a long-stemmed glass to the top with the bubbling pink beauty. She was going to drink the whole bottle. And then probably a second bottle. And she was going to eat an entire pizza on her own. A *cheese* pizza – no meat to get in the way of her cheese and carbs.

She deserved it.

'So,' Malika said, 'Rich People Church didn't bring you any new money, huh?'

Bee glared at the faded picture of Britney Spears on Malika's well-worn shirt. 'No.'

'Is that why' – she motioned at Bee – 'is that why this is happening right now?'

Bee looked down at herself. At her ill-fitting sweatpants and her oversized hoodie. Strands of hair fell loose from her topknot, and she pushed them out of her eyes. 'I am disgusting, and I like it. I'm going to wear clothes I can bloat in and drink until I pass out.'

Malika gestured towards the foyer of the Biscayne Bay manor Bee had kept in the divorce. 'You could always sell the painting.'

'The Degas landscape?' Bee covered her heart. 'Sell the one-of-a-kind Degas landscape? I would rather die.'

'Jeez, OK.'

'Besides' – Bee chugged down a gulp of her drink, bubbles tickling her throat, and burped behind her fingertips – 'I couldn't sell it even if I wanted to. It's stolen, and I'd need a fence. I'd have to sell it on the black market. I'd have to prove that I have the original and the one that's hanging up in the Met is a forgery of mine, and it's been so long now, I don't know what fence would take that risk. The whole point is doing this the right way. To show Oliver that you can follow your dreams the legal way. But it's so hard! It's like the system, like the *man*, wants you to fail.'

Malika piled three slices of pizza on a paper plate. 'Well, I don't know about that. But I do know that I'm going to eat this in the bathtub. Yell if you need me. But don't need me, cause I'm off the clock until tomorrow.'

Bee drained her glass and refilled it. Out the kitchen window, the last rays of sunlight reflected on her infinity pool and the open ocean, downtown Miami rising in the distance. Maybe she should take a dip in her infinity pool. Tipsy swimming was totally a thing, right?

Her phone buzzed on the counter. She silenced it with the push of a button and a sigh. Another unknown ID. Great, just great. Now on top of everything, she'd have to figure out how to change her number.

She shrugged and sipped her drink. Who was she kidding? She'd just get Malika to change it for her.

Oliver came running into the kitchen with clean pajamas and dirty hair.

Bee set her fists on her hips. 'Did you wash your hair?'

He shifted on his feet, his brown eyes sliding away from her face and looking at a spot behind her. 'Ye-ah.' His voice cracked.

'OK.' Bee got down on one knee to get a better look at him. 'That was a terrible lie. You went all shifty. Your hands got fidgety. You couldn't even keep your eyes focused. Let's do better this time. Keep still and keep your voice even. OK?'

'OK.'

'Now, Oliver, did you wash your hair?'

He opened his mouth and closed it again, keeping eye contact but unable to make a sound. He smiled at her instead.

She rose to her feet. 'Go wash your hair.'

'Yeah.'

Bee made sure he went up the stairs, following him as far as the living room. Once he was out of sight, she approached the end table next to the cream sectional and tapped the corners of the gold picture frames kept there. One held a picture of her mother and her uncle side by side on matching Harley Davidsons. The other was of Pinkerton holding a smiling, one-year-old Oliver. Those two pictures and the Degas landscape were the only memories she had of her old life. Every other bit of her retirement fund, every other bridge she'd ever built, was gone. Os had made sure of that.

That was the price you paid for getting out: everything.

Bee tucked Oliver into his bed and picked *Percy Jackson and the Lightning Thief* off the end table. He didn't need her to read it to him; he was an excellent reader, but it was something they got to do together. Bee cherished reading books at night because she knew all too soon, he'd grow out of it. He looked so young still. That could be due to his size. She worried he was underweight, wondered if she should give him those weird nutritional shakes for old people and kids, but the pediatrician was never concerned. His father looked young still too. The curse of the babyface. But with his Avengers blankets pulled up to his chin, his eyes heavy and Hogarth curled around his feet, he was her baby.

She finished reading about Grover's true identity when Oliver yawned so big half his face disappeared.

Bee closed the book and set it on his nightstand.

'One more chapter?' he begged. 'Puh-lease?'

'It's already past your bedtime.'

'Just one more page?'

She kissed his forehead. 'We'll read another chapter tomorrow.'

'That's the problem! I need to know what happens. I want to find out about Camp Half-Blood.' He sighed but it turned into another wide yawn halfway through. 'I'm not even sure how I'm going to sleep with all this suspense, Mom.'

She smiled. 'Say your prayers, yeah? I'll see you in the morning.'

'OK, Mom.' He rolled on to his side. 'Love you.'

'I love you more.' She switched his lamp off and grabbed the Percy Jackson book from his nightstand.

He groaned.

She winked. 'Just in case.'

Hogarth followed her, his paws noisy on the tile.

'And don't you think I'm giving you any more food,' Bee told the dog as the two of them trotted down the stairs. 'I saw how Oliver overfilled your bowl.'

Hogarth went off into the living room, tried and failed to jump on the couch.

'See?' She hoisted him up, surprised by how much effort it actually took. 'Wow, OK, you are going on a diet tomorrow.'

Hogarth turned three times in the middle of the sectional before plopping down.

'Yeah, that's how I feel about diets.'

Bee continued into the kitchen, determined to finish off the last of the rosé now that Oliver was in bed. She passed by the end table that had the two golden picture frames. Out of habit, she tapped each on the corner.

She grabbed the almost-empty bottle of pink loveliness and brought the glass to her lips, draining it in three good gulps.

The power went out.

Bee set the bottle down, burped, wiped her mouth with the back of her hand.

She strained her ears for the sound of distant thunder.

Nothing.

'Huh,' she said. 'What do you think, Garth? A brownout?'

The dog didn't reply.

Bee moved towards the in-law suite, already raising a hand to knock on Malika's door and check on her when she spotted the unmistakable beam of a flashlight outside the kitchen window.

'Malika!' She turned on her heels and ran for the foyer. '*Incoming!*'

She took the stairs two at a time, skidded around the corner to the master suite and jogged to the ensuite bathroom. She didn't bother with the switch – the window between the ornate mirrors of the double sinks let in enough moonlight.

She flung open the doors of a large storage cabinet above the toilet and pulled out an economy box of tampons. Buried beneath the surplus of regulars was a fully loaded, untraceable stainless-steel Colt 1911.

Bee checked the chamber. A copper bullet shone up at her. With shaking hands, she stuffed the box back and closed the cabinet. Her extra ammo was downstairs, in a Bisquick bottle in the kitchen pantry. Hopefully, she wouldn't need more than the nine shots she had.

She made sure the safety was on and stuffed the gun in her waistband at her back. She needed to grab Oliver and Malika, and the dog. Where was the dog? The emergency generator could keep the safe room secure if nothing else. But she had to get them all there before the intruders made it inside.

Bee's expensive face cream lay on its side between her porcelain sinks, its pale blue contents oozing out on the marble countertop. She flipped it upright, fingers sliding over a crack in the glass. Like someone had stepped on it.

The rings of the shower curtain scratched against the metal rod and a masked man appeared in the mirror.

'Oh shi—'

The crook of his arm was around her neck in an instant. She could see her eyes bulge out of her reflection's head. Bee grabbed his forearm with both hands and pulled, desperate for air.

He squeezed tighter.

This time when she pulled on his arm, she didn't bother trying to breathe. She took what space she could and bashed her head against his nose.

That made him let go, made him reach for his bleeding face.

She sucked precious air and ran to the door, shrieking, 'Malika!'

The intruder hit her hard on the back of her knees. She collapsed – smacked the cold marble floor. He covered her mouth with a gloved hand to stop her desperate scream, but she twisted in his hold, kicked him in the gut. He swore but held on tighter. She bit at his glove and lobbed a kick at his groin.

He fell to the ground, holding himself.

Bee screamed and scrambled to her feet. She grabbed the gun from her waistband but didn't even get a chance to switch the safety off before he had a hand over her mouth again, another clutching her wrist and bending it backward. The gun fell out of her hold, crashed against the floor.

Tears spilled out of Bee's eyes. She tried to pull away from her assailant, but he only held on tighter, wrenching her arm close to breaking behind her back.

He dragged her out of the room and down the hall. She called out as loud as she could for help, using all the air she had left in her lungs, and his grip tightened on her cheeks until her teeth cracked in her jaw.

He spun her around to face forward.

Another masked man had Oliver in his arms, the barrel of a gun hidden in his curly hair.

Bee instantly stilled.

'There's a good girl.' The man who held her spoke with a thick Eastern European accent. 'You're going to behave now, aren't you?'

She nodded, tears running down her face and over his leather fingers.

Her son's eyes were wide and terrified, his skin as white as paper, and she focused on trying to meet his gaze, on trying to make herself look braver and calmer than she felt.

Oliver and his captor went out the front door without so much as a peep. The emergency generator had failed to keep the alarm system on. Bee and her bleeding assailant went next. They descended the steps in near darkness. The outside lights were disabled, the full moon hanging in the sky the only thing illuminating the faded red pavers.

'In the back.' Her attacker opened the door of a white Honda Civic. 'Stay down. Try anything funny and we kill you both.'

She lay down in the backseat, gathering Oliver to her chest when he was thrust in after her. He cried on her neck. Warm tears rolled behind her ear and disappeared in her hoodie.

'It's OK,' she whispered, her voice hoarse. 'It's OK. It's going to be OK.'

'Broke my nose,' her attacker said to his partner before he closed the door, leaving Bee and Oliver alone in the vehicle.

Headlights streamed in through the back window. Bee shushed her son and rose on her elbows to sneak a glance in the rearview mirror.

The approaching car picked up speed, switching its headlights to their brightest setting. Bee held on tight to Oliver and sank into the cloth bench seat.

Two gunshots rang out, piercing the windshield of the oncoming car before it cut across the carport. It collided with the masked men in one loud thud. The tires screeched as the vehicle came to a sudden halt.

Bee couldn't breathe. She squeezed her eyes shut and held on to her son for all she was worth.

The door opened, humid air rushing in, and a familiar voice spoke.

'Come on, Shelby, love – it's time to go.'

THREE

Bee hadn't seen him in over a decade, but Adam Gage wasn't the kind of man you forgot. Tall and tan and broad-shouldered. A handsome, square face, with dimples that popped when he smiled. A chiseled jaw covered in stubble that was always the perfect five o'clock length. The bridge of his nose a wide, sturdy triangle in profile.

The only things about him that had changed were the wrinkles around his hazel eyes when he smiled, a new scar in the shape of a crescent moon at the center of his bottom lip, and a receding hairline he probably should have just surrendered to and shaved clean off.

She stared up at him, still clutching Oliver tight to her, shock and disbelief clouding her ability to move. To react.

He held up his empty palms. 'Hey, Shelby,' he said, dimples popping, eyes wrinkling, and her pulse buzzed in her ears.

'Stay here,' she whispered to Oliver, sliding out of the car.

He wasn't wearing a jacket, only a short-sleeved, white polo shirt, tucked into gray slacks. He didn't look like he was concealing a weapon, but she knew from experience that didn't mean he wasn't. 'It's been a while,' he said.

Her eyes stung. She tried to sniff the pain away. 'Are you here to kill me?' She kept her voice low so Oliver wouldn't hear. 'Or recruit me? Because honestly, I'm not prepared for either.'

'No.' He stuck his hands in his pockets. 'No, neither, Shelby. Can we talk?'

She had so many questions, all of them rushing over her tongue at once, that she couldn't ask anything at all. Instead, she managed, 'It's Beatrice now.'

'Oh,' he said. 'Wow.'

He stepped around her, glanced around the carport. The car he'd used to run over their attackers still had its lights on, casting shadows around them.

Bee smoothed out her top when his back was to her and

remembered what she was wearing. As quietly and yet frantically as possible, she unzipped her hoodie and threw it into her car, covering Oliver's face.

He ripped it off with a, 'Pfft!'

She hadn't changed much either in twelve years, not really. A little wider in the hips from childbirth, but the yoga and the board-certified plastic surgeon had kept her stomach more or less flat, her breasts more or less perky. And sure, her blonde hair now came from the salon chair, but she'd been born with it, so what did it matter if she needed a little bit of a color boost now that she was thirty-three?

Oh, for the love of God, she wasn't even wearing makeup. She licked the tips of two fingers, ran them over her manicured eyebrows. Wetted her lips. Pinched her cheeks to bring some color to them. And then she opened her blue eyes as wide as she could. They were naturally large, well spaced apart under those manicured eyebrows, and she'd never had to pay a surgeon to fix her nose. She'd always rather liked her button nose, the only physical feature she'd inherited from her mother. But large, doe eyes – especially blue ones – always made people think you were innocent.

And she didn't know what Adam was there to talk to her about. But any extra innocence she could bring to the moment wouldn't hurt.

She tugged the hem of her wrinkled red tank top down over her ill-fitting sweatpants.

This wasn't her finest moment. 'You could've called,' she said and realized as she spoke who those unknown numbers belonged to. 'You could've called from a number I would've answered.'

He grinned at her over his shoulder. 'Is there a number I could have called you from you would've answered?'

She smiled, checked her topknot. It was still there. 'Probably not.'

'It's a nice place you got here, Shelby.'

'It's Beatrice, Adam.'

'Sorry.' He turned so they were face to face, toe to toe. 'It's gonna take me a minute to get used to it. Beatrice it is.'

'What are you doing here?'

He wasn't supposed to be here. He was definitely not supposed to be here.

But neither was a third masked man, creeping up the carport with a machete in his hand.

'Adam!' Bee screamed. 'Behind!'

Adam ducked at her warning. The masked man swung his machete too late, lodging the blade into the car's doorframe.

Adam jammed a right hook in the man's gut. He cried out, folded over. And then ran full force, tackling Adam to the ground.

Bee dove back into the car, cradling Oliver to her chest.

'Jeez, Mom! Watch the nose!'

'Sorry!'

Fists pounded on skin, bones creaked, men swore in foreign languages and Oliver scrambled out of her grasp.

'Don't get out!' Bee hissed, clutching Oliver's pajama collar. 'Don't get out!'

'I'm not gonna get out, Mom! I just wanna see!'

The masked man had gotten the best of Adam, hips straddling his waist, raising a fist to punch him in the face.

There was the flat crack of a gunshot.

Bee gasped.

Another crack.

The masked man on top of Adam went limp, sagged like a puppet whose strings had been cut.

Adam pushed the dead man off and sat up, panting for breath, a Beretta Bobcat .22 in his hands.

'That,' Oliver said, 'was awesome! Holy cow!' He jumped out of the car.

'Oliver!' She swung her hands to grab him and missed, his Hulk pajamas sliding between her fingers.

'You killed all those guys by yourself! Who are you?' He bounced up on the toes of his Hulk slippers. 'Why'd you call my mom Shelby?'

'Oh, he probably meant to say Mrs Bee, and it just came out sounding like Shelby.'

Bee pushed him behind her, surveyed their savior still on the ground. 'Are you all right?'

'Yeah, I'm fine.' He slid the small gun into an ankle holster. 'Are you OK? Were you hurt?'

She shook her head and then winced. 'Only when I broke that guy's nose with my skull.'

His mouth curved in a grin. 'You broke his nose?'

'It sounded like it anyway.'

'Good. But listen, Bee. Those guys were Georgian. And I don't mean Atlanta. They don't mess around. We need to get out of here before their backup arrives.'

An evening rain started, cooling off the Miami street. She could hear water splashing against the high vaulted roof of her carport even over the buzz in her ears.

'What do you mean, we?'

'I'm here to get you guys out of town. There's some' – he glanced behind her at Oliver – 'there's some stuff going down.'

'Go wait for me in the car,' Bee whispered to Oliver.

He groaned but did what he was told, sitting in the backseat of her silver Mercedes S-Class.

She tilted her head and observed Adam. He seemed so relaxed now. Like dropping in out of nowhere after radio silence for a decade plus to save the day just in the nick of time and whisk her away was a normal thing to do on a summer evening.

'What stuff? You gonna be honest with me, tell me why you're here? Of all the McMansions in the world, you just had to walk into mine and all that?'

'Yeah, um.' He stood up, ran a hand over his balding head. 'So. Your ex-husband?'

'I've met him, yes.'

'He . . . well, he hired me. I'm supposed to take you and the kid to the beach house, any means necessary.'

'Oh-ho, is that so? And why would you do that?'

'To protect you.'

She tilted her head even further until her ear touched her shoulder. 'Protect me? From what?'

'Theo Alvarez.'

Bee didn't move. She kept her ear on her shoulder until her neck complained and her brain made a *wubba-wubba* sound.

'Well.' She straightened herself out, cracked the kink out of her neck. 'Well. Shit.'

'Yeah.'

'OK, um.' She pressed a hand to her forehead and tried to form a coherent thought. 'Well, let's get the hell out of here.'

'Yeah.'

'I've got the dog and the nanny inside. You watch Oliver?'

Adam nodded. 'Be quick. In and out.'

'In and out,' Bee agreed, already jumping over the dead man at her door. 'In and out.'

She crept into the darkness, steadied her breath. The light from the kitchen streamed into the foyer, and she followed the path it laid out before her, taking a quick glance around to try and shake off the feeling that something could pop out from behind the couch at any moment.

'Malika?'

Hogarth sneezed in the living room. She peeked over the couch and found him belly up, tail thumping against the cushions.

'Oh, good boy. Super helpful. Thank you for your service.'

Bee crossed the kitchen and cracked open the door to the in-law suite. Half of the small room acted as an office, complete with rusting, black metal file folders, a desk purchased from hell's Swedish labyrinth and a corner wall of bookshelves stacked with untidy novels. The other half was Malika's bedroom: a twin mattress under the window covered in messy purple sheets and a cheap folding table covered with top-of-the-line electronics. The closet door cracked open, and Malika poked her head out.

'Good!' Malika said, coming out of the closet. 'You're alive. And I'm glad you're alive, don't get me wrong, but how are you alive?'

'Um,' Bee said. 'Adam Gage showed up.'

Malika gaped at her, a whale looking for krill. 'What?'

'Yeah. I know.'

'Adam Gage? Your Adam Gage?'

'Yeah, I know!'

Malika shared a look with Britney's face on her shirt. 'Might I ask why?'

'Charlie sent him. Apparently, Theo Alvarez is after us.'

'*What*?'

'Yeah!' Bee tossed her arms up. 'I know! Get your go bag. We're fleeing.'

Malika dragged her desk chair to the closet and stood on it. She pulled a packed duffle bag out of the top of the closet. 'Do you know why Alvarez is after you?'

'No, I figured I'd ask about that after we got the hell out of here. I'll meet you out front.'

'Bee!' Malika jumped off the chair. 'Wait!'

Bee jogged to the kitchen and grabbed her phone off the counter.

She pressed Charlie's face with her thumb, but his phone didn't have the decency to ring, sending her straight to voicemail. She left a two-word, four-syllable swear on his voicemail and hung up the call.

'Don't you miss receivers?' She called back as she hurried up the stairs. 'I miss slamming phones down. Will you get Hogarth's leash?'

Malika grumbled but did as she was asked.

Bee ducked into her bathroom long enough to grab the gun off the floor. She shoved it back in her waistband and ran down the stairs.

Then she grabbed the gold-framed pictures of her mom and uncle, of Pinkerton and Oliver, off the end table. Bee tucked the frames under her arms and tried calling Charlie again.

Again, straight to voicemail.

She walked to the foyer and opened the coat closet.

Hogarth's paws clicked on the tile when he and Malika approached her, shoving her laptop in her go bag.

'Boss,' she said, 'don't you think Adam Gage showing up is a little, I don't know, convenient?'

Bee pulled out a large storage bin from the back corner. Standing on the box, she pushed the extra blankets to the side of the top shelf, revealing a hidden panel carved into the wall. She pressed it on the right side and popped it open.

'Of course I do. But I'm gonna worry about that when Oliver and I aren't in Alvarez's sights.'

'What if he's lying? What if he sent these guys in so he could, I don't know, kill them? In some sort of . . . like a big, freaking con? And now he's kidnapping you and Oliver, and shit's gonna get real.'

Bee reached into the hole and pulled out a stuffed black duffle bag.

'Watch out,' she told the dog before dropping the pack on the floor. She took a few more seconds to put everything back in its rightful place then stepped off the bin. Bee kicked it back inside the closet, shoved the pictures and the gun inside the duffle, and threw it over her shoulder. 'You think he's got an angle?'

'How can we trust him not to have an angle?'

Bee hoisted the strap higher on her shoulder. 'We can't.'

Malika gaped at her again, but what else could Bee say? Adam had never hurt her, not ever, and after risking his life in the carport, she doubted he'd suddenly change his MO now.

'I gotta get Oliver out of town, and I'll do what I have to do, Malika. I can take care of Adam. Trust me.'

Malika frowned. 'Yeah, I trust you. It's him I'm not sure about. He still the same – ugh, I hate this word – *dreamboat* from your past?'

She shook her head to hide her smile. 'Hasn't changed much.'

'I don't like this, Bee. Not even a little.'

'Me neither. But we gotta go. Come on.'

Adam stood at the trunk of her car, a license plate in his hands, and frowned when he saw her. 'How'd you both have time to pack?'

'We didn't,' Bee said.

Malika hopped down the stairs, a fierce glare on her face. 'We are not leaving this property until you and I have had a heart to heart, mister.'

Something grabbed Bee's ankle. She dropped her bag and fell to her knees.

Hogarth started barking and didn't stop.

Bee glanced over her shoulder. The man who'd attacked Adam wasn't as dead as previously thought.

Oliver screamed. 'A zombie! A zombie's got Mom!'

She kicked the zombie with her free foot, nailing him in the nose. Blood spurted from his face.

He flinched, and she pulled her leg free, the suddenness of freedom sending her ass first down the three concrete steps to her entryway.

He yelled something she didn't understand, blood trickling down his smiling lips, and rose to his knees.

Blood and grey matter shot out the side of his head. He fell over with the smile still on his face, much deader this time than before.

Bee heaved. She wrapped her arms around her stomach and closed her eyes. Bile hit the back of her throat, but she swallowed it down.

'Dude! You killed a zombie!' Oliver shouted. 'That was so badass! Say, what was your name again?'

She collapsed back on the red pavers of her driveway.

'Oliver, don't say badass.'

'Busted another nose. If you were a wrestler, you'd be the Nose Bleed.'

Bee opened her eyes and saw Adam above her, head tilted to the side.

He offered her his hand. 'Maybe The Face Wrecker?'

She closed her eyes again. 'Rhinoplasty.'

'It's good. Could see a lot of merchandise of a rhino with a bloody nose on it. Come on now. We gotta go before the neighbors call this in.'

'OK.' She let him help her to her feet. Then she unzipped her bag and pulled out the Colt. 'Here.' Her hands trembled. He took the gun, and she squeezed them into fists. These weren't her first dead guys. She couldn't afford to freak out now. 'This one'll kill them the first time.'

He checked out her gun, half his mouth curved in a goofy grin. 'This is yours? It's nice.'

She shoved the bag in his hands. 'Why are you surprised? I only have nice things.'

FOUR

Adam kept the gun in his hand when he asked, 'Who's got a phone?'

Malika glared at her, and she realized at once her mistake.

'Um,' Bee said. 'Well.'

His finger wasn't on the trigger. But it wasn't far from it either. 'Phones please.' He held out his empty hand. 'And in your bags, you got a laptop?'

Bee handed over her phone first, her protest stuck in her throat.

'Thank you,' he said. 'And you? I'm sorry, I didn't catch your name.'

Malika handed over her phone with her face twisted sourly.

'Thanks. Do either of you have a computer?'

Malika dropped her duffle to the ground and unzipped it, a steady stream of swear words on her lips. She pulled out her thin MacBook with reverence and handed it up to Adam with both hands.

He shoved the gun in his belt to take it. 'Thanks. Bee, you got a computer?'

'No,' she said. 'Just clothes and wigs and IDs and passports and some cash and—'

He raised the laptop and smartphones over his head and smashed them on the red pavers of the carport.

Bee jumped, a squeal escaping from her throat. Pieces of the devices splattered everywhere, covering the ground and their limbs like blood splatter at a crime scene.

Malika cried out – a strange, low hum of despair – and crawled on her knees to the destruction. She picked up her broken cell phone and whispered, 'Peggy.' She clutched her laptop's motherboard and held it against her cheek. 'Nat.'

Oliver scratched his head. 'Um. Why'd ya do that, Adam?'

'Anybody can track you if you got a smartphone or a computer.' Adam spoke to her son like a teacher to a student. 'Find out exactly where you are. We're trying to get out of here without being found.'

'You're a bad man.' Malika dropped the broken pieces of her

devices. She marched to him, her fingers in her face. 'You're dead to me. You hear me? Dead to me!'

'You better do as I say, or you'll be dead for real.'

She moved her pointing hand like she was going to slap him.

He grabbed her fingers. 'Knock it off. Get in the car. If I have to tie you all up to get you to safety, I will. I've got rope with me, and I'm not afraid to use it.'

Oliver punched the air. 'Yeah! Let's tie her up! I wanna write my name on her face!'

'You sonofabitch! I'd like to see you try!'

'Knock it off.' Bee tugged Malika away from the dreamboat of her past. 'We're under attack. We need to flee. You can hate each other in New Jersey. Tie each other up. Go full-on Tyson, I don't care, let's just get out of here before more guys with guns show up.'

Adam fixed his shirt, which had gotten untucked in the melee. 'Yeah.'

Malika grabbed Hogarth's leash and shoved the dog into the backseat. 'Sorry, Bee.'

'Aw, man,' Oliver said. 'Does this mean we aren't hog-tying Malika?'

Malika ruffled his hair. 'Hey. Maybe for Christmas.'

They'd barely made it out of the neighborhood when Oliver started bouncing in his seat. 'Mooooooooom! Mooooooooom! Mooooooooooooom!'

'Oh my God, what?'

'Hogarth and I have to pee.'

She rubbed her eyelids with the pads of her fingers. 'Can you hold it for a few more minutes?'

'Definitely not,' he said. 'Mom, there was so much action, like, all the pee went back up inside me. But now it's gonna come out, and it's gonna come out fast.'

'Ugh,' she said. 'Fine! Adam, can you pull over?'

Adam looked at her. He wasn't smiling, but his whole face was lit up in amusement, and she'd forgotten how much she liked that particular expression of his.

She tried very hard not to grin. 'What?'

'Nothing,' he said, and his voice was light. He pulled over to the shoulder of the road, a thick line of palm trees on their left. 'You're in full-on Mom mode.'

Oliver threw open the back door and grabbed Hogarth's leash, tugging the overweight animal out into the wilderness.

'Don't pee on each other please.'

'No promises!'

The two of them disappeared behind a tree.

Bee said, 'Malika.'

'Yeah.' She unbuckled her seatbelt and climbed out of the car. 'I'm on it.'

Bee stared at the tree in the headlights of the cars that drove by. Malika hovered in front of it with her hand over her eyes.

'Be honest with me, Adam. This isn't Os, right?'

His wasn't a name she said out loud often. Or ever. Once or twice in the past few years, scared the third time would bring him around like Beetlejuice.

Her father's gambling had gone off the rails when her mom died. Thomas Osbourn had shown up to collect payment, money they simply didn't have. But while he was in her home, he'd caught sight of her artwork and recruited her on the spot. How could she refuse, when her father would've been without kneecaps or a skull otherwise? She'd spent the majority of her adolescence with a paintbrush in her hand, which had led quite easily to forgery. Forgery had easily led to thieving. Os taught her how to use her pretty face and quick thinking to get anything she wanted. And all she'd wanted was to impress him.

Fifteen successful jobs, working with different crews under Os – the Mastermind.

Fifteen marks robbed blind.

Fifteen payments into her offshore bank account.

But it was the sixteenth job that had changed everything. He'd tried to send her back to her hometown, and instead, she'd ended up in the bed of a gangster.

Adam's hands were relaxed on the steering wheel. 'No.'

She nodded. Logically, she knew it couldn't be Os, that he was safe behind bars, where she'd put him. But it wasn't her logical mind she was trying to calm.

'So. What did Charlie do that's pissed off Alvarez?'

His grip tightened on the wheel. 'Well,' he said. 'Well,' he said again.

'Well?'

'He seems to have – now, he didn't confirm this with me – but the rumor is that he stole a bit of money.'

'How much of a bit?'

'Thirty-seven and a half million dollars.'

So stunned was Bee that it felt as if every fiber of her being, every synapse in her brain, simultaneously decided to separate from one another, pulling her from the inside out in every possible direction known to man. She slumped back in her seat, exhausted.

Adam said, 'Alvarez put out a hit. He wants you and your kid for leverage.'

Her stomach rolled. Bee grabbed the back of her head and held it between her knees. 'Oh my God. Thirty-seven. Oh my God.'

'Yeah.' He squeezed her shoulder and didn't let go. 'And a half.'

'And a half!'

'That's why I'm here. We're gonna get you guys out. Alvarez has a twelve percent finder's fee for whoever can bring you and the kid to him. But I'm not gonna let that happen, OK?'

'Four and a half million dollars,' she mumbled against her sweats.

His hand faltered. 'Huh?'

'That's twelve percent of what Charlie stole.' She glanced at him from her makeshift fetal position. 'How much is Charlie paying you that you aren't trying to get the finder's fee yourself?'

'Don't worry.' He tapped her temple. 'For an old friend, I'll take a loss.'

'Whatever it is. Whatever the cost. Charlie will pay,' Bee said. 'I'll make sure of it.'

Malika opened the door. Oliver pushed Hogarth into the backseat and climbed in behind. 'Sorry that took so long. Hogarth is too picky about what he pees on. What did I miss?'

Bee exhaled, eyes closed, and pulled herself together. She sat up straight and smiled at her son. 'Nothing, honey. We're just gonna go talk to your dad. You wanna go to the beach?'

FIVE

They didn't speak for the next few minutes. Traffic was light out of Biscayne Bay, moderate closer to the Turnpike. Bee kept turning in her chair to check on Oliver. He was on the verge of falling asleep, his head nodding forward until the movement startled him awake. Malika sat behind the driver's seat with her arms crossed tight over her chest and her death glare drilling into the back of Adam's head. And Hogarth slept between them in the middle seat, a big snoring lump of fat rolls and fur.

Adam tapped the brakes, slowing the car to almost a dead stop. Red brake lights lined the way to the row of police cars that had all northbound traffic completely stopped.

'Uh-oh.' Bee hit him on the arm. 'Adam!'

'Ow,' he said without feeling. 'Yes.'

'This isn't about us, is it?'

He frowned. 'Probably not.' He sat forward in his seat, craning his neck for a better look at what was in front of them.

Bee had an uncomfortable churning in her stomach. She shook her head, trying to will it away, but it sat in the pit of her intestine like a lump of unruly intuition. 'No, no. They've only stopped northbound traffic. They're questioning every car, and no one is getting out for drunk tests.'

Several cars were let through the blockade, and they rolled closer to the front of the line.

Bee opened her duffle bag at her feet.

'Half a dozen cars away,' Adam said.

'Where is it?' she muttered to herself, rifling around the bottom of her bag for a specific kit. 'Aha! Malika! Put this on Oliver. Oliver, hold very still and pretend to sleep.'

'Mmmmmmm,' he snored.

Malika laid the latex down over the side of his face and took the paintbrush from Bee.

'Five more,' Adam said.

Malika finished gluing the scar-shaped latex on Oliver's face and shoved the glue and brush behind her butt. Bee dug out a brunette wig from her bag and positioned it over her blonde hair, feathering the bangs to sit neatly on her forehead.

'Oliver, lie on Malika's shoulder,' she instructed.

'One more,' Adam warned.

'Pretend to sleep,' Bee said again. 'And if you can't do that, then pretend to cry.'

Adam rolled down the window. 'Here we go.'

A state trooper, dressed in various shades of brown and still wearing his wide-brimmed hat despite the moonlit sky, lowered the beam of his flashlight and peered into the car.

'Good evening,' he greeted, eyeing Adam. 'We've got an amber alert issued. Looking for a missing child. A young boy, Caucasian, about ten years old.'

'Well,' Adam said, with a calm, even voice, 'that's a shame. Sure hope you find him.'

The trooper almost smiled and leaned in further to get a good look in the back. 'You doing all right there, miss? How's your boy?'

The smile froze on the trooper's face when he caught sight of the scar covering Oliver's.

'Oh please!' Bee yelled. 'Please continue staring! Like he doesn't get that enough!'

Oliver hid his face in Malika's neck and cried.

The trooper backed away. 'Sorry for the confusion. Y'all drive safe now.'

Adam waved a hand, nodded and slowly rolled past the barricade.

The moment the window was back up, Oliver gave a loud laugh. 'I am never taking this off!' He traced his fingers over the scar on his face. 'Do I look like a badass?'

'Oliver!' Bee scolded.

He unbuckled and craned his neck to look at himself in the rearview mirror. 'I do! Look at me, Adam!'

'Super badass,' he agreed.

'Adam!' Bee scolded. 'Don't encourage him.'

Oliver reached over her shoulder to open her visor, the lights on either side of the mirror so bright he had to squint at his scarred reflection.

'I love it,' he said. 'I want it forever. I'm— Whoops!'

His constant toying with the latex had made the hastily applied glue come loose, and the top half hung limply down his cheek.

Frowning, he peeled it all the way off. 'Oh well, it was fun while it lasted.'

Then he flicked it at Adam.

Adam glared at him halfheartedly, plucking it out of his lap, then stuck it on his forehead.

'Oh, I see what you mean,' he said, 'I do feel like a badass now.'

'You, get in your seat.' Bee nudged Oliver with her elbow. 'And you,' she said to Adam, 'use appropriate language. He's ten.'

Oliver buried his hands in Hogarth's fat rolls. 'Yeah, and I had a gun held to my head tonight, Mom. Plus you made me totally lie to a cop.'

Bee sputtered, 'Now, that's not what—'

'It is,' Malika said. 'That's totally what.'

Bee pulled the wig off and shoved it back into her bag with a huff. 'Fine. You can say "badass" for as much as you want for the next twelve hours. But then that's it, you hear me?'

'Badass!'

Adam tossed the latex scar on to Oliver's lap.

'Hey!' Oliver picked it up. 'Don't be so mean to Scarry. It's OK, buddy.' He kissed the latex. 'I won't let anyone else hurt you ever again.'

SIX

Bee reminded Oliver to buckle up.

'Badasses don't obey the rules, Mom.' He clicked his seatbelt on. 'Just because the fuzz says you have to wear your seatbelt doesn't mean we gotta listen to 'em.'

'The fuzz?' Malika snorted. 'You're dumb, bro.'

'You're bro, dumb.' Oliver stuck his tongue out at her. 'I'm a badass.'

'A dumb badass.'

'Children!' Bee snapped. 'I need quiet to work.'

Oliver said, 'What kinda work? Adam's just driving to the hangar right now.'

'Yes, but I know where the hangar is. I'm, like, the map person. The guide. The . . . navigator! I'm the navigator!'

'The navigator is like the least badass position on the *Enterprise*, Mom. Don't be so excited.'

'Hey,' Adam said.

Bee smiled at him, shot a finger gun. 'Hey yourself.'

But two little lines had formed between his eyebrows.

She dropped her hands in her lap and let herself feel really stupid.

He gestured at the rearview mirror and clutched the wheel with both hands. 'Friends of yours?'

She looked at her mirror. It was a fair question. Three Harley Davidson motorcycles weaved in and out of traffic. She'd grown up in a small town overrun by her uncle's motorcycle club. But that MC was long gone now, even though she'd done the best she could to keep them safe. Os was an expert at finding weak points and using them for his own advantage. He'd learned hers quickly and pressed on it often.

'White guys on Harleys?' Bee shook her head. 'Oh, that's never a good sign.'

'Oliver and Malika,' Adam said, his voice a calm, commanding rumble, 'get down on the floor behind our seats.'

Malika frowned out the back window at the approaching motorcycles and did what she was told without argument. 'Come on, little badass. Let's make ourselves comfortable on the floor.'

'Aw, man,' Oliver groaned and yanked Hogarth down with him. 'If I gotta lie down here, you do too, Fatso.'

Adam pulled her gun out of the glovebox, his elbow brushing up against her.

She swallowed over the lump in her throat. 'They're probably not here for us.'

'Probably not.' He rolled her window down and set his gun-holding hand on her knee.

An older man rode up next to the passenger window, his long white beard catching the wind and fanning out behind his head.

Bee pressed her back against the seat as hard as she could.

'It's going to be all right,' Adam said without looking at her, his full attention on the road in front of him. One hand relaxed on the wheel, the other clutched around the gun in her lap. She could barely hear him over the wind screaming in through her open window.

She inhaled deeply through her nose. It shook over her lips when she released it.

Long Beard McWhitey held up a .38 Chief's Special outside her window.

Adam jerked the car hard to the right and fired.

Bee screamed, guarding her face with her arms. Burning gunpowder clung to her forearms, and the bullet exploded in her eardrums.

The side of the car smashed against the bike. The bullet hit the driver. He and his bike went down, skidding off to the shoulder of the road.

'Is he dead?' Oliver called out from underneath the dog.

Bee bobbed her head, wincing at the wreckage in her mirror. 'Yeah, probably.'

'He wasn't wearing a helmet,' Adam said. 'You should always wear a helmet on a bike, Oliver.'

She grabbed her hand rests. 'None of them are wearing helmets! *Why?*'

The biker on their left opened fire. Bullets pierced through the air, sailed across the inside as he sped along the length of the car.

Adam grabbed the back of her neck and shoved her face down into his lap. Bullets flew over her head and out her empty window.

He forced her hard against him, the fabric of his slacks against her cheek, his zipper on her nose.

'Oh God,' she said to the lump under her chin.

He fired his gun with his free hand, sending the rider down.

'Are you all right?' he asked when he let go of her.

She covered her open mouth with her fingers, breathing hard. 'Yeah, um. Uh.' *Never better*, she thought, her throat dryer than it had ever been in her life. She swallowed, her hand moving to cover her neck. 'Yep.'

The rider behind them fired three times. The second bullet shattered the rear window. The third whizzed through the windshield. It tore a hole through the glass, leaving cracks like ice over a frozen lake beginning to thaw.

Adam slammed on the brakes.

The bike hit the trunk with a thud. The biker rolled over the top of the car, screaming as he went. The screaming stopped when he hit the road in front of them.

Bee slid forward in her seat so hard her seatbelt engaged.

'Olly!' she gasped. 'You OK?'

'Dog butt! In my face!' He wrapped his arms around Hogarth and tried to take in an anus-free breath. 'So gross!'

'I'm fine too!' Malika called out from somewhere underneath Oliver and the dog. 'Thanks for asking, Boss!'

Adam put the car in reverse. He craned his neck to look in the empty space where the window used to be. The bike that had crashed into them screeched across the asphalt, sparks flying, their bumper pushing it to the side.

Cars honked and swerved to avoid them. One guy yelled at them in Spanish, his middle finger raised.

'Oh,' Bee shouted, 'I'm so sorry us trying not to die has minorly inconvenienced you!'

Adam sped up, steering the car through oncoming traffic backward.

An eighteen-wheeler laid on its horn.

'Truck!' Bee yelled.

'*Truck?*' Oliver demanded.

'Hold on!' ordered Adam.

'To what?' hollered Malika.

Adam yanked the wheel, spinning the car all the way around until they were face to face with the approaching truck. He floored the gas and sent them backward on to the grassy median, missing the eighteen-wheeler by mere feet.

It blared its horn in one long, angry burst as it passed by.

He shifted the car into forward and merged into traffic, now traveling the opposite way they had been.

'Everyone all right?'

Bee checked to make sure she hadn't swallowed her tongue. 'Mm-hum,' she said, panting hard. 'I . . . yeah. Yeah. Oliver?'

'This dog is too fat,' he groaned, his upper body hidden by Hogarth.

The dog looked up at Bee, content and oblivious.

'I'm gonna need a raise, Bee,' Malika said. 'You really don't pay me enough for this.'

SEVEN

Artie Bosh was waiting for them at the hangar. Cardello Industries owned several hangars on the private airstrip – not at the Miami airport, of course, but close. The other hangars were owned by middle-class, middle-aged white dudes who needed to pick up another hobby besides golf. Artie himself Bee had known for years. Charlie had employed him long before they were married. Artie, with his male pattern baldness and affable nature, was a big guy, far too big for the cheap suit he wore, but soft around the middle. He looked like he'd played football in high school then never worked out again a day in his life post-graduation. He had a friendly, wide face and all his teeth.

'Mrs C,' he greeted, wrapping her in a hug.

There were only a few Cardello men Bee would ever let hug her, and Artie was one of them.

More often than not, he'd been at the beach house with her when she, pregnant with Oliver, had been deemed by her husband too fragile to work. He was too friendly to be a good bodyguard, an attack dog who would lick an intruder to death, but he never complained about late-night ice cream runs. Or the occasional late-night spaghetti run. She'd sent him on a fair share of those in her third trimester.

'Hey, Artie. How's the family?'

'Rachael just turned eight.' He let go of her to pull out his wallet, flashed a school picture of a toothless brunette beauty. 'Looks just like her mom.'

'Well, small mercies,' Bee teased. 'You taking us to the beach house?'

He tucked his wallet away. 'Yes, ma'am. Jet's not much, I gotta tell you, but at least it's clean. How's it going, Malika?'

'You know, it's been worse, honestly,' Malika said.

Adam had Hogarth's leash in one hand and the duffle bag in the other. Artie didn't realize this until after he'd stuck his hand out in greeting.

Adam looked at the other man's hand, set the duffle bag by his feet and shook it.

Bee grinned at Malika, who rolled her eyes.

'Artie Bosh,' Artie said.

'Adam,' said Adam.

'Mr C told me you were coming.'

Oliver said, 'Hey, Artie. Is Rachael here?'

'No, sorry, buddy. But maybe you can FaceTime her in the morning.'

Oliver looked down at himself. 'Only after I change clothes at Dad's house. I don't need girls seeing me in my Hulk pajamas.'

'Girls? What girls?' Bee ruffled his hair. 'Let's keep that singular, huh?'

He ducked away from her hand. 'Can we go on the plane now? I'm so tired. And there were so many bullets. And so many farts in my face.'

Artie nodded, still smiling, but now it had taken on a confused quality, like he hadn't totally understood the conversation. 'Yeah, sure, go on ahead. I'll take the dog for a walk?'

'Please and thank you,' Bee said, and Adam handed the leash over.

He hoisted the bag over his shoulder. 'You ready?'

Bee yawned. He popped a dimple and she turned to the plane to keep him from seeing her face flush. 'Let's go.'

The Eclipse 500 was a small jet, but it was clean, the tan leather of the seats and the dark grey carpet spotless. The jet sat six, including the pilot and co-pilot, with the other four leather chairs facing each other. Two were reclining seats, the other two a bench in the back with a pull-down armrest and cup holder.

Oliver plopped down on one of the recliners and curled up on his side. Malika grabbed every pillow off the bench and plopped on to the empty recliner, buckling up and burying herself underneath the cushions.

The pilot was someone Bee hadn't seen before. A handsome Black man, about her age, taller than most, with a suit well tailored to his svelte form. He flashed her a pleasant smile and said, 'Mrs C.' He gave Adam a once-over but didn't offer his hand the way Artie had. 'I'm Jimmy White.'

'Nice to meet you, Mr White. You gonna get us home safe?'

'Yes, ma'am.'

'I'm gonna take your word for that.' She collapsed on the bench seat across from Oliver and yawned again. 'I'm fading fast, guys.'

Oliver was already snoring.

Adam put the bag in an overhead compartment and sat with her on the bench. Her stomach did a flip, tightened, and she rested her head next to the window so she could look at the runway and not at the ghost from her past solid at her side.

Artie and Hogarth came in last. The dog tried once to jump on Oliver's chair, but after failing, he sneezed and lay down on the carpet. Artie and Mr White took their seats at the helm.

Within minutes, they were in the air, flying away from all the forces Alvarez had sent after her and her son.

She watched the lights of the city fade, glimmering like stars beneath her. Maybe they were escaping the mess Charlie had made, but they were going into another mess. The beach house was a sanctuary, sure, locked down like a fort. But it was Charlie's sanctuary. Filled with Charlie's men. And the man next to her was one Charlie had sent her way.

Did that make him Charlie's too?

She closed her eyes. She needed to talk to Adam. She knew she needed to talk to Adam. But talking about feelings and communicating and blah blah ick. Bee shuddered, hugged herself.

How do you even start a conversation like that?

Hey, my dude. I know I've been married and had a kid and gotten divorced, but I waited for you to call me for, like, a super long time, so where did you go? Why did you drop off the face of the earth?

If she was honest with herself, it wasn't asking the questions that scared her. It was the answers she might get that kept her from asking. Os had often paired Adam and Bee up on assignments. But once they'd hooked up, that was it – they were never together again. Os had told her that Adam was the type of man who loved 'em and left 'em – as cliche as that was. That he couldn't have relationships, because those were weaknesses that could be exploited. And then he told her she should try to move on in that way of his that made it clear it wasn't a suggestion.

She shuddered again.

'You OK?' Adam asked, his voice quiet.

Bee opened her eyes and waited for them to adjust to the low lighting. 'Yeah,' she said. 'Just can't get comfortable.' She leaned back on the seat, rocking her head side to side against the cushion of the headrest. 'You know, Adam, and don't get me wrong here: I'm super happy that it's you my ex hired. But I was thinking, like, what are the odds that it'd be you my ex would hire?'

His elbow brushed against hers when he leaned against their shared armrest. 'It ain't much of a coincidence.'

'Oh?' Bee stared at him in the low fluorescent light. 'How do you mean?'

'Cardello, he's definitely your type.'

That didn't answer her question, so Bee didn't respond to it.

'Good-looking, big wallet, too trusting,' Adam continued despite her silence. 'He reached out for recommendations, got hold of a mutual contact. When I saw your face in the report, I figured I'd do an old friend a favor.'

'He sent my face out?' Horror crawled over her skin. 'My *face*?' She glanced at Oliver and dropped her voice back down to a whisper. 'To who?'

Adam shrugged. 'I don't know. Everybody.'

'That idiot.' She held her head in both hands. 'That big dumb idiot.'

'Yeah.'

'So now, it really doesn't matter what the threat was, does it? Because now some people who think I'm dead realize I'm actually rather alive.'

He said, 'That's why I'm here.'

Bee worried her bottom lip. Could this be Os after all? Could Os have sent Adam? Was this really all Charlie's doing?

But Adam had never hurt her. He'd ghosted her, alone and confused, sure, but never had he hurt her. At least not physically. But she'd been so young and all heart, it hadn't taken much to shatter it.

Back on Os's crew, Adam had been in charge of the heavy lifting. More than just the muscle, he cleared the way. He made sure that the people doing the job could get to the goods. It wasn't in his job description to save her life. And yet he had, again and again.

What choice did she have but to trust him? At least until she and Oliver were safely behind the gates of the beach house and Charlie was dealt with.

'Hey,' he said. 'You sure you're OK?'

She undid her topknot, combed her fingers through her hair. 'I'm fine,' she said. 'I'm just . . . I'm processing.'

'Yeah, there's a lot going on. A lot of missing pieces.'

'A lot of missing pieces,' Bee agreed. 'But we'll be in New Jersey in what, two hours? The only thing then is, how do we keep Charlie from finding out we know each other?'

'Lie?'

'Yeah, we're gonna have to lie. We're gonna have to lie our butts off. Lie 'em clean off.'

He popped a dimple. 'You're revved up right now.'

'Charlie doesn't know about my past, Adam.' She braved a look at Oliver and found him sleeping. Malika's face was hidden behind pillows, but Bee assumed the nanny was asleep too. And even if she was awake, Malika knew everything anyway. 'Charlie doesn't know about Thomas Osbourn, and I'd like to keep it that way. I picked him because Os didn't have any hold over him or his business. Because if he finds out, he's liable to freak out. Freak the F out. Freak out on everybody's faces. And that would be bad for everybody. Especially me. Because I need you around protecting not only my face' – she circled her face with her finger – 'but that of my son as well. And Charlie is likely to keep you away from us if he finds out.'

Adam relaxed against his seat, stretched out his long, muscular legs and crossed his ankles. 'He still doesn't know? You guys have a ten-year-old kid.'

'He's got no idea,' Bee said. 'Zero. At some level it's – it's like – am I really that good? You know? When I found him, I was fully off the grid, so to speak. I had to use the old tricks to get his attention. Fall into him and have him catch me. Smile every time he lit a cigarette so he'd associate my happiness with his nicotine addiction. Stare into his eyes and really listen while he talked nonstop about himself.'

Adam nodded. 'Classics.'

'I made sure to show him I was good at math and puzzles. And he really took that to heart and believes to this day that's why I was a natural at, you know . . .'

'Theft. Grifting. General disregard for law, order and authority?'

'Yeah, all of the above.'

He laughed, quiet and carefree, and Bee watched the way his throat moved.

'Speaking of which,' she said, 'how is your lifting?'

'Hm?'

'You were easily the worst pickpocket I've ever seen in my life,' Bee teased. 'Just zero finesse. No subtlety. Using your thumb all willy-nilly.'

His face brightened in amusement obvious even in the low light of the plane. 'I'm not that bad.'

'No?' She raked her hair over one shoulder. 'Take my necklace.'

'That's not fair,' he said. 'First of all, you know it's coming?'

'Mhmm,' she agreed, waiting anyway.

'Second of all, I'm one-handed.'

'You think most women will let you put two hands around their necks?' Bee guffawed. 'I think not.'

He lifted up the armrest between them and moved closer. 'Why would I need to be stealing women's necklaces in the first place?'

Their knees bumped. 'If you're gonna be around my kid, you should be able to lift. It's a necessary skill as far as I'm concerned.'

'Your requirements for employees,' he began, stretching his arm out behind her, 'are far from standard.'

His fingertips ghosted across the nape of her neck, sending a shiver down her spine. 'Tickles.' She grinned. 'And I'm not a standard employer.'

He pulled his arm away, and she smiled brighter to hide the weird disappointment that filled her stomach.

'I could teach you.'

'To steal necklaces?'

'First of all, it's more than stealing. Anybody can steal with the right equipment.' She turned her body to him on the bench seat and rubbed her palm over his forearm. 'It's sleight of hand. It's distraction. It's almost magic.'

Bee slid her teeth over her bottom lip and leaned further into his personal space. She watched him from underneath her lashes, seeking out his hazel eyes. A comforting wave of familiarity and nostalgia rushed over her when she realized he still wore the same cologne he'd favored over a decade ago. The musky citrus scent had filled the cab of the truck transporting a million dollars' worth of diamonds they'd driven right out of the airport in Amsterdam. Only her fourth job with Os, and her first with Adam. What an introduction that heist had been. He'd taken out three armed guards without ever brandishing a weapon, and her heart had sparkled like their stolen goods.

He let her into his space without any resistance, the corners of his lips twitching up.

She raised her free hand and toyed with the collar of his shirt. 'I'm an excellent teacher.'

He ducked his head, his stubble grazing the tip of her ear, and whispered, 'I don't doubt that.'

Bee's smile was quickly overtaken by a yawn.

Adam chuckled.

'I guess all that adrenaline is wearing off,' she said, stretching her arms above her head. 'I'm tired now. What time is it anyway?'

Adam checked his watch. 'All right,' he said. 'I'm impressed.'

Bee dangled his silver Rolex from her index finger. 'This is a really nice watch, Adam. You have great taste.' She put it on. 'It's a little big for me, but I think I can make it work.'

He tried to look annoyed. 'You're not going to give it back?'

'I earned this fair and square.'

'You cheated, and you know it.'

'Cheated?' Bee put a hand over her heart, his watch glinting in the moonlight. 'However do you mean?'

'You used your, you know' – he bobbed his head back and forth as he searched for the right phrase – 'feminine wiles.'

'Uh-uh.' She shook a finger. 'I used distraction. The fact that I'm a female with wiles is irrelevant.'

His flimsy annoyance broke with a wide grin. 'You know you're going to have to give that back.'

Bee yawned again, but this time for real. 'Oh jeez.' She knuckled her eyes. 'I really am tired.'

Adam sighed, held out an arm. 'Come here.'

'Are you sure?' she asked but did it anyway, her back against his side and her legs stretched across her seat. He wrapped his arm around her shoulders, and she held his hand over her stomach.

'Oh, you're warm.' She yawned and buried her head into his bicep. Underneath his trademark cologne was the smell of deodorant trying its damnedest and nearly succeeding.

It wasn't the most pleasant scent she'd ever smelled. But she was pretty sure she didn't smell like a bouquet of flowers either.

He squeezed her fingers. 'Get some sleep.'

She smiled. 'You should too.'

'Yeah. I'll try.' Adam inexpertly reached for his watch.

She grabbed his wrist and murmured, 'Too slow.'

He chuckled, and her head bobbed on his chest.

EIGHT

Charlie had arranged for an all-black Chevy Suburban to be waiting for their arrival at the private airstrip in Jersey. Mr White drove, Artie in the passenger seat. Hogarth, Malika and Oliver claimed the bench in the back so they could continue sleeping. That left the middle two captain's chairs for Bee and Adam.

The sun was on Bee's side. She held a hand over her squinted eyes and tried to think happy thoughts. Tried not to be irrationally angry at the sun for shining when it was Charlie who'd ruined her life. Charlie who'd done something stupid. Charlie who was burning too hot now that he didn't have her to direct his energy.

'Here.' Adam offered her his aviators.

She blinked at herself in their mirrored lenses. 'Are you sure?'

'Eh, sun's on your side.'

She smiled, fingers grazing his when she took the sunglasses. 'Thank you.'

Less than an hour later, the guard at the gate waved them in.

Oliver stirred in the backseat. 'Hey, we made it,' he said, his voice laced with sleep.

The Cardello Beach House was at the end of a secluded road, the only one around for a half mile, with its own stretch of shore that was accessible by a wooden ramp in the backyard.

The landscaping was minimal; seagrass and sand surrounded the two-story grey home on all four sides. The windows were large and open and framed in white. And standing at the front door, the door that Bee herself had painted green, was Charlie. He held a cigarette up to his lips and waved.

Like he was expecting them.

Like everything was OK.

Like her whole world hadn't just crashed down around her.

Her breath quickened, heart racing into high gear. She clenched her jaw and her fists, anger crawling up over her hands and arms and shoulders.

A lovely, young – *very* young actually – woman bounded out of the house. Her black hair was long and loose, her brown skin glistened in the sunlight like she'd recently spray painted herself with glitter and her sheer, purple lingerie dress left little to the imagination.

'Dad!' Oliver hollered from the backseat. He scrambled to leave the vehicle. 'Cassie!'

'Holy cow.' Sleep drenched Malika's amazed tone of voice. '*That's* Charlie's girlfriend? She's flipping stunning.'

Bee followed Oliver to the beach house.

Charlie pulled the cigarette away from his lips long enough to smile. 'Welcome home.' His hair was an unruly mop of un-gelled curls. He wore a white button-down shirt, the collar loose and the sleeves rolled up, tucked into a pair of belted dark grey trousers. 'You look like you could use a drink. Maybe a shower.'

Bee, glaring, marched up the front steps, her hands balled into fists at her sides.

'Hi!' Cassie chirped, holding out a hand. Oliver was still wrapped around her waist. 'I'm Cassie. It's so nice to meet you, Beatrice. I've heard so many great things about you!'

Bee begrudgingly stopped making a fist and shook the other woman's hand. 'Nice to meet you too. Please – call me Bee.'

'If you need anything, anything at all, let me know,' Cassie said. She put her arms around the Cardello boys at her sides, one happy family posing for a Christmas card picture. 'We definitely want you to feel comfortable in our home.'

The muscle above Bee's right eyebrow twitched. She met Charlie's eyes, the same color brown as their son's, and frowned.

He grinned back at her.

'Hi,' said Malika. 'I'm Malika.' She offered Cassie her hand. 'How are you? I'm the nanny. This is a lovely home. How are you? Oh, I said that already.'

Cassie giggled. 'I'm fine, thank you. How was your trip?'

'Eventful,' Malika said. 'Um. You wouldn't happen to have a phone, would you? Like a cell phone? Or a laptop? Both, honestly, would be great.'

Adam joined their group, the dog leash in his hand, and Charlie patted him on the shoulder. 'Good work, Gage.' He took a puff. 'It's nice when a man lives up to his considerable reputation.'

Bee did her best to smile at the young woman that her son was trying to turn into his jacket. 'Would you mind taking Oliver to his room, Cassie? He seems rather attached to you, and we've had a very trying day. Night. Whatever.'

'Of course!' Cassie ruffled Oliver's hair. 'Let's get you settled, huh? And we'll find you a computer, Malika.'

'Great.' Malika finger gunned Bee. 'I'm going with them. See you later.'

The three of them disappeared behind the green door, and Bee let the smile fall off her face.

It landed with a thud somewhere near Charlie's feet.

Charlie reached out with two fingers and lifted her chin, the smoke from his cigarette curling around her nose. His boyishly handsome face contorted into ugliness. 'No one was supposed to touch you,' he whispered.

She jerked away from him. 'What the hell is going on?'

He shrugged. 'It's kind of a long story and I'm hungry, so—'

'Why did you hire this man and not tell me he was coming?' Bee pointed a thumb at Adam. 'Why would you mess with Alvarez, of all people?'

'Ah.' He pointed his cigarette at Adam. 'So you told her the truth, did you?'

Adam said, 'I thought it was for the best.'

Bee stomped her foot. 'You're talking to me right now, not him!'

Charlie grinned. 'You're so cute when you're angry.'

'Shut up!' Bee pinched her nose. 'Oh, I'm going to kill you. I'm going to kill you so hard.'

'Look, let's talk about this over some food, OK?' He scuffed out the butt beneath his shiny brown Stefano Beyer wingtips. 'You guys have been traveling, and I started some ribs on the smoker a few hours ago to celebrate you coming home. You're welcome, by the way. Got up when there was just the moon and the mosquitoes outside to keep me company.'

He didn't wait for her to respond, instead walking into the house and leaving the door open for them to follow.

Bee was too angry to walk.

'Well,' said Adam, 'that went better than expected.'

She huffed. 'I'm serious. I'm gonna kill him, Adam. I'm gonna kill him.'

'As long as my check clears first.'

Bee turned and stormed across the threshold into her old home.

Nothing had changed; the Degas ballerinas hung in the same proud place above the fireplace. The same L-shaped grey couch in the corner. The same round dining room table next to the kitchen island with its white marble counter. The only thing different was the increase of men in cheap suits.

She counted four of them all spread out in the main part of the house. All of them in suits and ties. All of them with shined, black pleather shoes.

Oliver came bounding in from the back patio, a beaming smile on his face. 'Come on, Mom! Dad's almost done with the ribs, and then we're gonna go swimming!'

Bee chewed the inside of her cheek. 'Great. Just great.'

Charlie stood at the grill with tongs in his hand, platinum Cartier aviators on his face.

Cassie sat at the wooden patio table next to Bee, staring at him as if barbecuing ribs was the equivalent to painting a masterpiece. And as a painter of masterpieces herself – she only forged the best after all – Bee rolled her eyes in disagreement.

Adam and Oliver were in the background, running in and out of the waves, trying to only get their feet wet whilst simultaneously soaking the other. It appeared to be a contest that Oliver was gleefully losing.

Malika was upstairs, fiddling with whatever electronics Charlie's young girlfriend had managed to find.

Bee frowned and counted the men in cheap suits who stood outside. One behind the grill, one watching the beach, one hovering near the table and one facing the road. Three of them Bee had never seen before, but it was Mr White behind the grill. He'd taken off his jacket, exposing the Glock in his shoulder holster.

She knew, of course, that everyone her husband employed had to be packing, but seeing the gun and knowing it was there were two totally different things. And after their rather eventful day yesterday, she wanted Oliver to focus on playing rather than the fact that things were still dangerous.

'Mr White,' she said. 'Where's your jacket?'

He looked at her over the top of his Oakleys. 'Inside, ma'am.'

'Can you fetch it please?' Bee's lips parted in something vaguely resembling a smile. 'Before Oliver sees your weapon.'

Charlie opened the grill. 'Mrs Cardello is the boss when she's on the property, boys. Do as she says.'

Mr White walked into the house and Bee sighed.

'It's Ms, Charlie. Ms. I haven't been Mrs anything for the better part of two years.'

He picked up his empty glass and waved it at Cassie. 'How about a refill, sweetheart?'

'Sure thing!' She hopped out of the seat next to Bee. 'Would you like anything? I make a great cosmo!'

Bee blinked up at her. 'I'm fine, thanks.'

Cassie skipped over to Charlie, kissed him on the cheek and took his empty glass inside.

Bee watched her the whole time, her eyes stuck on the short hem of her dress. 'How old is she?'

'Twenty-one.'

'So at least she can handle refills legally,' Bee said. 'You're a pig.'

He grinned in agreement. 'I need something to keep me warm at night, Beebee.'

'She's barely older than Malika', Bee told the tabletop. 'She was barely eleven when Oliver was born. Gross.'

Mr White and Cassie walked back outside at the same time, each with the items they'd been tasked to retrieve. Cassie dropped hers off with another kiss on Charlie's cheek.

'Oliver!' Charlie called. 'Ribs are ready!'

NINE

Grilled corn on the cob and barbecue ribs piled high on silver platters sat in the center of the wooden patio table. Oliver bounded into his seat and dove into the ribs, wet sand clinging to his forearms and fingertips.

'Easy, easy,' Charlie urged at the same time Bee cried out for him to wash his hands.

But it was too late. A fine layer of sand coated the top three ribs.

'What?' Oliver pulled the ribs in question on to his plate. 'It's better with a little crunch.'

Bee mimed gagging, and Oliver laughed at her around a bite, sauce already on both of his cheeks.

'Isn't this nice?' Charlie watched Cassie fill his plate. 'A beautiful day with my family. It's been too long.'

Bee refused Cassie's offer of the tongs. 'Just what do you think is happening right now?'

Adam came out of the house with a damp hand towel. Oliver took it from him but then pretended he had no idea what it was for.

'Gage, pull up a chair,' Charlie invited with a wicked grin. 'You've earned your place at the table.'

Adam froze next to Oliver, his hands motionless above the damp towel, before he took a step back. 'I'm fine. Thanks.' With a nod, he moved to stand next to Mr White by the French doors.

'We were attacked in our home and fled here for safety,' Bee told her ex-husband. 'And yet you're acting like we came all the way to Jersey for a beach vacation. Are you really that delusional? What are you doing?'

Charlie sipped at his drink, studying her from behind the thick rim of his whiskey glass. 'Things are complicated.'

'I'm a pretty smart girl, Charles,' Bee replied. 'Lay it on me. I'll try to follow along.'

He leaned over to their son. 'Hey, Olly, why don't you take your lunch inside? Mr White over there has been going on and on about how he's better at *Halo* than everybody, but I know you could beat him.'

Oliver rolled his eyes. 'Yeah, OK,' he said and took his plate full of food inside.

'I'm gonna need another cigarette,' Charlie told his girlfriend.

She smiled brightly and went off in search of a box.

When they were alone – not counting the paid thugs who stood at all four points around them of course – Charles Cardello relaxed back in his chair.

'I got a little in over my head.'

Admitting any mistake whatsoever wasn't something Charles Cardello normally admitted to anyone, at any time, for any reason, so Bee was at a loss for words.

'Wha . . .?' she managed.

He sighed. 'It was an easy enough target at the end of the day. Things have been pretty quiet since the take. Somebody ratted me out. That's why all this is coming down now. All I gotta do is find the rat.'

'Alvarez is an easy enough target? Is that right? The biggest gangster Miami has ever seen since Pablo freaking Escobar is an *easy target*?'

'Look, I didn't actually think anything would come of it or I wouldn't have done it. The only reason he figured out it was me was 'cause of a rat.'

Her mouth fell open. Bee worked her jaw from side to side and snapped it closed. 'You think I care how he figured out it was you? You think I give a flying fuck how he figured out it was you? They came into my house, Charlie. My home. They took Oliver from his bed!'

Charlie frowned. 'Everything's all right now, Beebee. We're together, yeah? We can fix anything.'

She collapsed back in her chair, massaging her fingers along her temples. 'I'm gonna need one of those cigarettes.'

Charlie smiled at her, the wrinkles around his mouth – formed from years of chain-smoking – lining it like parentheses.

She wanted to punch him. Right in his parenthetical smile.

'What on earth were you thinking?' Bee asked, too tired to take a swing. 'Why the hell would you steal thirty-seven and a half million dollars from Alvarez, of all people?'

'The opportunity presented itself.'

Cassie came out of the house, a dark grey suit jacket over her arm. 'Here.' She handed him the coat and a red-and-white box. 'It's getting a little chilly out.'

He kept the jacket on the table but lit up a cigarette straight away. 'You still want one?'

Bee glared at him.

He shrugged and puffed.

Cassie settled into her seat, smiled at Bee and reached for Charlie's hand. He didn't refuse it but didn't quite accept it either, and Bee arched an eyebrow.

'Who are you?' she asked Cassie.

The young woman blinked. 'I'm sorry?'

'Daughter?' Bee guessed. 'Cousin?'

'Niece,' Charlie answered.

'Was this your idea?' Bee asked. 'Get a gangster in your bed and whisper in his ear until he helps you rip off your uncle?'

Cassie gasped. 'I did nothing of the sort!'

'It's not like that,' Charlie said. 'Alvarez and I are partners in some— Well, we handle a particular import from Cuba. Cassie and I met innocently enough.'

'Uncle Theo even gave us his blessing,' Cassie said. 'The theft fell into our laps.'

Bee laughed. 'Sure. Thirty-seven and a half million dollars just fell into your lap! That's how it works! Especially Alvarez's money! Super easy, am I right?'

Charlie took a big puff of his cigarette. 'You always said there was no such thing as security, only opportunity. And the opportunity arose.'

Bee curled her top lip over her teeth in a snarl and glanced over to where Adam stood stone-faced, staring down the beach. If he was listening, he gave no indication.

'You are delusional – as usual,' she said.

Charlie rose to his feet, leaning his hands on the table to put his face closer to hers. 'There is nothing delusional about me, Beatrice.'

Cassie rushed to take cover in the relative safety of the house, squeaking out, 'I, um, I think I'm going to go check on Oliver!'

'You are nothing but delusional!' Bee jumped to her feet. 'And now we're being hunted by Theo Alvarez, your girlfriend's uncle? I always knew you'd be the death of me, Charlie!'

She stormed towards the beach, passing Adam on the way. She caught him watching her from behind his sunglasses.

Charlie snatched his jacket off the table and trailed after her, sputtering. 'Death of you? Bee, I love you! I'd never hurt you!'

'Yeah, well, Anakin loved Padme too, but she still ended up dead in the end, didn't she?' She left her flip-flops on the ramp and kept walking barefoot. She couldn't stomp in any satisfying capacity on the sand, so she resorted to pacing up and down along the shoreline, let the waves skim over her toes.

Bee closed her eyes, searching for a way to communicate effectively with her ex. 'I love my life, Charlie, and I love my little family. Oliver and Malika. They're the most important part of my life. If you loved me, you wouldn't risk those things.'

'I am your family,' Charlie said. 'Oliver is your family. The girl who works for you is not your family.'

She walked up to him, one finger in his face. 'You're not my family anymore.'

Charlie's eyes crossed staring at her finger. 'We're always going to be family, Bee, no matter what a piece of paper says.' He blinked his eyes straight and looked at her with a deep frown between his parenthetical wrinkles. 'It's getting colder. Put on my jacket.'

She reached for it, but he first pulled out the red-and-white box of cigarettes and a small yellow lighter.

'Are you done?' Bee asked, arm still outstretched.

'Yeah, yeah.' He stuck the cigarette in his mouth and handed her the jacket.

'Thank you.' She curled her lips into a soft smile, her blue eyes seeking out his dark brown ones, and blinked prettily when he peered at her over the flame of his lighter. 'So thoughtful.'

Bee plucked the box of cigarettes from his hand, stuck them into his jacket pocket, sighed and then ran away.

'What—' Charlie called out, but it was too late.

She balled up his suit jacket and threw it into the ocean.

'Hey! That's a six-thousand-dollar jacket! What are you doing?'

The jacket washed back up near her feet with an incoming wave, and she waded further into the water to kick it into the current. 'Yeah, well, it will make for one well-dressed shark now, won't it?'

'Don't be ridiculous – sharks don't have arms!'

Bee shoved all her fingers in her mouth and screamed. The cold gray water lapped at her calves, soaked her sweatpants. She stomped through it to get closer to her ex-husband, reeled her leg back and splashed him for all she was worth.

'*You idiot!*'

He spat out ocean water, his cigarette a useless wet stick in his hand. 'I am *not* an idiot, Bee! I am an incredibly successful businessman.'

'Oh, is that right?' she shouted at the cloudy sky. 'That's what it's called these days! You're a businessman!'

'I know what I'm doing!' Charlie threw his cigarette down the beach. 'I always know what I'm doing. I'm always five steps ahead!'

'You are so stupid you don't even know how stupid you are! That's how stupid you are!'

'Hey!' came Adam's reprimanding voice. He jogged towards their fight and admonished both of them with a powerful glare. 'Oliver can hear you.'

Bee crossed her arms over her chest and looked away, not quite able to bear the full brunt of Adam's disappointment.

Charlie sighed down at his ruined wingtips.

'Now, come on.' Adam nodded towards the house. 'Let's go inside and handle this like adults.'

TEN

Bee followed Charlie across the patio, through the sliding glass door and into the main living area. Malika, Oliver and Cassie whispered to each other behind the island counter in the kitchen. It was mostly Cassie and Oliver whispering, and Malika staring at Charlie's girlfriend with a dazed expression, like at any moment little clouds shaped like hearts would appear around her and she would hover two feet off the ground.

'Baby,' Cassie said, closing in on Charlie the moment he stepped foot in the house, 'I think Oliver, the nanny and I are gonna head out and find him those books he likes.' She held out her palm with a smile. 'Please and thank you.'

Charlie pulled out his wallet. 'What books you reading?' His eyes were bright with interest, his wet clothes the only reminder of their screaming fight on the beach.

'Percy Jackson,' Oliver said. 'Me and Mom have been reading the first one, but we weren't able to finish it.'

Bee ran her fingers through his hair. She could still see the gun pressed to his temple if she looked hard enough.

Charlie handed Cassie three hundred-dollar bills. 'Buy him all of them,' he said. 'See if they have a collector's edition or something. Actually' – he pulled out another two hundred – 'stop somewhere and buy him some clothes. The ones he's got here are from Christmas and it looks like he's outgrown 'em.'

'You got it!' Cassie pressed a kiss to the corner of Charlie's mouth. 'Come on, Oliver. Let's go have some fun!'

Charlie motioned for Mr White to go with them. 'You don't look away for even a second.'

The four of them left, Cassie and Oliver's laughter audible even after the door closed.

Charlie diplomatically waved a hand at the table, and Bee rolled her eyes but took a seat. He dismissed Adam with a look.

Adam nodded once and moved to guard the entrance.

Charlie pulled out a flat silver container from his back pocket and removed a cigarette.

Bee groaned. 'Can we not smoke inside the house please?'

He froze, looked at the cigarette in his hand and back to her. 'This is my house,' he said, but she wasn't sure if he was talking to her or the cancer stick.

'There's a Degas on the wall, hmm? You remember?'

'Yeah,' Charlie sighed and put the cigarette away. 'I remember.'

'The ten-million-dollar irreplaceable painting? Maybe we don't ruin it with cigarette smoke?'

He held up his empty hands. 'I'm obeying you. You've won.' He sat down across from her and fiddled with the buttons on his shirt. 'You could've taken it with you. I did buy it for you.'

She stared past him, at the ballerinas dancing on the wall, and frowned. 'That's why I didn't take it.'

'Oh my God,' he said. 'I don't get you sometimes, Bee. I really don't. Is it because I bought it legitimately?'

'No, it's because you bought it to bribe me not to divorce you.'

He shook his head. 'That's not entirely accurate.'

'You also didn't buy it legitimately. You bought it from a fence. It was stolen. You just technically didn't do the stealing.'

'Eh. Semantics.'

Bee tried to rake her fingers through her hair but got stuck halfway on a knot. She blew out a loud breath through puffed cheeks and stared up at the ceiling. 'Can we get back on track please, instead of repeating this same stupid argument that we've had—' Bee stopped herself. She wasn't going to let him get to her again. 'Yes, back on track. OK.' She exhaled and inhaled several more times, eyes still closed, and focused on the way her stomach rose and fell.

When she opened her eyes, Charlie was staring at her like she was the ten-million-dollar Degas painting.

'Knock it off.'

'What? I wasn't doing anything.'

'I don't like the way you look at me.'

He shrugged. 'How was I looking at you?'

'Like you still love me.'

'I do! I've been— Have I not made myself perfectly, abundantly clear? I'm just waiting for you to get over whatever this' – he circled two fingers in the air – 'is.'

'Divorce,' Bee snapped. 'You're waiting for me to get over divorcing you.'

'Yeah.'

She closed her eyes and focused on her breathing again. In and out. In and out. 'OK,' she said, 'so what's your plan?'

'I hired the best man I could to keep you safe and get you to me.' He jerked a thumb at Adam. 'The very, very best. You should see his credentials, Bee. They're gonna make action movies about this guy.'

'Charlie,' she said, her voice tight, explaining something simple to a simpleton. 'Charlie, what's next?'

He scratched his nose. 'Well. We're here now. And this beach house is like a fort. We've got the only road in blocked off.'

'Yeah, which is great until Alvarez rolls up with triple the manpower. Or takes a couple of his go-fast boats from Miami and comes at us by sea.'

Charlie said, 'Yeah.'

She nodded hard. 'Yeah.'

He picked at dirt under his fingernail. 'So, I was hoping you'd be able to help with that. You know. With an exit strategy. We made such a great team, back in the day. Remember?'

She remembered. She remembered getting a courier drunk at a bar, lifting his wallet, sliding Charlie his credentials. She remembered the two of them stealing the courier's four million dollars' worth of untraceable gold nuggets – the heist that led to them buying the beach house.

She remembered Charlie, young and handsome, only needing her support and the barest of whispers to knock off the head of the family and take his place.

She remembered being locked away after, put on a pedestal with a sign that said FOR DISPLAY PURPOSES ONLY. Told she was too fragile for the bloody war he was fighting.

Charlie reached for her hand, and she yanked it away. He smiled all the same. 'You're always so good with that kinda shit, Bee. So good at solving problems.'

'That's why I got divorced,' Bee said, a harsh enunciation on every word. 'Solved the biggest problem right there.'

He collapsed back against his seat like he'd been shot. 'Why you gotta be like this? Huh?'

Bee's whole body started to quake. 'Are you serious? Are you *serious* right now, Charlie? *You* are the reason our son was pulled out of his bed at gunpoint!'

'I know, I know, I—'

'You were so busy getting it in, you didn't stop to think about the consequences of your choices! Like always, Charlie! You never think things through!'

'Now, that's not fair. Look at all this!' He flapped both arms around. 'All of this is because of me thinking things through.'

She wiped her mouth with the back of her shaking hand. 'You are out of your mind.'

'Oh, and I suppose you're not out of yours?' Charlie huffed. 'Let me remind you that you're a thief, Bee. Just like me.'

'I am not a thief like you. I am an exceptional thief. And I can't believe you just made me quote Hans Gruber!'

He laughed, a delighted, happy smile overtaking his lips. He looked at her, eyes shining again, and she felt something inside her skull snap. The click in her brain as audible as the sound of her shins skidding across the tabletop. As loud as his chair falling back from the force of her and hitting the ground. As persistent as him gasping for breath when she wrapped her hands around his windpipe.

'This isn't fucking funny!' she shouted from her position above him, straddling his chest. She reeled back one arm and landed a solid blow to his cheek.

Adam grabbed her under her arms and lifted her off Charlie. 'All right, you got one good one in.'

She kicked and flailed. 'I'm not done with him yet!'

'Oh, I think you are. Don't want Oliver coming back to his dad all beat up, yeah?'

And while Bee could understand that Adam had a point, the fury she felt pulsing through her brain kept her from calming down. 'Oliver had a gun to his head! A gun, Charlie!'

Adam set her down but stood directly in front of her, an immovable force not letting her anywhere near the object of her rage.

She tried to get around him anyway. 'We had bikers shoot at us!' she yelled around Adam's arm. 'Over and over again! They shot out the windows of my car! What you did wasn't only stupid, but it almost killed our son!'

Charlie sat up, elbows on his knees and head in his hands, and groaned. 'You think I don't know that? You think I don't hate that? I got selfish, Bee, and it cost Oliver. It cost you.'

He looked up at her from where he sat, so very small, his hair a mess, one cheek pink. 'There is nothing more important in this world to me than the two of you.'

Bee's eyes rolled so hard they almost got stuck in the back of her head. 'Except for money,' she said to the inside of her skull.

He hung his head. 'Like you're so different, right? That's why we make such a good team, Bee. We're the same.'

'*The same?*' Bee shook with anger. Flames engulfed her from the inside out. 'You have ruined my life and our son's life. I'm sure the house by now is burned. I haven't had a chance to check the security cameras, but how much do you wanna bet there are Feds parked outside? What about *my* paintings? Oliver's baby pictures are in the house, Charlie! Pictures of my brother. My mom!'

'I'll send someone,' Charlie said. 'It's not a big deal.'

'It's my house, Charlie! It's my life! And it's as good as over, so I'd say that's a pretty big deal!'

He stared at her, frowning, and it struck her then how little he'd changed since they'd first met all those years ago. How much he'd passed on to their son. A handsome, boyish face, far too young for the fancy suits and serious expressions he wore.

'We'll figure it out. Together,' said Charlie, sincere. Clueless. 'Just like old times.'

Her fists clenched at her sides, and she walked into Adam's chest.

'Ugh!' Bee shoved him. 'Why are you protecting him?'

Adam dipped his head low and caught her eye. 'I'm not protecting him.'

She frowned.

Charlie rose to his feet and grabbed the silver case out of his back pocket. 'I'm gonna smoke one outside, calm down before Oliver gets back.' He approached them, Adam still standing in between, and stared down at his shoes. 'I'm sorry, Bee. I hate what happened to Oliver and what happened to you.'

Bee watched him walk out on to the patio, still angry but not so blindly furious. Now all she could see was the impossible task before her.

'I have to somehow convince Theo freaking Alvarez to not kill us after my idiot ex stole his money.' She massaged her fingers along her forehead in a futile attempt to force her mind to work. 'You know, I heard that one time, one of his deliveries got intercepted, right? So he took the guy responsible and the guy's family.

His little kids, his wife, his sixty-year-old mom. And he made the family watch while he peeled the guy's face off. Guy was still alive of course. Because why would you peel the face off a dead man? What sort of point does that prove?'

Her stomach twisted. 'And then he killed everybody in that family. One by one. Oh God.' She bent over and grabbed her knees. 'Can you imagine how scared those kids were? Watching that happen to their dad? Watching their whole family executed? Oh God.'

She bolted around Adam and for the stairs, only to freeze in the hallway unsure of which room she should enter. Certainly not the master. Not anymore. Oliver's bedroom? The guest room?

She opened the hallway closet door and found the mink coat Charlie had bought for her years ago that she'd never been able to bring herself to wear. It was warm and terrible, soft and gross, and she closed the closet door and hid beneath it.

ELEVEN

A soft knock and a softer female voice forced Bee out from under the coat.

'Bee?' Cassie said. 'Are you in there?'

Bee wiped her nose on the soft fur. 'How did you know?'

'Oh, the crying,' Cassie answered. 'I mean, I can hear you pretty good. Not like super loud. I don't think they can hear you downstairs. But I was walking by and, anyway, can we talk?'

Bee slumped forward and searched the darkness for anything to bang against her head. When no hammer materialized, she thumped her temple against the wall. 'Sure, step into my office.'

Cassie opened the door a crack and peeked inside. 'Nice coat,' she said and shut the door behind her.

Bee lifted the fur so she could slide in next to her.

'Is this real?' Cassie pulled it on to her lap.

Bee nodded then realized the other woman couldn't see what she was doing. 'Yeah. Charlie got it for me when I was pregnant, but I cried about all the animals that died for it, so it's lived its life here in this closet.'

'Well, he has good taste,' she said.

Bee chuckled, empty. 'Yeah.'

The two of them sat together, cuddled under the mink coat, but neither spoke. Bee rested against the wall, eyes closed, and stretched out her legs as far as they could go in the cramped space. She heard Cassie's sudden intake of breath, the way she held it, then released it before trying again.

Bee waited.

'Why are you crying in the closet?' Cassie finally asked. 'Did – did something happen when I was out?'

Charlie's doomed us all, Bee thought but didn't say. *My whole life is over when I was so close to getting it started again*. 'No,' she said. 'Not really. It's . . . I feel like, no matter where I go in this house, someone is waiting to talk to me about their feelings. I need a break.'

Cassie's voice was very small when she replied, 'Oh.'

Bee said, 'Not with you. Of course. You know how men are. They won't shut up about their opinions, like what they think is the most important thing ever.'

'I see.'

Bee opened her eyes and tried to find Cassie's profile in the darkness. 'You said you wanted to talk?'

'Oh yeah. It's nothing,' Cassie said. Her shoulders scraped the wall when she shrugged. 'I was so excited to meet you. Charlie and Oliver only ever talk about how amazing you are, and I wanted to touch base with you and, well, make sure we're on the same page. I want us all to be a family. Together.'

Bee's opened eyes widened so much they almost bugged out of her head. 'Why?' she asked. 'Cassie, you're young and obviously kind and caring. You don't have to be mixed up with Charlie anymore. You can get out. You know where the money is.' Bee dropped her voice to a whisper. 'Go get it and give it back to your uncle, and claim you were taken advantage of. He'll forgive you. Or even better – take the money and run! Get out of the country. Have a new life away from men like Charlie.'

'Charlie is a good man,' Cassie said, voice stern.

Bee slunk away from her.

'He's a good man. And trust me, I know. I've lived my life in my uncle's shadow. He's an awful person. He deserved what we did. Charlie saved me from my uncle. He rescued me. He is a good man, Bee.'

'No,' Bee said, 'he's really not.'

Cassie stiffened, took in a sharp breath, and Bee decided to change the subject.

'I could use a shower.'

'There's fresh towels in Oliver's bathroom,' Cassie answered in a clipped tone.

Bee ran her fingers over the mink. 'I need pajamas.'

Cassie jumped to her feet, the coat falling on top of Bee's head, and darted out of the closet. 'I'll go get you some!'

A tank top, a hoodie, yoga pants, a comb and moisturizer had been carefully laid on the extra twin bed in Oliver's room while she'd showered.

They weren't her clothes, but they were close to her size. Bee felt a tug on her heart.

The gangster's niece was thoughtful, if nothing else.

'Fine. Whatever.' She dropped the towel and got dressed. 'She's a nice person. So what?'

She combed her hair, moisturized her face and arms and legs, and pouted her lips.

'I really needed this,' she told the lotion.

It didn't reply, for obvious reasons.

Bee rolled her eyes. 'Just because she thought I might need a little pampering doesn't mean I have to like her. OK?'

The lotion remained an inanimate object.

There was a knock on the door.

'Yeah!'

Adam poked his head in, then held up a bottle of champagne and two glasses. 'You look like you could use a drink.'

Bee loved the back porch of the beach house. She loved being away from the world, with nothing but the ocean before her, the moon shining on the waves as they capped white on the shore. But Charlie had given her everything she'd asked for in the divorce and more. His only request had been the beach house. And what could she say to that? She didn't plan on ever being in New Jersey again. Plus the house in Biscayne Bay was bigger and didn't come with stations waiting for hired killers.

'Why are you hiding in the corner?' The light of the mosquito-repellent torches silhouetted Adam's frame. 'Come sit next to me at the table.' Charlie's table. *Cassie's* table.

'I'm not hiding,' Bee said from her hiding spot. She sat against the wall of the house, stretching her legs out on the wooden patio. 'I just don't want anyone to see me drinking.'

She brought her skinny champagne glass to her lips and chugged until her throat burned. The champagne was nice but, between the two of them, disappeared quick.

Bee frowned. She couldn't remember how many glasses Adam had actually had. But she'd drunk her fair share of it. Not enough really, but a lot all the same.

'Maybe you should get to bed,' Adam said.

'Pfft,' Bee spat on herself. 'You.'

'Me what?'

'You bed.' Bee took a quick sip of her drink. 'You do it. I'm fine here. It's my house, isn't it?'

Adam tapped his finger on the table they'd eaten ribs at hours earlier. 'I suppose it used to be.'

Bee took offense to that. 'I take offense to that, Mr Gage!'

He huffed.

'This is my house! And she just, she just waltzes around like, like what?' Bee shook her head then stopped when the world started to spin. Her eyes grew wide, and she focused her line of sight on the flickering flame of the closest torch. 'You know what the worst part is?'

'Hm?'

'I like her.' Bee set her empty glass down and drank directly from the bottle. 'I like bubbles too.' She burped. 'Do you know what the first commandment of grifting is?'

Adam looked at her. 'Don't get drunk?'

Bee thought about it. 'No. No, it's be a patient listener. But don't get drunk is on there somewhere. I don't remember where.' She pressed the cool bottle against her forehead. 'I bring that up to say that if I were a little tipsy – which, I'm totes fine, bee tee dubs. But if I were, it's because I am one hundred percent . . .' She furrowed her brow against the bottle, struggling for the word. 'Authentic. Currently. Not always.'

'But right now.'

'Yep. Right now.' Bee held up the champagne bottle. 'To Vister . . . no. Victor. Ludwig. No, that's piano.' She blew a raspberry in thought. 'Lustig. That's it! Ha!'

She drained the bottle and dropped it, the clang of the glass on the wood louder than the waves rolling in on the sand. 'He sold the Eiffel Tower. And got away with it.' She burped again. 'A true hero.'

'That reminds me . . . where was it?' Adam took a long sip of his drink. 'Monaco.'

Bee giggled. 'Yeah.'

'You sold that bridge, Bee. You sold that bridge to the King of Monaco. His own fucking bridge.'

Bee waved like a queen in a parade. 'For twice what it was worth. Don't make me say the name of it though. It was something very French.' She tried to stand. 'Oh shit.' The house tilted on its side, and she held out her hands to steady it. 'Easy, girl,' she told the wall.

'OK.' Adam stood up. 'Let me help you.'

'I'm fine!' Bee jumped up straight, then wished for death when the whole ocean spun around her. 'Oh no.'

Her feet slipped. She grabbed for the wall but missed, stumbling into Adam's arms.

'I got you.' He helped her stand. 'You OK?'

She brushed him off. 'I told you, I'm fine.'

'Let me help you, Shelby.'

Bee tried to prop her hip against a chair. She overshot, landing butt first on the patio floor.

'Ow!' She hid her face in her hands in a feeble attempt to hide the sob that escaped. 'I don't know how to get out of this.'

'Hey.' Adam kneeled in front of her. 'It's OK.'

'It is not OK!' Bee wiped her nose. 'I'm blank. I've got no ideas. I can't even feel guilty about all the therapy Oliver's gonna need 'cause we aren't gonna live long enough to get it!'

'Maybe you're coming at this the wrong way.' He picked her up under her arms and hauled her to her feet. 'Maybe – maybe you should try to get Charlie to tell you where the money is. And then maybe, you grab it. And you get the hell out of dodge.'

She hung her head. 'I said the same thing to Cassie.'

'I can help you, Shelby. I can help you get the money. I can keep you and Oliver safe.'

He'd kept them safe so far. He protected them from the Georgians, saved the day when they were being pursued by white guys on bikes, stayed cool when questioned by corrupt troopers. But it didn't matter. He couldn't keep them safe forever. Nobody could keep anybody safe forever. Men like Alvarez, men like Os, once they had a hold of you, they held on tight and dragged you down. She couldn't go back to that world, couldn't fall back into that pit of an existence, so deep and so dark until the only way out was to stand on corpses.

'I can't do it, Adam.' Fat tears rolled off her chin. 'My friends, my . . . people I've loved. I've lost so many, and I can't do it anymore. I don't want Oliver to wind up like everyone else.'

His warm hand dried her face. 'He won't, Bee. He won't.'

'How can you know that?'

'Because now you've got me.'

Bee blubbered.

'Hey, hey.' Adam enveloped her in a hug, his cheek on her hair, a soft shush on his lips.

She wrapped her arms around his waist and held tight, buried her face in his chest.

He ran his hands over her back, tracing her spine.

'I'm scared,' she admitted. She pushed against him far enough to look him in the eyes. There were flecks of gold in his hazel irises. 'And I don't know what to do.'

'You need sleep.' Adam stepped back, offering her his hand. 'Come on.'

'Pfft.' Bee waved him away. 'I can walk. I'm not drunk!'

She negated her exclamation at the exact moment she tried to walk by swaying on her feet and grabbing at the air for balance.

'Easy, easy.' Adam held her hand. 'I've got you.'

Bee glared at him even as the earth spun under her feet; however, the ground moved too fast for her to assure him that he didn't have her. Not at all.

He swept her up in his arms and carried her into the living room.

'This is so overkill,' Bee complained, an arm around his neck, her head on his shoulder.

She yawned.

Inside the darkness, Bee could make out the almost corporeal figures of two of Charlie's hired guns, one at each entrance. Everyone else seemed to be asleep, but she could guess there were more men patrolling outside.

He opened the door to Oliver's bedroom.

Oliver snored away from the twin bed in the corner, tucked up to his chin in blue blankets, Hogarth sleeping between his feet. Malika slept on a cot placed between the beds, hands curled under her head and a soft smile on her usually grumpy face.

Adam pulled the blankets back on the empty twin bed and sat her down.

She lay down, too tired to even glare as Adam tucked her in. 'I haven't had a bedtime in years.'

He chuckled quietly, a soft exhale through his nose, and the mattress by her knees dipped when he sat.

She raised a hand to touch the half-moon scar on his bottom lip but changed her mind halfway there, holding her hand awkwardly in the space between them. Bee closed her hand and set it on her chest. 'Where are you sleeping?'

'The guest room's got cots in it,' he said with a nod towards the hall. 'The boys are taking shifts. Why? You want me to stay outside the door?'

'No.' Bee shook her head against the pillow. It was soft and cool beneath her head, and she turned her face to nuzzle deeper. 'No, go to sleep. I'll be fine.'

'Shout if you need anything.'

Bee closed her eyes. 'I'm drunk, not an invalid.'

He rose from the bed, and it squeaked from the loss of him. 'Yes, ma'am.'

TWELVE

'Aw, do you see the ice, little buddy?' Pinkerton showed Oliver the three-foot-tall ice sculpture of a cross. 'Seems, I don't know, a little sacrilegious, right?'

Bee tried to glance at the cross, but her eyes kept sliding off it. People filled the garden. Fresh, white flowers decorated every available surface. Twinkling lights hung in the air, crisscrossing above them, like the trails left behind by airplanes.

She could hear the band, but she couldn't see them. She couldn't see past the platform they were standing on.

Someone bumped into her shoulder; they mumbled an apology, breezed by and Bee realized they didn't have a face.

The swarms of people – dancing, laughing, eating – only Pinkerton had a face. Greasy patches of a beard that wouldn't grow in, freckles on his nose. Her Pinkerton.

'Hey,' he said. 'You OK?'

Bee didn't know.

She took Oliver, hugged him close, kissed his head. She breathed in deep to take comfort in his baby scent.

But he smelled like nothing.

She set the baby in the crook of her arm, dread filling her heart. She tried to get her tongue to move. 'Something's wrong,' she wanted to say. But it came out garbled. A whisper.

'G-Get get behind me.' Pinky didn't touch her, but he forced her back all the same. 'Stay.'

Her body quivered. Her heart pounded so loudly in her ears she almost couldn't hear anything else. Anything at all.

Anything but his voice.

'You took some tracking down.'

There he stood, unchanged from their last meeting. Still short. Still round around the middle. Dark hair. Darker eyes.

Bee opened her mouth to scream for help. But the only thing that came out was a mousy squeak.

'Get outta here, man.' Pinky's mouth twitched. 'It's not safe. For anybody.'

'Oh.' Thomas Osbourn grinned from ear to ear. 'I think I'll be just fine.'

Bee wetted her lips, found her voice. 'What do you want?'

'Only to chat.' He sipped champagne. 'To catch up. I've missed you dearly, Shelby. Or I'm sorry. I apologize. It's Beatrice now, yes?'

Oliver wiggled in her arms. She bounced him lightly. 'You know exactly what it is.'

'Hm.'

'What do you want?'

His brown eyes burned red. 'I wanted to reassure you. I thought this lovely celebration would be a perfect time to set your mind at ease. Perhaps settle your conscience.' He turned his attention to Oliver. 'Congratulations, by the way.'

Pinkerton blocked him from view. 'Come on, man. Somebody's gonna notice. These aren't the type of guys you wanna mess with.'

Os drained his glass, set it on a passing tray. 'I am unconcerned with these types of guys. I wanted to reconnect with the both of you. As it stands now, neither of you have outlived your usefulness.'

'Dude,' Pinky said. 'We're retired.'

'Yes. I see that.' Os smiled again. 'I know that we parted on less than pleasant terms. But your mistake, dearest Bee, only put me off schedule. I still found a way to get what I wanted. It just had to be more inventive. Messier.' He licked his spiked teeth clean. 'Did you know that your uncle Frank is highly allergic to peanuts? Oh, I guess I should say "was".'

Her heart crawled into her throat, blocking her airway. She tried to swallow it back down. 'Frank is dead?'

Os didn't hear her. 'And it was such a shame when their meeting place caught fire. Faulty wiring – officially. Tsk. Lost everything.'

Bee took a shuddering breath.

'It's a much quieter town now.' Os put his hands in his pockets and smiled at the faceless people all around them. 'Clean.'

Pinkerton's mouth twitched again. 'So much' – he shrugged, at a loss for words – 'for money laundering? You need a hobby.'

'Making money is my hobby. And I do believe the three of us have an opportunity to make some of it together again.'

The whole world spun around her. She closed her eyes to steady herself.

He spoke again. He sounded like he was whispering in her ear. He sounded like he was shouting from across the garden. 'Knocked up by a gangster, Bee. Do you know why you do this to yourself?'

She refused to open her eyes.

'Do you know why you seek out these kinds of men? That you turn yourself into a subservient little woman for anyone with the barest whiff of authority?'

Oliver hit her in the chin.

Bee looked for him. His smile distorted in her watery eyes. She held him to her cheek.

'Because my father hated me,' she said.

'Hated you?' Os laughed. 'Bee, dearest Bee. No. Your father didn't care about you at all! He didn't care if you lived or died. Oh, my poor girl. The opposite of love isn't hate. It's indifference. And because of his indifference, it's so easy for men, men like me, men like your husband, to mold you into whatever shape we want you to take.'

She blinked and tears fell on her son's white outfit. She blinked and the ground broke under her feet. A small crack, a fissure, growing bigger and bigger.

She wished it would hurry up and swallow her whole.

'This doesn't have to be your life. That's what I'm offering you.'

Bee stood on nothing but darkness. The sound of her racing heart echoed in the empty void.

'You crafted a web and caught yourself. I can set you free.'

Charlie appeared at her side and brought solid ground with him.

Utter relief filled her body. She leaned against him, swaying on her feet.

'What's going on?' He gave Os a once-over. 'Who are you?'

'Oh, just an old friend of your lovely wife and brother-in-law. Actually, a former employer, I should say. They both interned for me back in their youth.' Os pulled a thick envelope out of his coat pocket.

Charlie took it with a smile.

Bee opened her mouth to scream. Her voice was gone. Tears clouded her vision until everything blurred in front of her.

'I wanted to pay my respects to your son. And maybe – if you're up for it – discuss a business opportunity.'

Charlie pocketed the heavy envelope and shook Os's hand. 'I'm always up for business. Let me get you a drink. What did you say your name was?'

They disappeared into the crowd of apparitions.

'Come on,' Pinky said, but he sounded far away. 'Let me take the baby.'

Oliver was gone.

He was gone.

He wasn't in her arms.

Her baby was gone.

Her sweet baby. She'd lost her baby. She'd lost her baby! How could she lose her baby?

Os, visible again, set a hand on Charlie's shoulder and smiled at her. Horns grew on the top of his head.

Charlie laughed.

'No,' Bee cried, arms empty. 'You're supposed to protect me. You're supposed to protect me!'

Bee shot awake. Her heart pounded in her chest. She set a steadying hand on her forehead, pushing her hair out of her face.

Breathe in. Breathe out.

Breathe in. Breathe out.

The dream started to fade away.

She kicked her legs free from the tangle of blankets and glanced around the room. Malika, Oliver and Hogarth were gone, their beds unmade and disheveled. On her nightstand sat a glass of water and a bottle of Tylenol.

Bee sank to her knees and pulled her go bag out from underneath the bed. She hadn't bothered going through it since highway patrol had stopped them. She knew what she had in there. Wigs, makeup – both regular and theater – an extra passport, a bit of cash, some credit cards, an old flip phone and dry-clean-only clothes weren't super helpful for where she found herself now. But it wasn't a change of clothes she was looking for.

The picture of Pinkerton, smiling, greasy in the sunlight, a laughing one-year-old Oliver in his arms, had wormed its way to the bottom of the bag.

A drop of water splattered on the glass. Bee sniffed, wiped it clean with the sleeve of her hoodie, wiped her face with the same sleeve. She'd met Pinkerton on her first job with Os. He was awkward and weird, but he was good at what he did and respected her in the field. More than that, he always had her back. Pinkerton had stuck by her side when everyone else had fled. Pinkerton had been her family when she'd had none. He was the reason she was alive right now. And she was the reason he wasn't.

He'd expect her to solve this. He'd believe in her. Support her. Order her a rocket launcher.

A rocket launcher probably wouldn't be her best choice for dealing with Alvarez, but she'd call it Plan B for now.

There was a soft tap on the door.

Bee rubbed the hem of the sleeve across her face again. 'Yeah.'

Adam came into the room, clicking the door shut behind him. 'Hey, good morning. I made breakfast.'

Bee set the picture on top of her brunette wig. 'I'm up. I need coffee, but I'm up. Thanks for the Tylenol by the way.'

He stared at her go bag, head tilted to the side. 'Is that Pinkerton?' Adam picked up the picture in question. He smiled so brightly his eyes wrinkled. 'Shit, it is. He really stayed with you until the end, huh?'

The three of them had worked together multiple times on Os's crew. Pinkerton worked every job with Bee, but Adam was more transient. Freelance, where she and Pinky were salaried. The best jobs, though, her happiest memories of her past life, were when she'd had both of them on her team. 'What did Charlie know him as?'

She sighed and used the bed to climb to her feet. 'My brother,' she said.

'Right, right.' He set the frame in the open duffle bag with care. 'Got it. He was still called Pinkerton though, right?'

'Pinky.' Bee zipped up the bag and pushed it under the bed. 'Mob guys love a nickname after all.' She raked her fingers through her hair. 'Now, about that breakfast.'

THIRTEEN

Bee stumbled into the kitchen behind Adam.

'Here.' He handed her a hot mug of coffee. 'Cream and extra sugar.'

Just the way she liked it.

Bee took a sip and a seat at the island. 'How long have you been up?'

'Not long.' He flipped a pancake in a cast-iron skillet. 'Thought you might be hungry for real food.'

She nodded and watched him. He seemed at home in a kitchen.

Bee wiped the blush off her cheeks. 'Where's Oliver?'

Adam nodded at the glass patio doors, and she swiveled her seat.

'Oh.' She caught sight of her son running on the sand with Cassie. 'She's frolicking.'

Charlie sat on a patio chair, a cigarette in his mouth, Hogarth in his lap, and watched the two of them play. In fact, a number of his guys had gathered on the patio to watch the scene before them.

'It's cute,' Bee said. 'She's cute.'

She was also wearing a teeny tiny purple bikini that made Bee feel ridiculously overdressed, but hey, she wasn't the one frolicking on the beach. *Her* beach. This was Cassie's home now. Even if Bee had helped secure the funding for it. Even if Bee had decorated it, raised a child in it. Charlie's home with his new girlfriend.

And she was trapped there with them.

For how long?

Malika walked into the kitchen emitting an audible growl. 'Have you seen this, Bee?'

Bee looked away from her ex's frolicking girlfriend to find her nanny holding a twenty-pound laptop in her arms.

'This – this is what they give me. Watch.' She set it on the counter and opened it up. 'I have to plug it into the phone line, Bee. The *phone line* because there's no Wi-Fi here! It connects to the internet with a modem. Have you heard this? Listen to me! *listen!*' Malika mimicked – rather spot on – the screeching sound of a modem connecting to the internet.

Bee laughed. 'OK, OK, I get it. We'll have Charlie buy you a new one from the Apple store.'

Malika slammed the laptop closed. 'Maybe Butterfingers over here should pay for it.'

The plate rattled against the marble countertop when Adam set her stack of pancakes and a hearty serving of bacon before her. Bee turned away from Malika and picked up a knife and fork with a, 'Thank you,' directed at Adam.

'Butterfingers?' Adam said. 'I destroyed that thing on purpose.'

Malika's face twisted into a terrifying glare.

Bee chewed her cheek to keep from laughing again. 'Did you get a smartphone from Cassie at least?'

'Yes, thank God. Better than nothing. I was having to hand crank a radio to listen to Britney.' Malika twisted her hair into a sloppy braid. 'Well. I'm gonna go upstairs and see if I can get any work done. But I expect to be taken to an Apple store as soon as possible because this is downright *inhumane*.'

Bee watched her leave and thought it wouldn't be a bad idea to get her equipped sooner rather than later. Charlie was his own sinking ship, and Bee had no intention of going down with him. Him and his young, frolicking, kind-hearted girlfriend.

'Finish up,' Adam said. 'You're gonna need your strength.'

Bee swallowed and stared at him, thoughts of what she'd need her strength with him for filling her mind. Her cheeks warmed again. 'For what?'

He smiled and even his gum-to-teeth ratio was perfect. 'I'm gonna teach you how to defend yourself.'

She pushed a bite of pancake around a puddle of syrup with the back of her fork. 'I think I'll stick to yoga.'

'You should know how to defend yourself, Bee.'

'If I can defend myself, what will I need you for?'

Adam poured himself a fresh cup of coffee and drank it black. 'I'll let you teach me how to lift.'

'Deal!' She grabbed his hand and shook it so hard coffee splashed over the side of his mug. 'You can't go back on it now.'

'I won't.'

She ignored the way her hand tingled when he let her go. 'You're too easy, you know that?'

His mouth opened in a lopsided grin. 'No one has ever said that to me before.'

After breakfast, they went to the gym, located in a room downstairs off the hallway from the kitchen. Adam locked them in. And then he grabbed the back of his shirt with his fist and pulled it over his head in one move.

He was shirtless.

They were alone.

She swallowed.

His muscles had been formed from fighting, and formed they were. He was *lean*. Not someone who would pull a truck by a rope tied around his neck, but someone who could scale the wall of a building and take out a hidden horde of assassins or snipers.

Of course, checking out his well-defined abdomen and biceps would be more fun if he wasn't standing in a room that smelled like sweaty dudes.

Scars puckered his skin. Slashed along his biceps, mottled over his ribs, crisscrossing his back.

A large, torn circle underneath his collarbone. The last job the two of them had done had started in a café in Ibiza and ended in a hospital. He'd taken a bullet to the chest to save her life and then promptly abandoned her, like she'd never existed, like it was all just a job to him in the first place. The scar beneath his collarbone made her heart feel heavy. The incredible guilt and disbelief at witnessing a man jump in front of a gun for you. Followed by the overwhelming confusion when he'd no longer accept your calls.

Now he was here, in her ex-husband's home, after saving her life all over again.

Bee tossed off her hoodie and pulled her hair into a messy ponytail. 'So,' she said, smiling too big, 'what's first, Coach?'

He picked up a small black bag with handles. 'This is called a melon. We're gonna hit this and not each other.'

She pouted.

'Let's start with something simple. Here.' He gave her the melon. 'This is an open hand strike.' His palm struck the bag with so much force she stepped back.

'Jeez, Louise!'

He let out a soft chuckle. 'Sorry. But, see, it's more than pushing forward with your hand. You have to pivot with your feet. You ready?'

She nodded and braced herself.

He struck the bag again. This time she stayed still.

'Pivot with your feet. Get your power from your lower half. And hit with the heel of your hand. See?'

'Yep,' she lied.

'Your turn.' He took the bag and held it up by his head. 'Go on.'

'Just don't want to hurt you,' she said. And then she struck the bag.

'Good. Again.'

She hit it harder this time.

'Again.'

Harder still.

'Good. Let's work on a groin kick.'

Her eyebrows shot clear up to her hairline.

'With the bag,' he reminded her, failing to hide his grin. 'The important thing to remember is to kick the bag with the top of your foot. Where your shoelaces would be. Yeah?'

'Kick the bag,' she repeated.

'Yeah.' He held the bag in front of his groin. 'Just the bag.'

She kicked the bottom of the bag with the top of her foot as hard as she could.

'Good! Again.'

She kicked again. And again. And again.

'Now, you take the sole of your foot and aim for the kneecap.' He lowered the bag in front of his leg. 'The kneecap is one of those places that's really hard to protect. And injuring a knee can slow an attacker down.'

'Because of the limping?' Bee guessed.

'Right,' he said. 'Because of the limping. Now, kick.'

After she'd tried out the move with both feet, Adam tossed the bag off to the side.

'OK.' He rubbed his hand over the top of his not-quite-bald head. 'Let's work on what to do if you've been grabbed. You can strike and kick when an attacker is approaching. But what do you do if you don't see them coming in time?'

'Scream for you?'

'Yes. But you can escape too. Turn around.'

She frowned so deeply it was almost a glare. 'OK. But I'm not happy about it.'

He wrapped his arms around her, lifted her off her feet and against his slick chest.

'So, hold on to my arms,' he said, his voice almost a whisper in her ear.

She gulped. His arms were damp from sweat, but it didn't keep her from holding on tight.

'What you want to do is create an opportunity to use your body as dead weight. Jerk your head back and connect with my nose. Use the heels of your feet – or your high heels – and dig into my shins. Anything to shock me into dropping you. And then grab on to me for all your worth.'

Not wanting to actually hurt him, she rubbed her heels against his shins.

'Good. So, when I let go, tuck your chin to your chest and fall forward. It's gonna happen quick. You ready?'

Her ear rubbed against the stubble on his jaw when she nodded. She dug her heels into his shins.

He gave a cry of pain and dropped her.

She didn't let go of his arms.

Bee tucked her chin to her chest and fell forward. Adam fell over her, bracing himself because he knew it was coming, and pratfell on his face.

She rolled off him and forced herself to smile so big her vision blurred. 'That was fun!'

He grinned up at her. 'Yeah, you did good. One more?'

She bit a cuticle.

'It'll be easy, OK?'

The spot below her belly button quivered, her entire lower body turning to jello. Tingling, wiggling, useless jello. 'OK.'

He rolled on to his stomach and did a push up to standing, the veins in his forearms so pronounced that any nurse would clamor to take his blood.

Her heart pounded away in her chest, and she blew out a breath from puffed cheeks.

'This time you're gonna see me coming.' Adam spread his arms wide. 'When you see me get close, you're going to duck.'

He approached faster than she expected. She ducked, and his arms closed in over her head.

'Now, you're going to spring up, aiming the top of your head for my chin.'

She sprang up. He moved his hands under his chin to block her incoming blow.

'Good. Now, I go back.' He winced in pretend pain and stepped back, holding on to his face.

Bee laughed, in a super convincing, not awkward at all way.

'Grab me by the shoulders and knee me in the stomach.'

She pulled him down by the shoulders and brought her knee up to his stomach as fast as she could without harming him.

'Ugh!' he cried. 'Again.'

She obeyed.

He cried out again, clutching his stomach. 'Bring your hands together above you and hit me on the back of my head.'

She clasped her hands together above her head and brought them down on the back of his.

He fell to the ground at her feet with a glorious thump.

Bee laughed again, this time sounding more natural, even the slightest bit real.

But when had real ever mattered to them?

He rolled over on to his back and grinned, sweat running down the ridges of his stomach, along the V that disappeared into his shorts.

'Toss me that towel?'

She grabbed it off the bench press and threw it underhanded. It landed squarely on his nose.

'Thanks,' he said behind the rag and wiped the sweat off his brow. 'You did good, Shelby.'

'You'd make a great TV wrestler.' She offered him her hand to help him up. He took it, even though he didn't need her help. 'You're great at exaggerating blows.'

'That was my dream,' he said, still holding her hand. 'As a kid. I wanted to be Hulk Hogan. But I could never get the hair right.'

She giggled, nose crinkling, and laced her fingers through his. His hazel eyes were lined in gold and shining bright.

Her giggle died in her throat. She froze, an open smile on her face, and absolutely no air passing between her lips.

She dropped his hand. 'I have to go,' she said. 'Shower. I have to go shower. Sweaty.' She wiped her palms on her yoga pants and started walking backward. 'Better get cleaned up for lunch! What is for lunch by the way?'

'Sandwiches.'

'Oh, that sounds delicious! So I'll see you in— Ow.' Bee rubbed her shoulder, wincing. 'There's a door there.'

He stepped towards her. 'You OK?'

'Ha ha, just fine!' She clutched her throbbing shoulder. 'Barely felt it. I've got another one anyway! See you at lunch!'

Bee didn't head straight for her room after her lesson with Adam. She snuck into the garage, hands in her pockets, carefree, and took a look at their options. Lots of different entry-level Sedans to choose from. But only two were unlocked. And of those two, only one had a key in the visor. Bee took it with disdain, not for the moron who'd do such a thing, but for her husband for employing such a trusting thug.

Back in her room, Oliver was in the shower, the bathroom door cracked open and his spirited rendition of a Britney Spears song his nanny had taught him filling the space. As quietly as she could, she pulled her go bag from under the bed and gathered up all the cash she had. Seven thousand dollars.

It wasn't much, but it would have to do. She was getting out of Charlie's home ASAP. She could hide from Alvarez on her own. Her and her nanny and her son. Maybe Adam. So not really on her own. But hiding out in some Canadian RV park was better than living under her ex's thumb.

Bee found Malika in the fridge. 'Psst,' she whispered – badly.

Malika looked at her, mouth full and cheeks round.

Bee placed both the keys and the cash in Malika's hands.

'Go and get whatever you need. We gotta get the hell out of here. I'm not staying here forever.'

Malika swallowed and counted out the money. 'What? Why? It's only been a day. And Cassie is so nice, and she smells so good. Why the big rush?'

'A day? A *day*? It's been twenty-six hours – 1,560 minutes in my ex-husband's home with his good-smelling girlfriend and I can't go out like this, Malika. I refuse to die here.' Bee raked her fingers through her hair. 'I refuse to die here with them! I won't do it! I won't!'

Malika popped another grape in her mouth. 'Jeez, fine. I'll get to work. Any requests?'

Bee sighed. 'My own pajamas would be nice.'

Malika shoved the cash in her pockets and rattled the keys. 'What about Butterfingers? He coming too?'

'I haven't decided yet.'

'OK. Cryptic, but OK. I'll be back in a few hours. Don't wait up.'

FOURTEEN

Bee donned another pair of someone else's yoga pants, someone else's tank top and the same hoodie she'd been in all morning. She twisted her wet hair into a topknot and left the bathroom she shared with Oliver and Malika.

'Hey, buddy,' she greeted. He was in his bed, a Nintendo 3DS in his hands, Hogarth on his feet. 'Oh, that's new!'

'Yeah, Cassie got it for me.' He didn't look up. 'It's super awesome.'

'Nice.' Bee smiled. The video game system would keep him occupied and happy in his bedroom. 'She's a thoughtful one, that's for sure.'

Oliver kept pressing buttons.

She shook her head and walked out of the room. 'Love you, buddy.'

'Yeah, love you too.'

The door to the spare room was cracked open, light pouring into the hallway, and two hushed voices were speaking.

She came to a stop outside it, careful of her shadow, and tried to discern what the voices were saying, and who they belonged to.

'I don't know, man. I don't like this. The two of you, rolling around, getting all sweaty on each other. It's bound to lead to other things.'

'What?' Adam's disembodied voice replied. 'You don't know what you're talking about.'

'Don't know what I'm talking about?' the other man said. 'I know you. You took a bullet for this girl. I know you think your relationship gives you an advantage here, but maybe she's the one with the advantage. Maybe you forget what you're doing because all those old bullet-taking feelings come back.'

They were talking about her. Bee held her throat. She needed to hear what they were going to say. She needed every last bit of information she could get. But that didn't make listening any less miserable.

'You really gonna bust my balls about this?' Adam replied, exasperated. 'There's no feelings. This is business. Bee's gonna find where the money is. That's the kinda thing she's good for. All we gotta do is keep her and her son alive.'

Her brain grew twice its size, filled up her skull then collapsed in on itself. She held her breath, scared if she exhaled it would come out in a cry.

'Then she'll lead you to the money.' The other man's voice she recognized as belonging to the pilot, Mr White.

'Yeah. Eighteen million apiece.'

He'd been lying the whole time. Adam had sought her out, plied her with alcohol, preyed on her desperation – all in an attempt to get the money Charlie had stolen. He'd lied. To her! And she'd believed him. Believed him, hook, line and sinker. Adam had been running an angle the whole time. She should have listened to Malika.

Mr White chuckled. 'I'm gonna buy an island, man.'

'I think islands cost more than that.'

'A small island. A small one. I can get a small one for that. With just the one house.'

Her shaking hand covered her mouth. She snuck inside the hall closet without making a sound. The fur coat was still a heap on the floor. She collapsed to her butt, pulled the soft fur to her mouth and smothered her cry.

She needed him. She needed him! Oliver was still in danger. Even though they were currently safe, hidden away in Charlie's beach house, Alvarez wasn't going to forget about them.

She couldn't hide in her ex-husband's fortress. She could pretend like they were safe, but the illusion wouldn't last forever. She had to get out before somebody slipped up, or switched sides, or worse.

And she needed Adam. For Oliver's sake, she needed Adam.

Adam had always kept her safe. Adam had always protected her, even when other men in his position had left her to fend for herself. That's the way jobs worked. Os assembled a crew, and everyone worked towards a common goal. But if somebody went down, they were cut loose, not reeled in.

Her job was to put on a dress, speak in an accent. Sometimes she'd get called in for forgery. But those guys, those professionals, never took grifting seriously. She was expendable. There was always someone to be a pretty face around to distract a mark.

But Adam had cared about her. Or at least, she'd thought he did.

He'd risked himself for her. That wasn't something she'd ever had before.

Bee closed her eyes, and she could remember seeing him, victorious in his violence, and yet still trying to shield her from the gore.

The elevator doors had slid closed. Another job well done.

Bee caught Pinkerton's grin.

'That was great, Shelby,' he said. 'You totally owned that place.'

'I fired that guy. Did you see?' she asked Adam on her other side.

He had one hand in his pocket, the other holding a briefcase, and was watching the floor numbers click down. He smiled at her.

'He just walked out.' Bee rested against the handrail. 'He didn't even question it.'

'He packed a box and everything!' Pinky dug his index finger in his ear. 'How long until he realizes you don't have that authority?'

She shrugged. 'I've never fake fired anyone before.'

'Forty-eight hours,' Adam said. At their combined looks, he continued, 'From my experience.'

He didn't say anything else, instead focusing on the floor numbers again, and the elevator descended in silence.

'Just gonna let that one sit there, I guess,' Pinky mumbled. 'Hey, what are we doing tonight?'

Bee couldn't resist. 'Same thing we do every night, Pinky,' she said in the most Wellesian voice she could muster.

Pinky squinted his eyes. 'What?'

'You know. From the cartoon.'

His eyes stayed squinted.

'With the rats,' Adam offered. 'The rats who try to take over the world.'

'We're gonna find some rats and take over the world?' Pinkerton shook his head. 'That seems like a really weird plan, dude.'

Bee clicked her tongue. 'That's not—'

'How would rats be of any use? You know?' Pinkerton leaned a palm against the wall. 'Seems like you'd need some sort of massive weapon. I can't think of any offhand that's rat powered.'

'No, it's from a show,' Adam said. 'From a kids show.'

Pinkerton opened his mouth, but Bee held up a finger.

'Let's drop it. This was my fault. I apologize.'

The elevator came to a halt. The doors slid open, and Bee went to step through them but froze in place instead. With wide, unblinking eyes, she stared at the dozen or so masked men holding automatic weapons and the business-casual-dressed hostages tied up on the floor, her brain unable to process what it was she was seeing.

Adam cleared his throat. 'Just trying to go to the lobby.'

He pressed the lobby button, and the doors slid closed.

'Two robberies in the same building?' Pinkerton asked. 'What are the odds?'

Adam dropped the briefcase and spun Bee around, pushing her against the wall. His yell of, 'Go flat!' to Pinkerton was lost in the sound of bullets piercing the metal doors. He covered her with the full weight of his body, arms around her head, forcing her face into his throat. The spray moved upwards as the elevators descended.

'Are you OK?' Adam whispered in her ear. He moved back far enough to run his hands through her hair, over her neck, down her arms, checking her for injuries.

'Yeah,' she panted. She darted out her tongue to lick her suddenly dry lips. 'Yeah, I'm OK.'

'I'm fine!' Pinky said, climbing to his feet. 'Jeez, how did they miss all of us?'

The elevator stopped at the lobby in time for the three of them to witness a man dressed as a security guard dragging the obviously dead body of another man dressed as a security guard by the ankles.

Adam reached around her to press the door-close button.

'What,' Bee said, 'the hell.'

Adam pulled off his jacket and handed it to her, eyes trained on the ceiling.

'I know! Right? Crazy.' Pinky pulled out a flip phone. 'Imma call Os and see what we should do next.'

Adam pushed the emergency stop on the elevator. 'Pinkerton,' he said and rolled up his shirt sleeves.

'Yeah, yeah.' Still on the phone, Pinky got on all fours. Adam used him like a step and slid the emergency hatch aside. He hauled himself up into the elevator shaft. 'Your turn, Bee.'

She kicked off her heels and stepped on Pinky's back. 'Sorry about this,' she said, but he was too busy talking to Os.

Adam grabbed her arms and pulled her out. She could see the building's second elevator ascending next to them. Thick black cables held what she stood on in place, and she refused to look around. Bee didn't need to know how far she'd fall to her death, thank you very much.

Pinkerton hung up the call and Adam helped him out.

'Os says we're a go.'

The elevator doors for the floor above them were at chest height for Adam. He wedged his fingers between them and yanked, veins bulging in his forearms, in his neck, his face red. When he parted the doors, Bee shoved the briefcase in to keep them propped open.

Adam shook out his hands and smiled at her, but it didn't reach his eyes. 'I'm gonna need lights out.'

Pinkerton nodded. 'I can do that.'

'What do you need me to do?' asked Bee.

'Wait here,' Adam said. 'This is too dangerous.'

'I can help.' Bee rolled back her shoulders, rose to her full height. 'I can.'

But Adam shook his head. 'No, I can't risk it. If you're out there, I'm gonna worry about you the whole time. Stay here. Stay where it's safe. OK? Let me do my job now.'

There were an awful lot of men with guns down there. 'Can you do this, Adam?' She touched his hand.

He glanced down at her fingers on his knuckles, looked her in the eyes.

'You aren't armed,' she said. 'Are you sure you should do this? It's dangerous for you too.'

'You worried about me, Shelby Lynn?' He caught her fingers, gave a squeeze. 'My job is to clear the way.'

She rolled her eyes. 'Fine.' Bee snatched her hand back. 'I'll be here. Alone. In a creepy elevator shaft. Awaiting my knight in shining armor to rescue me.'

'Cool,' Pinkerton said. 'Can you be the table this time? 'Cause I gotta get out of here.'

Bee glared at him. 'No.'

He shrugged and struggled to get out of the shaft. Adam cast her one last lingering look before he followed.

Bee curled up in the corner, tucked out of sight of the emergency hatch, and pulled Adam's jacket over her like a blanket. It smelled like him. Like dandruff shampoo and his musky, citrus cologne.

The lights went out, casting the elevator shaft into complete darkness. What if the elevator plunged to the ground? Should she try to get out or at least get closer to the propped-open doors?

But if the elevator suddenly crashed to the ground, she doubted her abilities to jump to safety, no matter how close she was to the exit.

Gunshots sounded, dozens of them. Screams of terrified people echoed from beneath where she hid, bouncing up the shaft.

Bee pulled his jacket over her head, clutched her hands over her ears. A child again, hiding under the covers of her bed, while her drunk mother and even drunker father shouted at each other, broke anything they touched.

It felt like hours before she heard footsteps. Bee kept herself under the protection of his jacket. She was safe from reality under there. Adam was neither dead nor alive. Pinkerton was neither missing nor found. Everything was just as it had been before she hid herself away.

But it was Adam who cleared his throat, Adam who croaked out, 'Bee.'

And it took all of her nerve to climb out of her hiding spot.

He was filthy. Covered in blood. Bright scratches on his head, over his ear, running over his neck and down his right shoulder, which was out of socket, hanging too far down his side.

Adam eased himself on to the roof of the elevator, wincing all the while, and crouched down next to her. His voice was a whisper when he said, 'It's over.'

She wiped the tears off her face. 'You're hurt.'

He glanced at his arm. 'Yeah.'

'Pinkerton?' She sniffed. 'The hostages?'

'Everybody's out,' he said. 'The police are on their way so we gotta get going.'

Bee tried to huff derisively. 'Some response time, huh?'

He smiled, and this time it lit up his eyes, made his dimples pop. 'They didn't know until we let them know.'

He was so close she could see the beads of sweat on his forehead, how they ran down his skin and over his wounds and polluted his blood. She wanted to touch him. She wanted to feel him, to make sure he was really there, that he was alive. That she wasn't dreaming. That this was real. He was real.

She offered him his jacket, her hands trembling around the fabric. 'I kept it safe for you.'

'I knew you would.' He stood and didn't take it back. 'Listen, Bee . . . the only way out is through.'

Bee nodded, shrugged on his jacket and stood up. Her legs were shaking.

He helped her out of the elevator shaft, and then she dropped to her knees and helped him.

Adam yanked the briefcase out, and the doors slid shut.

He offered her his hand. There was blood on it.

'Don't look,' said Adam. 'Please.'

She clutched the jacket to her chest. After all that, and he didn't want her to see the carnage he'd left behind? Well. She supposed she could do that for him.

Bee took his hand, and his palm was wet and warm. 'OK. You lead; I'll follow.'

She opened her watery eyes. There she was, hiding under yet another coat. How long could she hide for? Charlie wanted her to clean up his mess so he could keep the money he'd stolen. And Adam wanted her to clean up Charlie's mess so she could lead him to the money Charlie had stolen. She wanted to burrow under the coat and never leave the closet again. She wanted to transport herself back in time, home in Biscayne Bay, watching the sunrise over the open ocean. She wanted her biggest problem to be Rosalie Waters refusing to even listen to her business proposal.

The front door slammed, and a deep male voice yelled something unintelligible.

Bee startled in the darkness.

Someone screamed in sheer terror.

She ran, out of the closet, down the hallway to the stairs.

Adam and Mr White caught up to her before she could get to the bottom.

'Bee! Wait!' Adam grabbed her arm. 'Don't go out there alone.'

'Oliver!' She wrung her arm out of his hold. 'Oliver's in his room.'

Adam pointed at Mr White. 'Guard his door. No one in. No one out.'

He crept up the stairs and down the hallway without making a noise.

Adam took her elbow. 'Come on,' he said, sounding like he would much rather not go anywhere at all. 'Stay behind me.'

FIFTEEN

Artie Bosh was on his knees in the middle of the stark white shag carpet of the living room.

His nose broken. His face bloody. His hands clasped in a desperate prayer.

'Please,' he sobbed. 'Please, my daughter, Rachael. She's sick. I couldn't buy her medicine. Please, Mr C, I'm so sorry. I'll do anything.'

Charlie stared out the large window overlooking their bit of ocean, hands behind his back, shoulders straight.

The hairs on the back of her neck stood up. She pushed past Adam, but he grabbed her arm again.

'No,' he said. 'There's six guys out there, all armed.'

'They aren't gonna shoot me.'

He didn't let go. 'Not on purpose.'

Charlie faced the man before him. He eyed him up and down, contempt etching itself across his boyish face. 'Why didn't you tell me about your daughter, Artie? Surely you know, you must know, that I'm a compassionate man. A father myself. We're a family, Artie. Why not come to me with this? Why not ask me for help?'

Artie held his face in his hands. 'I was ashamed. I gambled all our money away. Our house was in foreclosure. I was too ashamed to come to you, Mr C. I'm so sorry. I thought, I thought . . . I thought no one would ever know, what I'd done.'

Charlie sat down in an armchair. 'How would no one have known? Alvarez is coming after my family now. My wife. My child. You decided that your pride was more important than my flesh and blood? How can that be, Artie? After everything we've been through together. How could you think such a thing?'

Bee searched out Adam's eyes. 'Let me in there,' she said. 'I know him. I can help.'

He frowned so deep his lips touched his jaw, but he let go of her arm and stepped back.

'Ah, here she is now.' Charlie gestured at her like a car salesman pointing out the nicest vehicle on the lot. 'The woman you decided should die.'

Bee shook her head at his over exaggeration and stood to the side of his chair, blocking Artie. She was Esther, beseeching her husband, the king on his throne.

'Let's hear him out, Charlie.' She needed to step lightly. Charlie didn't respond well to being told what to do. It all had to be suggestions. Gentle encouragement. Put him in room-temperature water and slowly, slowly turn up the heat, so he wouldn't realize he was being boiled alive. 'Artie might have information that can help us.'

He wiggled the end of his tie at her, annoyed. 'Go ahead, Artie. You speak now because of the kindness of Mrs Cardello.' He arched an eyebrow at the man. 'Make every word count.'

'I'm sorry, Mrs C. I'm so, so sorry.' Artie clutched his hands in a desperate prayer again. 'He paid off Rachael's medical bills. He pulled strings at the bank and kept my house from going under. I didn't have a choice. Please believe me. I didn't have a choice!'

Charlie fiddled with his shirt cuffs. 'We always have a choice, Artie. And you chose to be a traitor. You've been with me long enough to know how I handle rats. I can't make exceptions.'

Artie fell to all fours. 'Please! My daughter! My Rachael! She's only eight!'

Charlie stood.

Bee stepped in front of him, one arm raised. 'No, don't!' She needed time to think. She needed time with Artie. Something smelled rotten, didn't make sense, didn't fit into the puzzle in her mind's eye she was carefully piecing together. This man she'd known for years – why would he do this?

But Charlie's eyes flashed, his jaw tensed so hard it clicked, and Bee's heart raced.

She'd overstepped.

'Oliver is upstairs.' Bee pressed both hands to his chest and looked at him from underneath her lashes, demure and soft. 'He can't hear this, Charlie.' She toyed with a button on his shirt. 'There has to be a better way.'

Charlie took hold of her shoulders, caressed his way to her neck and kissed her forehead. 'Not for this,' he said. He slid his hands down her arms and held on to both of her wrists. 'Get her out of here.'

Two men came barreling up to her. Each had over a foot on her, each at least a buck fifty bigger. One man kept a hand on the gun at his side, but he took hold of her elbow with the other and jerked her into his chest. The other man grabbed her by the waist, a fist in her borrowed hoodie, and if he pulled any harder, he would've stripped her naked in her own living room.

'Let go of me!' Bee wrung her arm free. 'I am *not* going anywhere.' She planted her feet and glared at the men daring to touch her. 'Charlie, listen to me. Charlie! This is Artie! He brought me ice cream when I was pregnant. You trusted him to look after me when you were working. He did something bad. he made the wrong choice, but that doesn't make him a bad man! He's never done anything like this before, Charlie. Doesn't that – doesn't that give you any pause? Make you wonder at all?'

'Out of here,' Charlie ordered. He stood between her and Artie. 'It's for your own good, Beebee.'

The man with the gun pressed his chest against her again. 'Let's go, Mrs C.'

She stood her ground. 'Back off me. Now!'

'Easy there, tough guy,' Adam said, his voice a low growl. He pushed the man back with a flat hand. 'She doesn't want you so close.'

'And Mr C doesn't want her here at all,' the man growled back. 'She needs to get out of here.'

Adam turned all his attention to Bee, offered her his hand. 'There isn't anything else you can do,' he said. 'Come with me. Please.'

She looked from his open palm to Artie crying on her carpet to the thinly veiled rage burning across Charlie's face. Her stomach clenched, but she took his hand and let him lead her back to the stairs.

She refused to go further than the second step.

Adam understood even though she hadn't spoken a word. But he used his body as a blockade to keep her from going back in the room.

Artie still cried on his knees. 'Please. She's only eight. Please.'

Charlie stroked Artie's thinning hair, a small snarl on his face. 'As a favor to you, my old friend. I will not let your daughter know that her father died a rat. That will stay with us in this room. It will never leave here.'

Artie wailed.

'Unfortunately, you won't be leaving here either.'

Bee pressed her face between Adam's shoulder blades.

A gunshot.

Once, twice.

Quiet. Suppressed.

But she flinched anyway.

'It's over,' Adam murmured. 'Cleaning it up now.'

Bee didn't look. She ran for the nearest bathroom.

Bee gripped the toilet seat, heaving over and over again, her eyes clamped shut. Droplets of sweat covered the back of her exposed neck. Her abdomen tightened with every retch, released with every shaky breath.

She flushed the toilet with her eyes still closed, groaning as she stood on shaking legs. Trembling hands held on to the sink, and she studied her reflection. Underneath her blue eyes were dark purple half-moons, accentuating the crow's feet that Bee spent a good deal of money injecting away.

Bee opened the medicine cabinet and kept the mouthwash in her mouth for longer than the directions indicated, swishing it back and forth behind her cheeks and lifting up her chin to look at the purple bruises on her throat.

To think, less than 48 hours ago her biggest problem had been Rosalie Waters not investing in her bookstore. But Rosalie had been right, hadn't she? Charlie was the devil. A gutter rat, a snake *and* a serpent. She should thank the woman for her prayers. She'd been right about that too – Bee really could use all the extra prayers she could get.

There were two knocks on the door. 'Bee?'

Bee glared at the ceiling like it was at fault for all her problems and spat out the mouthwash. 'Yes, Adam?'

His severe widow's peak appeared first, followed by his handsome face, then his broad shoulders, and before she could even turn the full force of her glare on him, he was in the bathroom with her.

Adam shut the door and leaned against it. 'You all right?'

She smiled, guarded and grouchy. 'Peachy.'

'I wanted to, um' – he rubbed the back of his neck and couldn't quite look at her – 'I wanted to talk to you.'

Oh, did he now? This oughta be good. Did the lying liar who lies want to lay more lies on her? Did he want to use her obvious loneliness, their past relationship, her clear attraction to him for his own personal gain?

Bee tipped her head all the way back. What was wrong with her? Why did all that just make her more attracted to him?

'Yeah?' She sat on the countertop. 'What about?'

Would he come clean? Experience told her no. He was in here to get a read on what her thoughts were. To try and keep her under his thumb. He wasn't about to admit to anything. Not when the money was nowhere to be found.

Her chin trembled, and she bit her lip to steady it. She'd certainly done this to other people – maybe she deserved to see what the other side felt like.

'I just wanted to make sure you're OK. I know that guy was your friend.'

'He wasn't my friend.' She kicked her heels against the cabinet, over and over, one at a time. 'Just some guy I used to know.'

'Still, it was good what you did.' He was whispering, for effect, she figured. And so he'd have an excuse to move closer to her. 'Trying to find out the reason he betrayed you.'

Bee fiddled with the sink faucet. If Artie could turn on them, Artie who she'd known for over ten years, Artie who'd held her Oliver as a baby – if *he* could turn on them, there was no hope. There was no safe place.

Her eyes stung, and she gazed up at the nearest light fixture. 'There isn't any way out of this. They're going to keep coming. They're going to kill us. They're going to kill Oliver. They're going to kill me and—'

'That's not gonna happen,' Adam said, and any distance between them was gone. His hands hovered above her knees. 'I'm on your team, Bee.'

Her legs parted, ever so slightly, making room for Adam's hips.

He wasn't touching her, not really, but she could feel him all the same. Heat radiated from him and gathered in the pit of her stomach. His fingertips ghosted over her quivering thighs.

'We're going to figure this out.' His eyes were on her mouth. 'Together.'

She clutched the countertop, willed herself not to reach out and touch him. He was right there, so close. It would be easy to move the slightest bit forward. So easy to wrap her legs around his waist.

Bee swallowed down the urge to kiss him.

He was using her. He was lying to her.

'Thank you for telling me the truth, Adam,' she said. She pushed him back with the flat of her hand. 'I appreciate it. We gotta be able to trust each other. We're a team, right?'

'Yeah.' He ran a palm over his thinning hair. 'Yeah, we are.'

She jumped off the counter and hoped he couldn't see how wet her eyes were. 'Glad to hear it.'

She peeked into the living room to double-check the mess was gone before she allowed Oliver out of his room. Her attention was drawn to the painting Charlie had bought for her all those years ago.

Blood splatter covered the dancing ballerinas, their white tutus stained red.

Bee stared at the painting. Unblinking, mouth agape.

Degas ballerinas. She'd always been able to see the movement on the canvas. To see the fluidity of each dancer's steps.

But now all that remained was a massacre.

One of Charlie's men stood next to her, yellow gloves on his hands, cleaning blood off the wall with a damp sponge. The rug in the middle of the room and the man who'd died on it had already been disposed of.

He waved his sponge at the painting. 'Mr C said you'd know how to fix that.'

The priceless, one-of-a-kind, original work by Edgar Degas.

Ruined.

She'd know how to fix that.

She'd know how to fix something Charlie ruined. Destroyed.

Brutalized.

Bee covered her mouth with both hands and watched the dancers succumb to their demise.

Mr White opened the bedroom door for her.

Oliver didn't look up from his Nintendo. 'Lunch ready, Mom?'

She exhaled a smile. 'Not yet. Soon though.'

He flashed her the quickest thumbs up on record and got back to his game.

Her sweet boy. He had no idea what his father had done. They were so close to dying, the two of them. All because of Charlie. Charlie and his half-assed plan. His impulsive theft. His arrogance.

When Oliver was younger than two, Charlie had shot a man in their living room. She'd been upstairs in the nursery, trying to put their son down for the night. When she'd left to investigate the noise, only to find that Charlie could be so violent – so brutal – mere feet away from their sleeping child, she'd snapped back into herself. She'd realized what she'd done. That she'd tried to hide from Os but had only ended up hiding from herself.

She'd left that night and called Pinkerton for escape.

And Pinkerton – her best friend in her old life, her brother in her new one – he'd died trying to save her.

Bee kissed Oliver on the forehead. He wiped it off but grinned up at her. 'You OK, Mom? You look like you're gonna sneeze.'

She rubbed her nose with her knuckle. 'I'm – I'm fine. Let's get ready for church, huh? We'll go visit the church where I married your father and where you were baptized. Would you like to see it?'

He sighed and snapped his Game Boy closed. 'Fine, but only if I get to drink the blood of Christ.'

'I don't think they'll have the communion wine available on a random Tuesday evening, but I'll get you a Coke on the way there.'

'Deal.'

SIXTEEN

Oliver slurped the last bit of Coca-Cola from his medium-sized cup in the back of the Suburban.

'Wow, you drank that fast,' Mr White said. 'Bet you won't be thirsty for a while now.'

'Shows what you know! I'm still thirsty.'

Mr White held out his cup. 'You want the rest of mine? Just gotta switch straws.'

'Badass!' Oliver grabbed the half-full paper cup and switched the straws. 'Can I take it into church, Mom?'

Bee looked out the window at Saint Nicholas's. A large red-brick castle on a corner street, the church covered their car in shadow. 'I mean, I know your dad still tithes here on the regular, so probably. But don't spill anything.'

She didn't want to stay for long, didn't want to have to have a conversation with the priest. She wanted to light a candle for Artie, say a prayer for his daughter. She'd had no idea Rachael was sick. And now the little girl, only eight years old, would grow up without a father.

All because of Charlie. If Charlie hadn't taken Alvarez's money, if he hadn't taken Alvarez's niece into his bed, she'd still be in her home in Biscayne Bay, saving every dime she could to open her dream bookstore. Artie would still be alive to take care of his toothless, brunette beauty.

Adam slid out of the car and opened the passenger door for her. He didn't know that she knew what his true intentions were, and she was going to keep it that way. She hated him, hated him for lying to her, hated him for getting her drunk and trying to talk her into stealing stolen money.

But people were coming after them. Artie had turned on them. Men had shown up at her house, state troopers had blocked the road and white guys on Harleys had shot at them. People were going to keep coming after them as long as Alvarez was willing to pay for his revenge. Oliver was in danger, and Alvarez wasn't going away.

Bee had no choice but to keep Adam close.

So she'd put up with his perfect smile, and his hazel eyes, and his strong hands. She'd put up with his barreled chest and broad shoulders and the five o'clock shadow covering his square jaw. She'd put up with it with a giggle and a fluttering of eyelashes. Because he might be playing the game, but the master of the game had taught her all his tricks.

The inside of Saint Nicholas's never failed to take her breath away. Dark wooden pews lined the cream tiled aisle to the organ at the front of the sanctuary. High, domed ceilings painted pastel colors, the walls as bright as an Easter egg, delicate stained-glass windows filling the room with a rainbow of sunshine.

This was the church where she'd worn a white dress and pretended she wasn't pregnant. Where Pinkerton had taken her arm and given her away. Where she'd stood before God and vowed to love a man she didn't.

Os had terrified her into it. He'd always been controlling, and in the beginning, it had been worth it. Under his guidance, she'd learned to lie and steal and cheat like an expert. She'd told herself they were only robbing the rich anyway. What did it matter? But he'd grown more and more controlling of her every movement, refused to let her visit her only remaining family and had even started devising plans to target the men who shared her DNA to test her loyalty. She'd needed somewhere to run, somewhere safe, somewhere with enough manpower that Os couldn't simply walk in and destroy her. Charlie had been a mid-range mob guy when she'd discovered him. He'd had the boss's ear but none of his power, ran his own loan business as well as running supplies for the family. She'd spotted his potential immediately, not just as a mark but as someone able to climb the ladder. All he'd needed was a little push, and she'd have all the protection she could ever want.

Yeah, that had turned out perfectly, hadn't it?

Bee lit a candle for Artie and Rachael. And then she lit one for Oliver too. But when she bowed her head to pray, she found her thoughts quiet. What could she ask of a God she'd let down so many times? The God her mother had loved and taught her about and clung to when the cancer stole her ability to breathe.

In the end, she prayed for health.

She'd always been able to steal everything else.

'Mom,' Oliver whispered. 'Mom, I have to pee. I have to pee sooooooo bad, Mom. Mom. Mom!'

Bee opened her eyes with a sigh.

'I'll take him to the restroom, Mrs C,' Mr White said. 'I don't mind.'

She nodded her consent and took a seat in the nearest pew. Buff Jesus hung on a crucifix above the organ. Or was the whole thing called the crucifix, Christ and cross and all?

Adam sat down beside her but kept his hands to himself, and disappointment both at that and the fact she was disappointed that he didn't try to touch her washed over Bee at once.

'This is a swanky place.'

'Heavily funded.' Bee tugged her skirt hem lower on her crossed legs. 'Alvarez and his ilk see to that.'

'Even though he's in Miami now?'

She shrugged. 'He hasn't found a church he likes in Florida yet. He seems to think as long as he writes a check, God will forgive anything he does.'

'At least he believes in something,' Adam said. 'Gotta admire a guy with principles.'

'Help!' Mr White screamed. '*Help!*'

Adam was on his feet before she'd even processed what the other man was shouting, pulling a matte black Beretta M9 out of his shoulder holster.

Mr White limped down the aisle, one eye swollen, his nose busted and bleeding. Oliver was nowhere in sight.

Bee jumped out of the pew and ran, but Adam wouldn't let her pass. He held on to her arm and kept the gun in his hand, a critical eye sweeping over the injured man.

'Three men – they showed up,' Mr White said. He held on to a pew to stay upright. 'Pulled the little man out of the stall! I tried to stop them, but they took him!'

Bee's legs gave out from underneath her.

Adam helped her to her knees before assessing Mr White again. He still hadn't put his gun away.

'If three men came into the bathroom to snatch Oliver, what are you still doing breathing?'

Mr White inhaled, nostrils flaring, knuckles turning white on the pew. 'I tried, man. I tried to stop them. Look at me. I'm lucky they didn't shoot me. But I tried, I really did.'

Bee collapsed in on herself, forehead pressed against the cold tile. Tears fell one by one on the very aisle she'd walked down to marry the man who'd done this.

The father of her child had done this. Selfish and stupid. He'd risked Oliver's life.

And now Alvarez – Theo Alvarez himself – had her sweet little baby boy.

Someone was wailing, and it took Adam's hand stroking her spine, pulling her up into his arms, whispering comforting words in her ears to realize it was her.

Charlie already knew about Oliver by the time they made it back to the beach house. His eyes were red rimmed, his gelled hair pulled out at odd angles, sloppy sleeves pushed up above his elbows. He ran to the Suburban the moment the car pulled into the driveway and threw open Bee's door.

She hated him. She hated him with every fiber of her being.

He pulled her out of the car and held her tight.

'I'm so sorry,' he cried into her hair. 'Please believe me. Please. I'm so sorry.'

She set her jaw and stared straight ahead. Cassie stood on the front porch, wrapped in a shawl, tears streaming down her pretty face. Malika sat on the steps, her head in her hands.

He fell to his knees and wrapped his arms around her waist, pressed his face into her stomach. 'My son. They took my only son.'

'This is *your* fault.' The words fought their way out of her throat. They scratched her tongue and rattled her teeth. 'This is all your fault, Charlie.'

'I know.'

Bee moved away from him, and he let go of her without objection. But he didn't get off his knees in the middle of the driveway. He cried where he kneeled, Charles Cardello, the gutter rat, the serpent. The snake.

Bee touched the crown of Malika's head as she walked up the stairs, made eye contact with Cassie as she stepped into the beach house. The house she'd taken newborn Oliver home to from the hospital. There were men hovering about, but she paid them no mind. Nobody had been able to protect Oliver. Not Charlie and his redshirts. Not Adam and all his twisted promises.

Not her. Saying a prayer and lighting candles and pretending like this wasn't her fault too.

Bee locked the bathroom door and leaned against it, knees shaking under her. She didn't recognize her own reflection.

Who was this woman? Scared? Disheveled? Dark purple circles under her eyes, worry lines around her lips?

What was she doing?

She watched her reflection pull the hair tie off her bun. Ran her fingers through it, raked it back. She splashed cold water on her face and looked again in the mirror.

Oliver needed her. He needed her to get her shit together and clean up Charlie's mess.

Bee adjusted her boobs in the tank top, fluffing up her cleavage and her courage.

'Let's get to work.'

SEVENTEEN

It had only been a few hours since Oliver was taken, the moon still high in the sky, but it felt like a lifetime to Bee. Malika sat on the twin bed Oliver slept in, a brand-new laptop on her lap and a collection of iPhones fanned out on the bedspread. 'This hasn't been easy, given what I have to work with. But I did manage to dig up some dirt. You are not gonna be happy, boss.'

She was already not happy. She hadn't been happy in a long time.

'What'd you find?'

'First things first. Alvarez has Oliver. Best I can tell, he's taking him back to Miami.'

Bee nodded. She'd figured that.

'Now. Brace yourself.' Malika spun her new laptop around, a picture of Theo Alvarez getting into the backseat of a Lexus on the screen.

Mr White was behind the wheel.

Adam was holding the door open for Alvarez and a cell phone to his own ear, scowling.

Bee plopped down on to her bed, too stunned to move her gaze away from the screen.

'Malika,' she said. 'Wait.'

'Hmmm?' Malika recoiled. 'What? You gonna barf?'

Bee frowned and thought about it. She was a little queasy but nothing imminent was on its way. 'Is he still working for Alvarez?'

'Best I can tell?' She shook her head. 'This picture is four years old.'

Before Bee had even moved to Miami.

'Since then, I've been able to find him popping up in different places. But often with our pilot friend.' She pointed at Mr White and then tapped at the keyboard again. A low-resolution picture of the two of them walking on to a private jet popped up, mountains in the background. 'Looks like they get hired as a package deal. Adam does the heavy lifting. And White is transportation. Driving, flying, boat . . . captaining, or whatever it's called.

'I did go ahead and pull Adam's CIA file. You know, for fun.' It slid on to the screen, and Bee leaned in to read it, but before she could, more documents popped up. 'And FBI file. MI6 has a super-detailed report on him, and by that, I mean here is a piece of paper that's redacted.'

A small picture of Adam's scowling face sat at the top of the paper, followed by nothing but blacked-out lines of information.

'Oh, Interpol's in on it too, don't you worry. But I'm assuming you know a lot of this stuff already. Or at least it doesn't surprise you.'

'No.' Bee looked down at the floor and seriously considered floundering on to it. 'The Alvarez gig does surprise me though. I should've listened to you, Malika.'

Malika leaned across the divide of the beds to set her fingertips on Bee's shoulder. 'Are you gonna need a hug? Because I'm not really a hugger, but—'

'I'm OK.' Bee tugged on a loose string of her shirt. 'I'm just processing.'

'How do you feel about him?'

Her cheeks warmed. 'Every time I look at him, he makes something inside coil.' She put her hands on her stomach, below her belly button. 'Right here. Every time. A weird, twisting, turning, tingling sensation and I can't get it to stop.'

'In your bowels,' Malika said.

Bee looked away, unable to look her friend in the face anymore.

'You're so attracted to him that he makes you want to crap your pants,' Malika sighed. 'Well, I don't understand it, but let's get his take on things then, huh?'

She hopped off the bed and threw open the bedroom door. 'Hey, Butterfingers! Get in here!'

Hogarth waddled into the room first, followed by Adam, with his hands in his pockets and his eyes on the ground. Said eyes went wide and then squinted at the sight of himself plastered on the screen.

Hogarth barked, and Adam swore.

'Yeah, that's right.' Malika closed the door. 'We're on to you. We know all about you. You've got some explaining to do.'

The dog tried valiantly to jump on to Bee's lap but was simply much too fat, so he curled around her feet instead.

She shook her head at him.

'Huh,' Adam said, peering closer at the monitor, 'I look good in that one.'

Of course in the picture indicated he was shirtless and holding an older flip phone to his ear, squinting off into the distance, directly at the camera spying on him.

Bee rolled her eyes.

'Take a seat.' Malika sat next to Bee and left her supplies covering the other bed.

Adam looked around at his lack of seating options. 'I'm good thanks. But how – how did you do all this? Is that my MI6 file?'

Malika crossed her arms over her chest. 'Obviously.'

Adam's gaze zeroed in on Bee, who couldn't quite make eye contact back. 'This is your nanny?'

'I'm a hacktivist,' Malika said. 'I'm good at it. I search for terrorists online, then I tattle on them to the CIA. It's all kind of a grey area in terms of, like, it being legal or not. So I have some leeway as far as personal inquiries go. I understand their systems. I can get in, I can get out, and they aren't looking for me anymore.'

He adjusted the silver Rolex on his wrist. 'A hacker nanny. What are the odds of that, Shelby?'

Bee sat up straight and looked directly into his hazel eyes, doing her best to ignore the way her lower belly tingled. 'You're still on good terms with Alvarez, aren't you?'

His brows creased in surprise, those two warning lines making an appearance, and he nodded.

'I'm going to need you to contact him. I have a plan.'

'A plan?' Malika repeated. 'That involves the guy who wants you dead?'

'Yep,' Bee said. 'We're gonna do lunch.'

'Lunch,' said Adam, his whole face furrowed. 'You're gonna do lunch with Theo Alvarez?'

'We've done it your way,' Bee chirped. 'With all guns blazing. And car chases. Now we're gonna do it my way.'

He held up his hands in surrender.

'I've got Claire Brown's passport and credit cards in my go bag,' Bee said. 'But you and Adam are gonna need something.'

Malika nodded once and stood, bumping her shoulder hard into Adam's chest when she grabbed her duffle bag from the foot of Oliver's bed. She rifled through it for a moment then said, 'Here,' and tossed Adam a badge. 'Congratulations. You're an air marshal.'

He studied the air marshal badge. 'This is real.'

Malika looked like she knew this already. 'Yeah.'

'How did you get an air marshal badge?'

Malika covered her heart. 'I routinely hack into the CIA, that's how—' She rubbed her temples. 'Look, I'm a big help, you know? But I'm off the books. So sometimes they go out and grab some coffee and leave me alone with gadgets and junk.'

He held it up. 'This is junk?'

She shrugged. 'I haven't had a use for it until today, so it's been sitting around, taking up space.'

Adam stared out the window. 'What's happening to me right now?'

'Everybody, take a breath,' Bee said in her mom voice. 'We've got work to do. Malika, I'm going to need everything you can find on Alvarez and his guys. I mean, absolutely everything. Even if you think it's inconsequential, I want it. OK?'

'You got it, boss.'

'Be honest with me,' she said, twisting the knife he didn't know about. 'Yeah, Adam?'

'Yeah, Bee. Yeah.'

She hugged herself. 'Who told you about the robbery?'

Adam scratched the stubble on his chin. 'His name is Delgado. He works for Alvarez.'

A smile spread across Bee's face, so big she couldn't see anything but her own eyelashes. She had her own Delgado back home. Liliana, who'd painstakingly helped her dress for her church ambush on Rosalie Walters. 'Delgado?' She wanted to be sure. 'Martin Delgado?' Before she started celebrating, she wanted to be sure.

'Yeah, Martin Delgado.'

Her smile hurt her cheeks. 'Fantastic!' Bee rubbed her palms down her thighs and stood up. 'We leave for Miami as soon as possible. I have to gather supplies in the city.'

Adam asked, 'What are you gonna do?'

'What I do best,' Bee said. 'I'm going to find a man in need and give him exactly what he wants.'

EIGHTEEN

She crept out of the bedroom with her powder foundation compact shoved in her bra and moved on tiptoes down the stairs to the kitchen. Redshirts were around, but none of them were interested in her, and she couldn't see Charlie.

Thank God. She hadn't talked to him since he'd broken down in the driveway. An entire day spent hiding and stewing and planning. Waiting on Malika to find information before she struck. Even though they'd started before Oliver had been taken, they were still so far behind.

She ducked into the kitchen, grabbed a cheese stick from the fridge and a paper towel off the counter. She bounded up the stairs and stood stock-still at the end of the hallway, ears trained for the sound of approaching footsteps.

Sure she was alone, she tiptoed to the master bedroom. The door creaked when she opened it, and she held her breath.

No one materialized around her.

Bee slunk into the dark room and ate half the cheese stick while she waited for her eyes to adjust. Everything seemed to be exactly as she'd left it. The same blackout curtain covering the glass balcony door. The same bedding set. The same ridiculous number of pillows. The same pictures on the wall.

Bee frowned. How could Cassie sleep in here when the ex-wife was smiling down at her?

Weird.

The forgery of Van Gogh's *Sunflowers* – one of her own, thank you very much – came off the wall easily, revealing a small safe. The safe had two locks: one that opened with a traditional code punched into a keypad. The other only opened for a matching fingerprint.

Bee held up the powder and blew. Loose particles drifted down like snowflakes over the safe's fingerprint scanner.

She pushed the rest of the cheese stick on the scanner, covering it in her makeup, before wiping off the device with a paper towel.

Then she entered the code on the number pad, frowning when it was correct.

'Still my birthday, huh? Also weird.'

She put the made-up cheese stick on the scanner. It read her husband's fingerprint, and the lock opened.

Bee clucked her tongue and grabbed three stacks of $10,000.

Cheese stick disposed of and money stashed in her go bag, Bee found Charlie sitting on the back porch, Cassie on his lap.

Her body shook from head to toe. 'May I speak to you,' she said and didn't ask. 'Privately.'

Charlie tapped Cassie's thigh and rose from his seat.

'Oh, Bee.' Cassie grabbed her hand. Her dark eyes shone in the sun. 'Oh, Bee, I'm so sorry.'

Bee's heart froze in her chest. Had something happened? Was Oliver— She couldn't even think it.

Charlie shook his head. 'Alvarez's got him, but he's alive. In Miami. Banks sent word.'

Banks was Charlie's number two, in charge of running most of the logistical aspects of Cardello Industries. Charlie was the charisma, the public face and – terrifyingly enough – the ideas guy. Banks was everything else.

Somehow, Malika had gotten hold of that information before Charlie. Even though her nanny continually impressed Bee, Malika's skills were never a surprise.

'Would you give us a minute?' Charlie asked.

Cassie dropped a kiss on his cheek and shut the glass doors behind her.

Charlie still had a mark on his cheek from where she'd decked him.

She wanted to punch him again. At least so he'd be symmetrical. But she wrapped her hands around the back of the patio chairs. Let the cold metal bite into her palms, her knuckles turning white.

'I'm leaving soon. Me and Gage and Malika.' Bee watched the waves roll in. 'We're heading to Miami.'

'Miami,' Charlie repeated. 'Into the lion's den.'

She nodded once, willed herself not to cry. 'Yeah, into the lion's den. I'm going to Miami, and I'm going to recruit backup. I'll rescue Oliver, Charlie. I'll clean up your mess for you. But you're gonna have a part to play in this too.'

'What?'

'I don't know yet,' Bee said. 'But when I call, you answer.'

Charlie turned away from her, leaned a flat palm against the wall of the house. 'You'll need cash.'

She shrugged. 'I already stole some money from your safe. You really should consider changing your combination. And cleaning your fingerprint scanner. That wasn't difficult.'

His eyes widened, a grin playing at his lips, and Bee wanted nothing more than to break his mouth so he'd never be able to smile again. He pulled out his wallet and handed her a wad of hundreds anyway.

Bee licked her lips, dithered.

'Go on,' he said. 'Take it.'

She snatched the money out of his hand.

'I miss you, Bee. A lot.'

She stashed the cash in her cleavage. 'I haven't gone anywhere.'

'You know what I mean. We were a team. Partners. I miss that. I miss you.'

Bee closed her eyes. Bloody ballerinas stuck to the back of her eyelids; turned into a limping, bleeding Mr White screaming for help. She let go of the chair and tried to rub the image away.

'Maybe when all this is over . . . maybe you and me, we can open up that bookstore you want.' Charlie stepped closer to her. 'Oliver would like that. The three of us, in business together. A real business, you know.'

Bee pursed her lips and stared him down. 'I don't want anything from you.'

He covered his heart with his hand. 'You wound me, Beebee. Why? Why do you hate me so much when all I've ever done is love you?'

'Love?' She laughed. 'You don't love me, Charlie. You love yourself.'

'What do you know about it?'

'You're a bad man, Charlie. You thought you saw enough good in me that it could help change you. That there was something in me that could redeem you.' Her eyes burned. She blinked the pain away and forced herself to look at him even though it made it worse. 'But there's nothing good in me. There never was. It was all a lie.'

'Don't you dare try to tell me that none of it was real,' Charlie said with a measure of panic in his hushed voice. 'I know you, Bee. Whether you like it or not, I know you. You loved me.'

She looked away from him, watched the waves crash on the sand. 'The first time we met.'

His shoulders stiffened. 'Yeah. What about it?'

'I'd planned it. Far in advance. I waited in the alley for you to walk by and then tripped into you so you would have to catch me.'

Charlie patted his pockets and pulled out a box of cigarettes and a lighter. 'So what?'

'I altered who I was. I pretended to be someone you could save. In a bad job, too poor to chase such a grand dream of becoming – what was it now? An accountant?' She chuckled and shook her head. 'Once I had you where I wanted you, I started whispering in your ear about all the scores the two of us could pull off. It shows how little you learn from past mistakes that you let this new girl do it to you again.'

He puffed on a cigarette, his lips parted around it in a feeble imitation of a smile. 'That's called dating, Bee. Everyone lies to get people's attention. Everyone schemes to start a relationship. But we were together for eight years. Don't pretend you spent the entirety of eight years conning me. Besides, stealing from Alvarez was my idea, not Cassie's. She's innocent.'

'Then why even bring her into it?'

'Jealous?'

Bee rolled her eyes.

'You don't need to be jealous, Beebee. She's around to keep me warm at night. What am I supposed to do? Be cold while you go through this phase?'

She sighed. 'We've been over this. This is not a phase. I don't love you, Charlie.'

'Ah, but you used to.' He pointed his cigarette at her. 'And you will again. That kind of stuff, it comes and it goes. And I'm a patient man.'

'Get it through your thick head,' Bee ground out between clenched teeth. 'I never loved you.'

Charlie stepped into her personal space. His eyes burned into hers, his cigarette-filled puff soft on her lips. 'For eight years, you shivered every time I touched you.' He caressed her cheek with one knuckle, and she proved his point despite herself.

He smirked, emboldened. 'For eight years, you never turned me down once. For eight years, you came in my bed willingly. For eight years, you initiated kisses, you reached for my hand, you sought out my eyes and my approval. You praised me every chance you got.' Charlie leaned in closer still, breathed her in, and when his chest expanded, it grazed her own. 'You got on your knees and worshipped at my feet, and you mean to tell me that you never loved me?'

She swallowed down the urge to back away. 'I mean to tell you it was a lie. Tell me, Charlie,' she said, braving his brown eyes. Oliver's eyes. 'Using that impeccable memory of yours, how many times in eight years did I ever say "I love you" first?'

Bee watched him process the question. 'Because I'll give you a hint – the only times I ever said it first were when I wanted something. I got pregnant because I wanted your protection. I wanted to get married because I wanted your money. I got on my knees and worshipped at your feet because I wanted you to trust me. And it worked. Because you let me leave with more than what I came in with. And all I had to do was make sure you got to see your son every once in a while. I got the house, and I got half your money, because you believed every one of my lies.'

He took the last drag of his cigarette, his gaze stuck on her mouth. 'I was wrong. We aren't alike.' He dropped the butt to the ground, snuffed it out beneath his shoe. 'What you do is messier.'

Charlie slid open the glass door but paused at the threshold. 'Be safe, Bee.' He clutched the handle tight. He still wore his wedding ring. 'I'll be praying God grants you the same protection he granted Daniel in the lion's den.'

He didn't look back.

Bee covered her mouth to block the sob that threatened to call after him.

NINETEEN

'Ugh,' Bee groaned. 'Really?'

Adam looked at her, earbuds in, a finger on the touch-screen. 'What?'

'Our lives have been a constant stream of senseless violence these last few days and you're going to unwind with an action thriller?'

He glanced at the screen in the airplane seat in front of him and back at her. 'It's just a movie.'

'But it's also been our experience. Wouldn't, like, the opposite be more relaxing? Like a musical or something.'

'A musical, huh?' He didn't smile, but his face looked more delighted than confused now. 'What would you recommend?'

Bee wasn't exactly up on her theatrically released musicals. 'Uh.'

'*Grease*,' Malika said. '*Grease 2*. That's all I've got.'

'I doubt they've got old movies on this thing,' Adam said. 'It's a domestic flight.'

'Why are you watching movies anyway?' Malika swiped through apps on her phone. 'Shouldn't you be air marshalling?'

'I'm not actually an air marshal.'

'Malika's right.' Bee chose to ignore Adam's facts. 'I don't want any plane-related incidences. We've already had a car incident and a motorcycle incident and a house incident. I'd like to survive this flight with only minimal turbulence and no one trying to kill me 30,000 feet in the air.'

Adam took the earbuds out and settled into his seat. 'No one's been trying to kill you.' He clasped his hands behind his head. 'Take you as a hostage and kill you later at a time more convenient for the Big Bad, yeah.'

'Right well, that's all.' Bee bit her lip to keep from smiling too big.

'Where'd you find that anyway?' Adam waved his elbow, not unlike a chicken wing, at her drop-down table. 'Steal it off a toddler in the airport?'

'It's an adult coloring book,' she snarked. 'I *bought* it at the airport. And as you can see, I'm staying in the lines.'

'Good job.' He grinned. 'Is there anything you can't do?'

Bee opened her mouth to reply, but Malika beat her to the punch with a rather accurate exclamation of, 'Cook!'

Bee closed her mouth and nodded.

'Sing.' Malika fired off a list on her fingertips. 'Though she keeps trying for some reason. She gave up on tennis super quick.'

'I wanted to get into it, you know, for the cute outfits.' She bumped Adam's knee when she reached for a different coloring pencil. 'But I never surpassed mediocre, and the coach I hired spent half the time talking about the script he was writing.'

'Ooh, I remember that.' Malika turned her attention back to her phone. 'How many more movies do we need of a no-longer-violent man whose wife dies off-screen coming out of retirement to get revenge? That's almost every dude movie ever made. I mean, talk about toxic masculinity.'

'Toxic what?' Adam asked. 'What are you talking about? It does sound like a movie I've seen, but you never know, maybe he had a different take on it.'

Bee took a delicate sip of her soda. 'He did not.'

'Toxic masculinity is a belief in our culture that the most negative, harmful stereotypes about manliness are somehow part and parcel with the male gender,' Malika ranted. 'They're unavoidable. They're even desirable. It leads to problems with men being able to express their, let's say, softer emotions without ridicule or judgment. It works against them in custody cases, even if the mother is unfit. Male victims of rape are often ignored or told hey, what's the big deal? Etcetera, etcetera, dudes, dudes, dudes for all eternity. I'm bored now.'

Adam said, 'Huh,' and his whole face went blank.

'Actually, you could be the poster boy for it, seeing as how you're a balding man who's paid to be violent—'

Adam scowled. 'I am not balding. It's called a widow's peak.'

'—but I've yet to see you brood, and you smile way too much.' Malika put her earbuds in. 'I'm going to watch pimple-popping videos now until we land, and I'd appreciate it if no one talked to me.'

Bee gagged. 'Hide your screen.'

'Where?' Malika looked around. 'Where would you like me to hide it? I'm jammed into the window seat.'

'Pimple-popping videos?' Adam leaned over Bee to get a better look at the phone. 'Stuff like that is on the internet?'

'Literally everything is on the internet,' Malika said and played one.

Bee covered her mouth and closed her eyes. Her gut flopped around inside her like a dying fish.

Adam said, 'There's a whole boiled egg in that guy's arm!'

'Switch with me.' Bee bopped Malika on the elbow. 'Switch. Switch. Quick! Come on, come on.'

'All right, all right, hold your horses.' She unbuckled and rose. 'It's natural – you don't have to be so crazy about it.'

Bee lifted the armrest and scooted beneath her. 'You two have fun.' She did her best to disappear into her coloring book.

Malika handed Adam one earbud, and the two of them sat close, heads together, watching all the horrible things that the inventor of the internet – thanks a lot, Al Gore – had unleashed on the world.

Bee grinned despite herself. She flipped to the back of the last page, folded it over so she could use the blank side and took out the black pencil.

Malika and Adam's laughing profiles took the rest of the flight to sketch. She'd give it to Oliver as soon as she could. He'd love it.

Adam set his small suitcase down on the shiny white floor of baggage claim. 'Don't know why you had to check a bag,' he said.

'They weren't gonna let me carry on my taser,' said Malika. 'There's my bag now, so don't get your panties all in a twist.'

Adam sighed. 'You know, I've got sisters.'

'That's great,' Malika said. 'Can you take my bag?'

'I'm not a pack mule.'

'Yeah.' She rolled the suitcase next to his feet. 'You aren't an air marshal either, and yet, here we are.'

He raised the handle, set his bag on top. 'Two sisters.' He held out his palm to Bee and smacked his fingers against it when she hesitated. Bee handed over her duffle bag. 'Fraternal twins. Pain in the ass, both of them. You guys would all get along.'

Malika hummed. 'You know I'm young enough to be your daughter, right?'

He wrinkled his sturdy nose. 'What's that got to do with anything?'

'Excuse me, ma'am?' A TSA agent approached Bee. He had a mustache that looked like he'd grown it as a homage to Hercule Poirot, and the pallor of someone who lived in Miami but was allergic to sunlight and beaches and fun. 'Can I see your ID?'

Bee smiled easy. She glanced at her companions and pulled her wallet out of her purse. 'Of course, but can I ask what for?'

Mustache Vampire checked over Claire Brown's ID, looked at Bee's face and back again. 'You came up as someone matching the description of a— Well, it's best if you come with me for a minute.'

'Description of a what?' Adam positioned half his body between her and the agent. 'Go with you where?'

He gave Bee back the ID. 'It'll only be for a minute. There's a small detention center—'

That caused both Adam and Malika to squawk in protest.

'*Detention center?*' Malika exclaimed. 'You are out of your ever-loving mind if you think Claire needs to be detained!'

'You don't need to detain anybody,' Adam said at the same time. He pulled out his badge. 'I can vouch for Claire. She ain't done nothing that needs detaining.'

Mustache Vampire offered them what he must have thought was a reassuring smile.

It wasn't.

'It's fine. There's plenty of magazines to read. It'll only be for a minute while we make a few phone calls.'

'Phone calls?' Malika repeated like they were the vilest words ever uttered. 'Oh, you won't be the only one making phone calls, mister!'

'It's all right. Calm down.' Bee rubbed Malika's arm, caught Adam's eye.

Them overreacting wasn't doing her any favors.

'It'll be a minute.' She arched an eyebrow. 'I only need a minute. OK?'

'Fine,' Malika pouted.

Adam nodded. 'We're not going anywhere.'

'I do apologize for the inconvenience, Miss Brown.'

Mustache Vampire didn't sound sorry.

He led her to a small corner room that reminded Bee of a hospital waiting area. Uncomfortable chairs lined three walls, and random magazines were scattered every few feet. There wasn't a door. But there was a lady TSA agent standing at the entrance with her hands on her belt. She was younger than thirty, Black and looked like she could use a cup of coffee.

'Airport police say you match the description of someone who's been coming in here and stealing luggage.' Mustache Vampire gestured at the chairs.

Bee looked at them and didn't sit. 'I match the description of a luggage thief?' She willed the muscle above her eyebrow not to twitch. 'What a coincidence.'

'I'm sure,' he said. 'But I need to make a few phone calls. Can I have your ID again actually? I'll need to run it. I'm sure this is a simple misunderstanding. But I do have to be thorough.'

Bee dug out her ID and handed it over with a tight smile. 'Of course.'

He left, and she sank down into an uncomfortable chair.

'What a coincidence.'

The TSA agent left to guard her offered a sympathetic nod.

Bee picked up a fashion magazine. Between flipping pages, she observed her guard.

The woman's top pulled at her chest, too small for her bosom. A single diamond ring hung from a gold chain around her neck.

Bee shared a look of surprise with the model in the mascara ad. She peeked over the magazine. The guard's ring finger was ringless.

'Hmm.' She turned a page.

The guard's shoes were sensible, but she shuffled on her feet and leaned against the wall, frowning.

She knew what she had to do, and she wasn't proud of it. But Oliver was somewhere in this city, taken hostage by a gangster, and if she had to lie to and manipulate a pregnant woman to set up his rescue, then so be it.

Bee set the magazine down. She stretched her arms above her head and yawned. 'It's quiet in here.'

The agent nodded and closed her eyes.

Bee stood and walked across the room. She made a big show at the magazine rack, tapping her finger against her chin and clicking her tongue, before finally grabbing a *Vogue*.

She sat down across from the entrance. Bee flipped a page or two and counted to fifty in her head.

'Oh!' Bee gasped in surprise. 'Did you see that?'

The TSA agent opened her eyes.

Bee covered her mouth. 'A family walked by with a newborn baby.' She hung her head and sucked in a shuddering breath. 'Oh, I know I should be happy for them. But I feel like I'm being punished.'

She sobbed. Tears rolled down her cheeks, and she made no effort to wipe them away. 'All I wanted to do was bring his ashes to the ocean. That's all I wanted. Oh, my poor baby. My poor baby!'

The TSA agent sat down next to her. She took Bee's hand in her own. 'I am so, so sorry for your loss.'

Her crying came out more like a squeal. Snot ran from her nose, and she let it. 'I was seven months. Seven months and— Oh God!'

Bee collapsed on to the agent's shoulder. 'He was perfect! My baby!'

The agent put an arm around Bee and squeezed her tight.

She let herself cry, good and long, before she sat up and sniffled. Bee used her whole palm to wipe her face clean. 'My mom never got to meet him, you know? So we were going to go out on her boat. And say goodbye.' She closed her eyes and blubbered.

The agent *oooh*ed and squeezed Bee again. 'That sounds like a sweet thing to do.'

'But now they're holding me in here. Like I'm a terrorist.' Bee inhaled through her nose, loud and wet. 'They're saying I'm a luggage thief at this airport? I don't even live here. I'm from New Jersey. How could I be stealing luggage from the Miami airport?'

The agent shrugged. 'Sometimes computers get things wrong. I'm sure we'll be able to sort this out and prove you're innocent.'

'I want . . .' Her voice shook, and her eyes filled with tears yet again. 'I want to get my baby's ashes. And I want to be with my momma!'

The agent stroked her hair. 'There, there. Would you like some water? Get hydrated. Maybe it'll help you find some calm.'

'Yeah.' Bee pulled her quivering lips into a smile. 'Water would be nice.'

She patted Bee's hand and winked. 'I'll be right back.'

Adam and Malika were waiting for her outside the sliding doors of the airport.

'I'm going straight to hell,' Bee announced.

'Why?' Malika twisted her hair into a messy braid. 'Whatcha do?'

'I may have told a pregnant TSA agent that the reason I was here was to scatter my stillborn baby's ashes in the ocean with my mother.'

Malika paused in mid wrap of her hair tie. 'That's dark.' She blinked and remembered what she was doing. 'Even for us, that's dark.'

'Hey.' Adam hailed a cab. 'It worked.'

He'd started to sweat in the Miami heat.

'Little warm for ya?' Malika teased.

He opened the trunk of the taxi and stuck their luggage inside. 'If I take off my jacket, somebody'll take me down. People don't like seeing shoulder holsters at airports for some reason.' He slammed the trunk shut and opened the car door for them. 'Doesn't change the fact that the sun has set and it's still ninety degrees out.'

'Well, Claire Brown is burned,' Bee said before she slid inside the cab. Her brunette wig collected all the humidity in the air and caused condensation to form on her scalp. She pulled it off and held it in her lap. 'We're gonna have to figure something else out for lodging options.'

Adam sat in the passenger's seat.

'Where to?' the driver asked him. He wore a golf hat and spoke with a thick Cuban accent.

Adam turned halfway in his chair to look at her.

She fiddled with the hair in her lap. 'What's the fanciest hotel around here with a super-nice bar?'

Malika held the compact open while Bee applied makeup.

'I don't understand why this is necessary,' said Adam from the front seat.

Bee closed her red lipstick and tossed it into her purse. 'Do you or do you not want to sleep in a bed tonight?'

He raised a shoulder. 'Don't matter to me.'

'It matters to me,' Malika said. 'We need a home base with plenty of outlets and room service.' She sniffed. 'And you need a shower.'

He let out something between a groan and a chuckle.

Bee took off her leggings. Her dark blue tunic covered her bum and not much else. She pulled out a pair of six-inch pumps that were nude on top and red on the bottom.

Bee gasped in delight when she slid them on. 'Oh, how I have missed you ladies!'

The taxi pulled into the drop-off of the Biltmore Hotel. The hotel looked as if the Big House from Percy Jackson had undergone refurbishment to be more Mediterranean. Grecian statues and fountains decorated every empty spot that wasn't the massive golf course surrounding it on three sides.

'Can you wait for us?' Adam asked the driver. 'What do you think – twenty minutes?'

Bee scoffed. 'Ten.'

'Twenty minutes,' said Adam. He handed the driver a fifty-dollar bill. 'Keep the meter running.'

'Yes, sir.'

The three of them stood outside the lobby doors with bellboys and valets politely not looking their way. The hot air swayed the palm branches of trees above her head, filling her lungs with humidity when she breathed in deep.

Strange to be back in the place she called home without her son at her side. She missed him so much her body ached, but he didn't need her worry or her tears or her pain. He needed her to do what she was best at.

'I'll be right back.'

Adam shook his head. 'I don't want you going in there alone.'

'What?' She grinned. 'You wanna be the flirt?' She tapped his chest as she walked by, an older gentleman opening the door for her. 'See you in ten!'

She chose the more upscale restaurant option in the hotel (the Biltmore had six) and scanned the bar.

Few patrons sat underneath the warm lighting, sipping drinks. A man towards the end had a Scotch in his hand and several empty glasses in front of him. He was a white guy in his mid-forties, well dressed and bald.

Bee took the seat next to him.

She ordered a glass of rosé and caught his eye.

His gaze stuck on her chest.

She turned to give him a better view and smiled. 'Hi.'

The same older gentlemen opened the door for her upon her triumphant return to the hotel's motorcade.

Malika pulled out her phone. 'Nine minutes. Nice.'

She and Adam gathered around Bee, the three of them forming

a small circle, and she held out her palm to display her treasures away from prying eyes.

'OK, I got his ID' – Bee nudged it with her fingertip – 'and I think he's a great match for Adam.'

Adam took the card. 'Are you kidding me? Look at this guy.'

Bee snatched it from his hand. 'Don't look too close.'

'He's got a solid fifty pounds on me!'

The game of hot potato continued when Malika took the ID from Bee. 'He's like your twin. He's a white dude; you're a white dude. He's bald. You're bald.'

'I am not bald.' He rubbed his hand on his head. 'See? I've been growing it in. Give it time. It'll come back.'

'You lost some weight, OK?' Bee rubbed his arm, up and down, her voice soft. 'You started working out. You bought some Rogain. It's a midlife crisis. That's why you're taking two girls to a nice hotel. I also have his credit card—'

'Ooh, a black one!' Malika took it too. 'Those are my favorite.'

'—and he had his wedding ring in his pocket.' Bee held up the solid gold band between two fingers. 'So I don't feel so bad about taking his stuff.'

She still had one card left in her hand.

'Why do you have a hotel key for this place?' asked Malika.

'Oh, he gave it to me.' Bee tugged at the hem of her makeshift dress. 'Yeah, he thinks my affections are negotiable. Anyway. Where's our cab? Let's go. I'm tired.'

Adam waved their taxi driver over, and the three of them piled back inside.

Bee said, 'Take us to the Four Seasons please.'

TWENTY

'I'm sorry, sir,' the young woman behind the counter said. She hadn't bothered to check her computer. 'As you can see, we're very busy. Our only available room is the presidential suite, and it's $6,650 a night.'

Malika leaned on the counter and dropped her voice to a conspiratorial whisper. 'There are an awful lot of nerds here.'

She and Bee flanked Adam. Bee held on to his elbow, but Malika had opted to walk herself through the Four Seasons lobby. The lobby itself was impressive, furnished with many comfortable places to loiter. A high, lit ceiling worked in the favor of the many prints of upscale artwork framed along the walls.

A wide variety of bespectacled individuals milled about. Several had opted to drink in front of the life-sized bronze statue of a naked woman and were not so discreetly taking pictures of each other tweaking her nipples.

'Pharmacists,' the woman whispered. 'There's a convention right now.'

Adam dropped his stolen ID and credit card on to the counter. 'We'll take the suite for two nights.' He pulled out Charlie's cash from his jacket pocket, being careful not to flash his gun, and counted out $14,000. 'Keep the change. Only use the card for incidentals, yeah?'

Her green eyes grew as wide as a turtle's shell. 'Of course, Mr Lynch. Let's get you and your guests checked in right away! Will you be needing help with your luggage?'

'Yeah. I'm done being a pack mule for the night.'

She waved over a bellboy who sprang into action, taking the few small bags from next to them.

'Good for you, Mr Lynch.'

Malika flung herself on to one of the four large couches in the living-room area of the suite. 'This,' she exclaimed, 'is the only way to travel. Mortimer! Be a dear and fetch my slippers.'

'Oh good, you found your bed,' Bee said. 'I'll take the king.'

Malika stuck out her tongue.

Adam tipped the bellboy and shut the door. 'I gave that kid twenty bucks for pushing three bags in a cart.'

Bee shrugged. 'At least it's Charlie's money.'

He rocked his head from side to side in reluctant agreement.

Malika shot off the couch and raced to the large bag on the floor. She pulled out her laptop and hugged it tight to her chest. 'Hello, beautiful.'

'We gotta do this stuff now?' Adam glanced at his watch. 'It's late.'

'We don't have to do anything.' She pulled out more computer-related accessories. 'But I am gonna get connected before I sleep. Also, here.' She handed him a box of .45 caliber bullets. 'I've got your nine-millimeter in here somewhere too. And— Ah! Howard!'

Malika kissed a black taser, a loud pop in the hotel room. 'It's good to see you again.'

Bee set her bag on a couch and rifled through it for something to wear to bed. Malika had been in charge of getting her some casual clothes in New Jersey, since her go bag was long ago packed for escape and not for sleep.

'You named your taser?' Adam flung his duffle bag over his shoulder and followed Bee. 'Howard?'

'Howard Sparks.' Malika dumped her belongings on the stately desk by the window. She opened the curtain to let the Miami skyline light up the dark night. 'He's the father of Tony Sparks, our country's most lovable douche of a taser.'

He threw a confused glance in Bee's direction. 'I don't wanna know.'

'Malika,' she said, 'there's no underwear in here.'

'Hmm?' said Malika. 'Oh, that's because I forgot to bring you any.'

Bee tossed her arms up. 'You forgot underwear but remembered a sweater? It's ninety degrees outside!'

'Sometimes it gets chilly in the AC!' She flopped into a chair. 'I guess I don't spend enough time thinking about your ass, I'm so sorry!'

Bee pinched the bridge of her nose. She'd used up all her underthings at the beach house and for whatever stupid reason hadn't done a load of laundry before hopping on the plane. 'Oh well. I'll just be wild and free.'

'Wild?' Adam didn't laugh. But he did come close.

She grabbed her bag and marched for the bathroom. 'I don't have to explain myself!'

Showered and mostly clothed, Bee left the bathroom with a comb in her hand.

Adam gathered up a few belongings for his turn in the bathroom.

'Wait, wait, wait.' Malika grinned. 'Wait. I got something for you guys that you're gonna dig. Or hate. Doesn't matter to me. But I got them ready to go.'

She opened a small brown case and slid it to the edge of the desk.

'Contacts,' Bee said. 'You got us a pair of contacts?'

'No. I got you each one contact. Go on – put them on.'

Bee shook her head. 'No. It's a trick.'

Malika's mouth fell open. 'It is not a trick! It's a gadget! Come on – try them on, then we can go to sleep.'

Adam plucked one out of the case. 'Let's get it over with.'

'That's the spirit!'

Bee acquiesced, frowning, and struggled to put the contact in her eye for a solid minute and a half.

She blinked, expecting to be blind in that eye, or at least for her vision to improve. But there was no discernible change.

Malika opened a program on her computer, and two different views of almost the same scene – herself, sitting at the hotel desk – were side by side on her monitor.

'Ta-da! Those contacts are cameras! I can see what you guys see tomorrow. I can also send you relevant information through them.' She drummed her palms on her desktop.

Bee braced herself. 'Oh, here we go.'

Adam flinched so hard he rocked back on his feet. 'What the hell was that?'

'That was a screaming succubus!' Malika cackled. 'You gave me such an old man face.'

Adam took the contact out of his eye and set it back down in the case. 'Old man face? I don't have an old man face.'

Malika mirrored his flinch, eyes wide yet furiously blinking, chin tucked to her neck.

'If anything that was a surprised face,' said Adam. 'I wasn't expecting it. I'm not a big computer person.'

'You don't say.'

Oliver would've been delighted by the image and the fallout, proud of his nanny, joining in on making fun of Adam.

Bee waved a hand between them. 'All right now. You show me what they can do. And no screaming monsters.'

'You are no fun. But OK.' Malika typed on her computer, and blueprints appeared in Bee's vision. 'See, now, those are the blueprints to the Louvre. Which isn't relevant to what we're doing, but still cool, am I right? If I find something you need to see, you can see it instantly.

'And here.' She opened another case in her pile of electronics. 'Virtually invisible inner-ear comms. We can talk to each other no matter where we are, and we can hear what's happening around the other person too.'

Bee picked one up between two fingers. Made of a see-through, plasticy material, the inner working electronic parts and wires were the skin tone of a pale to light tan person.

'Nifty.' She tried it on and motioned for Adam to do the same. 'Testing, testing.'

He nodded. 'It's good.' And she could hear him in her head and right next to her. 'Good work.' He set the comm back in the case and headed for the bathroom. 'You still get third shower though.'

The door clicked shut. Malika rubbed her nose with the back of her hand and sniffled. 'I need to ask you, Bee.'

'Yeah?'

'How . . . how much do you want Alvarez to know about you?'

Bee propped a hip against the desk and stared down at the keyboard. 'I think,' she said slowly, 'we should let my reputation do some of the work for me. But don't make it too easy.'

'Me? Never.'

When Malika took her turn in the bathroom, Bee pulled out the extra bedding stored in the suite's closet.

'You sure you don't mind the couch?' The pillow fell on her face, and she pulled it out of the way with her fist. 'The three of us could always sleep in a W formation on the king bed.'

He took the soft bundle from her, his hands feather-light on her forearms, but the warmth of them stayed behind even after he dumped the bedding on the couch facing the door.

Adam wore sweatpants and nothing else. 'This'll do fine,' he said, and the puckered skin of his back looked silver in the hotel-room light.

She rubbed away the goosebumps on her arms. 'You know, it, uh, it pulls out into a bed.'

He shoved a pillow on one end then shook out the comforter over the cushions. 'Easier to roll off the couch than climb out of a bed.' Adam checked to see if his guns were loaded, one after the other, then set each one down on the nearest end table.

Bee stared at them. His Beretta M9 and her Colt 1911. One matte black and one stainless steel. And then she thought about Adam, rolling half naked off the couch, grabbing the guns and firing away at whatever attempted to break down their door.

'Well.' She swallowed. 'That's a thought that's gonna linger.'

He grinned, half his mouth first, and then the other – a happy, slow-blooming smile. 'Get some sleep, Bee. I'll see you in the morning.'

'Yeah. Yeah, OK.' Bee touched her neck and watched him busy himself with his ammo, fingers tracing her suprasternal notch as he made sure everything was in order. 'Hey, Adam?'

'Hm?' He glanced over his shoulder in time to see her heading for him.

She set her hands on the sides of his face and kissed the corner of his mouth, lingering for a heartbeat too long.

Adam didn't touch her, didn't respond, but she could hear the hitch in his throat. She pulled away only slightly, ran her thumb along the crescent-moon scar in the center of his bottom lip.

He exhaled and she breathed in.

'We're gonna get him back, Bee,' he whispered. 'I promise.'

She nodded and tried to believe him. 'Goodnight, Adam.'

'Goodnight, Shelby.'

TWENTY-ONE

Bee set her heel on the chair to moisturize her foot. Her borrowed robe fell open, and she tucked the wayward flap under her bum.

'Quit wiggling,' Liliana ordered. She stood on a step stool behind Bee, a heated curling iron in one hand and a round brush in the other, and waved them both at her reflection in the mirror. 'I'll burn your neck.'

Liliana's closet was the size of a decent starter home. Designer dresses, shoes, purses and jewelry were the only decorations in the massive room, displayed more as a shrine to wealth than as a functional organization system. Inside was a pale pink vanity with every feasible accessory for beautifying oneself available. Makeup of every color and kind covered the countertop. Hairdryers and straighteners and brushes lined the wall next to the lighted mirror, waiting to be called into service. She had lotions and potions and hair-removal waxes: everything stacked in neat rows on or under or beside the vanity.

Bee checked her modesty once more. 'I'm sorry but I don't feel like flashing the whole world.'

'I'm the only one who'd see anything.' Liliana went back to styling Bee's hair. 'I mean, unless you flashed the mirror. And then I guess Anastasia could see it. And the guy you're in love with – whatshisface.'

'Adam.' Bee switched to her other foot. 'I'm not in love with him. So back off, OK?'

Liliana spat a laugh. 'Shut up and let me do your hair. You're almost as bad as Anastasia.'

Bee put the lotion on the vanity and grabbed a vial of ruby-red nail polish. 'Thanks for doing this by the way.' She shook the bottle. 'I wouldn't be able to get through this without you.'

Liliana wrapped a strip of red hair around the curling iron. 'It hasn't happened yet. I can get the horse to water and all that.' She let the soft wave fall over Bee's shoulder. 'But I can guarantee you're going to be the best water that stubborn horse has ever seen.'

Bee started painting her fingernails. She caught her friend's eye in the mirror and smiled. 'I owe you one.'

'You owe me wine,' she corrected. 'A lot of wine. You'll think, "Is this too much wine?" and then you'll still buy more wine. And then it will be enough.'

Bee laughed. 'OK. Deal.'

'Would you stop?' came Adam's grumpy voice. 'No. No. Would you—' He giggled. 'Knock it off.'

Bee and Liliana turned in sync. Adam and Anastasia had entered the master bedroom. He wore a white tuxedo with a black bow tie and a scowl.

Anastasia towered over Adam barefoot. She poked his side.

He twisted away from her, an angry giggle escaping at being tickled. 'Can you do something about this?' he asked Bee.

She shook her head, too stunned to form words.

Big bad Adam Gage was ticklish.

'He fits fine into my husband's suit,' Anastasia said, sneaking one more poke into Adam's side. She walked into the closet and watched her reflection play with Bee's red wig. 'It is a little tight for him. My husband, he is so weak. But it will do the job.'

Adam adjusted the coat. 'If I move my arms too much, a seam will bust.'

'Then don't move your arms too much,' Liliana said. 'Beauty is pain.'

'That is what I told him,' Anastasia said. 'Everything I wear is too tight.'

Liliana nodded. 'What are we supposed to do? Wear something that fits every day?'

Adam rolled his eyes.

Bee chuckled and set the vial down.

Anastasia sorted through the giant black makeup case that took up over half of the vanity and said, 'Makeup now. This bank will be so impressed with your new look.'

'Banks,' Bee said.

Adam cleared his throat. 'I'm leaving this here until we go.'

Anastasia and Liliana leveled him with their best glares.

But he shrugged out of the jacket and hung it up on the back of a pink leather couch. 'I'm gonna check in with Malika.' He peered in through the doorway at Bee. 'You, uh, you need anything?'

She shook her head. Liliana and Anastasia scolded her.

'Sorry, sorry.' She blew dry the red polish on her nails and wrinkled her nose at the chemical scent. 'I'm OK. Thanks though. And it's not a bank, Anastasia. It's Banks. He's Charlie's second in command. I gotta get him on my side. If I go to Alvarez alone, I'll be swallowed alive. Having Banks there gives me validity I wouldn't have on my own and should keep Alvarez from simply killing me outright. And I gotta talk to him face to face. The last thing I need is more hitmen tracing a phone call, finding out where I am and coming after me.'

Anastasia set her palm on Bee's forehead. 'I'm bored now.' She nudged Liliana with her elbow. 'I am bored. Tell her. It will make things less boring.'

Liliana said, 'Well—'

'She screwed the swim coach!' Anastasia exclaimed, working the beauty blender around Bee's nose.

Liliana gasped in indignation. 'I was just about to—'

'In the pool!'

Bee covered her mouth with her hand, hoping to drown out the sound of her snort.

It didn't work.

Liliana glared at both of them in the mirror.

Anastasia patted the blender over Bee's forehead, grinning.

'Liliana!' Bee tried with all her might not to laugh. 'Liliana, he's in high school!'

'He's eighteen,' she said, attention on the mound of hair she worked on. 'He graduated this year, thank you very much. He's spending his summer working at the pool before he goes off to college.' Her gaze shifted to a far-off place. 'It was really romantic. He lit candles all the way from the parking lot to the ladder.'

'So' – Bee's lips quivered as she fought a smile – 'the public pool?'

'Yeah.'

Anastasia said, 'I didn't know you could have sex in water. Wouldn't water be pushed into places it should not be pushed?'

'I've done it in water lots of times,' Liliana said. 'It's fine. The penis is a natural plug.'

Bee lost herself to laughter. The Anas scolded her. 'Sorry. Sorry. Oh man, I needed that.' She wiped a stray tear away from her nose with the pad of her pinky finger, careful of the damp polish.

Laughter receded, and worry filled the empty space. 'I don't know what I'm gonna do if this doesn't work, guys,' she said. 'Oliver . . .'

Liliana held eye contact with her reflection. 'Oliver is going to be fine,' she said. 'Because his mother is the best there is at this. You're gonna get him out, Bee.'

'You must focus.' Anastasia stuck Bee's right eyelashes in a bright pink curler. 'If you do not focus, if you do not do your job, then he will not be fine. But if you do what you must? You will get him back.'

Bee nodded, and the Anas made a squawking noise of disapproval as the eyelash curler fell to the floor. 'Sorry, sorry.'

They were right. She had to go into this with a clear head. For Oliver's sake, she had to do her job. She had to be the grifter she was and not the mother she'd become.

Bee looked at herself in the three-paneled mirror. Liliana had picked out a red dress with a plunging neckline and a severe slit over the right leg. The straps were sturdy enough to keep anything from slipping out, which was good, because the dress itself didn't allow for a bra.

Or underwear really.

Which worked out.

'I want to be buried in this dress.'

Anastasia said, 'I can arrange that.'

Bee bit her tongue between her teeth and giggled then turned to face her audience. The Anas sat on stools, tall green glasses filled with bubbly water in their hands, appraising her like they'd been tasked with assigning a score.

Adam leaned a shoulder against the doorframe, hands in his pockets, one foot crossed over the other.

She met his gaze and smoothed the fabric down over her hips. 'What do you think?'

'It's good,' he said.

Liliana twirled so fast in her stool it wobbled underneath her. 'Good? That is a seven-thousand-dollar gown!'

'So what?' Adam planted both feet flat on the ground and stood straight. 'You could dress her like Ronald McDonald. I got seven bucks in my wallet. I could buy her a muumuu at the Good Will. She'd still turn every head.'

Liliana thrust her glass into Anastasia's hand and hopped over to Bee, ran her hands over Bee's bare arms. 'It's a good thing he's cute because he's very annoying.' She squeezed her shoulders. 'He is right though. I'm thinking silver shoes. How high a heel can you handle?' She dropped her hands and disappeared into the shoe section of her closet.

'Like, medium.' Bee turned back to the mirror. 'I know how hard you worked on my hair, and it is amazing. But I'm wondering about wearing this wig with this dress. I look like Jessica Rabbit. You know, except for the boobage.'

Liliana chuckled from around the corner. 'You're welcome. Here.' She reappeared, silver high heels in her hands. 'These are Jimmy Choo, and you can keep them forever. I never wear them.'

Bee handled them with care. 'Thank you again, girls. This means so much to me.'

Anastasia drained her bubbly water. She covered her mouth with her pink-and-white fingertips and burped. 'It is no problem. We stick together.'

'That's right,' Liliana said. 'Now, what are you wearing tomorrow? I was thinking something like this.' She grabbed a denim miniskirt and white long-sleeved blouse off an ottoman. 'Some sensible kitten heels. Or ballet flats. What do you think?'

Bee held the skirt up over her dress to gauge where the hemline hit her legs. 'It's skimpy.'

'Well, what do you want? A business suit?' Liliana set her fists on her hips. 'Because I have one. It's Chanel. Gorgeous! You want it?'

'I don't know.' Bee put the skirt down and looked around the room, at the unlimited options available to her, and drew her mouth into a thin line. 'He's expecting an ex-mafia wife. What do they look like?'

Anastasia said, 'Big lips. Big tits.'

Bee pointed at her. 'Right. I don't have time for that though.'

Adam rubbed his forehead and stepped forward. 'Look, Bee, I know you got a process. I know what you wear plays an important part in that process. I don't understand it, but I get it. But maybe you're coming at this from the wrong way. Maybe instead of focusing on what he's expecting, you focus on what you need to be when you're in the room.'

'That's a good point.' Liliana tilted her head and observed her. 'What do you need to be?'

Bee faced the mirror. She set her hands on the small of her waist and focused on her breathing. In and out. Finding center. She wasn't plotting against a drug lord. She hadn't escaped death however many times in a week. She was on her yoga mat, on her dock. Breathing in and breathing out.

Instead of the ocean stretching before her, it was her own blue eyes that filled her vision, scared but determined.

'A weapon.'

Liliana said, 'Helpful. Truly.'

'No. No, it is.' Anastasia jumped up, her stool falling to the floor with a bang. 'I know exactly what you need!'

Anastasia spoke to herself in furious Russian, a whirlwind of discarded clothes piling up in front of them.

Liliana sighed. 'You know, you could leave what you don't want on a hanger.'

But Anastasia paid her no mind, reappearing with a dark green mini sundress, a delicate lace-up bow in the back, and gold accessories.

Bee looked at the dress, looked at Anastasia, looked back at the dress. 'This is what a weapon would wear?' Then she game-show-host gestured at her Jessica Rabbit outfit. '*This* is what a weapon would wear.'

'No, no.' Anastasia held Bee's chin in her hand. 'He will never see you coming.'

Anastasia had a point. Having the element of surprise on her side certainly wouldn't make things worse. Instead of the deafening .45 caliber slugs from her 1911, she'd be the unheard missile launched from a submarine.

Liliana's rear started buzzing. She pulled out her cell phone and sighed. 'It's for you.' She handed it to Bee. 'Good luck getting that horse to drink, Mama.'

Bee tossed her borrowed hair over her shoulder. 'That's why they pay me the big bucks.'

TWENTY-TWO

'Invitation only.'

Bee frowned out the overly tinted window of Liliana's diamond-white Mercedes-AMG GT Coupé and surveyed the busy dock on the Hollywood Intracoastal waterway. Sure enough, a sign out front proclaimed the casino ship closed for a private party. 'Shouldn't be too hard.' She checked her teeth in the visor mirror. 'You ready?'

Adam left the car as an answer, fixing his black bow tie and walking around to open her door. He offered her his arm, and she placed a hand on his elbow, twisting her lips into the barest of smiles.

They sauntered into the well-dressed crowd waiting in lines to board the ship. Security guards were checking invitations at the two points of entry on the docks.

She nodded at the couple walking in front of them.

He grunted in reply.

She let go of his arm and pulled a tube of lipstick out of her silver clutch. Bee applied the lipstick as she walked, her pace faster than the couple. Once she was in front of the woman, she dropped it on the dock.

It rolled under the woman's shoe, and she tripped. Her male companion grabbed her to keep her from wiping out. He stopped so suddenly that Adam bumped into him.

'Sorry, mate,' he said, but the man waved him off.

'Are you all right, darling?' he was saying, and Adam walked to Bee, already waiting in line.

He held up the two invitations he'd lifted out of the man's jacket against his chest.

She patted his arm like an owner praising a puppy's first outside piddle. 'Good job.'

'I especially liked the "mate" part,' Malika said over the comms. 'Are you in character as an Australian tonight, Mr Gage?'

Adam wiggled his finger in his ear. 'This thing's gonna drive me nuts.'

Bee grinned and moved up the ramp. 'Malika or the earpiece?'

'What do you think?'

They neared the first security checkpoint, and Adam offered her his arm again. 'You ready for the easy part?'

She sagged forward. 'Oh for— Ugh.' She took his elbow and forced a smile for the security guard. 'You had to jinx us, didn't you?'

Behind them, the couple they'd stolen from were bickering. 'You had the invitations, Chad! Don't tell me you forgot them!'

'I didn't forget them, darling. They were right here. I swear, I had them in my pocket!'

Adam handed over their stolen invitations, whole face bright with suppressed laughter, and set his hand on top of hers. 'This is gonna be fun.'

'I've never actually been in here,' Bee said as they boarded. 'So, you got any info?'

Malika *mmhmm*ed and a picture of the ship appeared in Bee's eye.

Adam rubbed the corner of his.

It looked in the picture as it did from her real-world perspective: a cruise ship shrunk down to fit inside canals.

The picture changed to blueprints and Malika narrated the tour she forced them on. 'There are about six hundred people on board at a time, between guests and crew. One fancy restaurant that requires reservations. Two different buffets, both operating during the lunch and dinner trips. There are three levels available to guests. The first one, the one you're on, is the gambling floor. One up and you hit the food options and a couple balconies. The life rafts. And the top floor is open air, bands play, old people dance. Not a bad way to spend your rent money.'

Bee looked around with a deep pout. No one manned the tables. 'No gambling at the dock, I see.'

Adam said, 'Well, not gonna case the joint standing here.'

At that, she motioned behind them with her chin. 'And yet there are the offices. I can see six cameras from right here.'

Half his mouth opened in a grin. 'I got seven.'

'Of course.'

'Let's go check out the rest of the ship.'

'After you, Mr Gage.'

Adam winced, braced himself. 'Malika, can you show me the fastest way up?'

'I want eyes on Banks,' Bee added. 'I need him at my side tomorrow or Alvarez is never going to take me seriously.'

'Yeah, yeah. You guys get to do the fun stuff. I might've liked to dress up and gamble. Eat some fancy food.'

Adam must have got directions to the stairs because he started walking away from where most of the patrons waited for an elevator.

'You can order room service,' Bee said. 'Lynch's card is on the room.'

'We're gonna make him pay for our food too?'

She held on to a banister and followed Adam up the skinniest flight of stairs she'd ever seen.

'He thought he could negotiate for my affections – plus, wedding ring in the pocket, remember? He deserves it.'

Up on the top deck, a band was playing to a crowd of people who were more interested in their first round of drinks than dancing.

Adam and Bee accepted champagne from a passing waiter and hung out near the railing to watch the ship depart. And to scout all the guests on the deck of course.

The song ended and the band reset. The lead singer, a shorter man with dark, slicked back hair wearing a well-tailored black tux and a bright yellow bow tie, took the mic out of the stand and began to sing.

Well, croon.

He crooned in a beautiful voice that would've made Ricky proud.

Not Martin. The other one. That would never let Lucy in the show.

'What's Ricky's last name?' Bee asked.

'Martin,' Malika answered in her ear.

'No. The other one.' Bee stared up at the stars for answers. 'You know. The one that was in black and white.'

She could hear Malika's look in the silence.

'For some reason, I'm thinking Ethel, but that can't be right.'

'Ricardo.' Adam drained his champagne, licked his teeth. 'Ethel was the neighbor.'

Bee snapped her fingers. 'Right! That's who the singer's reminding me of.'

'Yeah, he's good.' He cleared his throat. 'You wanna dance? It'll be a minute until they open the tables.'

She pressed her smiling lips together. 'Yeah, that, um, that'd be fun.'

'OK, you two do you,' Malika said. 'I'm gonna order room service.'

Adam offered Bee his hand, and she took it, her dumb smile taking full control of her face. He led her to the outskirts of the dance floor, then his hand was on her waist. She could feel it through her dress, warm above her hip. So large it covered her whole side.

Bee tried to pretend she wasn't hyper-aware of the feel of him against her. That she wasn't in awe of how gently his hands held her when she'd seen what he could do with them.

She held her clutch over his shoulder, behind his neck, and regretted not flinging it into the ocean when he asked her to dance. It had only had lipstick in it, to begin with, and she'd dropped that on the dock.

But then again, it was Yves Saint Laurent.

And it did complete her look, Jessica Rabbit though it was.

Adam pulled her closer. She squeezed his fingers and let him. It would be out of character to not enjoy this moment of closeness, so damn it, she was gonna enjoy it.

He smelled much better now, like dandruff shampoo – for all his luscious locks – and a hint of Liliana's father's cologne.

Bee curled her arm around his shoulders. His hand slid to the small of her back. Every time he exhaled from his nose, it puffed against her cheek.

She would only have to shift her face a fraction and her lips would be on his.

Adam must've had the same thought. He moved his face towards hers, temple brushing temple.

Bee's heart thudded against her breastbone.

'You know what this reminds me of?'

His question sparked the memory of the last time they'd danced cheek to cheek, under the stars, while a short, well-dressed man crooned in Spanish.

'I liked Ibiza,' Bee said.

He grinned. She could feel his stubble against her skin. 'It was a good job. Well, the first half.'

'Yeah.' The tip of her nose ghosted along his jaw. 'The second half wasn't my favorite.'

He caressed her back, a slow, soft circle obviously meant to torture her. 'Nobody likes being the bait.'

'I don't mind being the bait. Getting stuck in the trap with the mark is another story.'

'Hey, I took a bullet for that mistake, in case you forgot.'

Bee shook her head. 'If only forgiveness came that easily.'

He chuckled, low in his throat, and she watched the muscles move in his neck.

Once again, she thought about tossing the clutch into the Atlantic. At least then she might be able to sneak a touch of him.

She didn't think he'd let her run her fingers through his gorgeous mane, but she was willing to sacrifice Saint Laurent to Trident if it meant she'd get to tug on it.

'I haven't been back,' he said, and his voice pulled her out of her daydream. 'I thought about it. A lot. But it didn't seem right.' He shrugged. 'Not without you.'

Her heart stopped its assault on her bones to unleash hell on her stomach.

Why did he make her seasick?

Bee pressed her cheek against his to gather her courage. 'You never called.'

It might have been her imagination, but his steps faltered a tiny bit.

'I waited. After you got out of the hospital, I thought . . .' She chewed her lip. 'But you didn't call. And Os said he reached out to you for a few jobs, but you turned him down. I tried calling, but the number I had for you was disconnected. I figured you changed your mind.'

He pulled back far enough to look incredulously in her eyes. 'Thomas Osbourn is a lying sack of garbage. I never changed my mind. You hear me?' He bent his head until they were practically nose to nose, his eyes wide.

She could see the sincerity in them so clearly, she had to look away. He was a liar, she told herself. Him and Os both. Look where trusting liars had gotten her.

'He told me things would get bad for you if I didn't back off.' His hand slid to her hip again. He felt so far away and far too close. 'That was the last I heard from him until you burned all his bridges down. I never shoulda believed him,' he said. 'That's on me.'

'Lots of people believed him.' Bee twisted her mouth into a sad smile. 'That was kind of his thing.'

He held her hand tighter. 'I thought, you know – I thought I was over it. It's been so long.' He shrugged and sniffed and looked away from her at the same time. And then his hand was on the small of her back again, pulling her in.

Other couples swayed around them. She could see them, see them holding each other, whispering in each other's ears. One sweet blue-haired lady had her head nestled on her companion's hunched shoulder. But Bee couldn't hear them. She couldn't hear the whispers. And she could barely hear the band play, barely hear the singer croon into the handheld mic.

Her blood rushed through her veins, buzzed in her ears.

She grazed her chin on his cheek and held her breath, willing her heart to slow down before she fainted on the dance floor.

'I have to be honest with you.' He held her tighter. 'I thought I could use our history together. I thought I could take the money and run and that all those old memories, all those old feelings, they wouldn't come back.'

Adam tilted his face towards her, so close she couldn't see his eyes. All she could see was his stupidly square jaw and his annoyingly perfect cupid's bow.

'But they came back, Bee.'

He licked his lips, and her tongue darted out to wet her own.

She wished she'd brought a backup tube of lipstick.

'It all came back.'

The music stopped. The couples around them parted to clap, and Ricky took a bow.

They stood still on the dance floor. Staring at each other. Bee couldn't remember the last time she'd blinked.

She blinked four times.

Had he just confessed? Had he really just told her that he was planning on using her to get to Alvarez's money?

Her swallow clicked in her throat. Bee took a deep breath and raised her eyes to meet his. 'Did you really think I didn't know?'

'There you are!'

All emotion fell off Adam's face. Bee let go of him. She turned around, confused, stunned. Uncertain.

But there they were.

Anastasia and Liliana, arm and arm, wine glasses half filled with Pinot Grigio in hand, dressed to the nines.

Bee laughed because there was nothing else she could do. 'How did you guys get here? It's invitation only. And I'm pretty sure you weren't dressed like that when we left.'

Liliana shrugged. 'My old man has a standing invite for this dinghy.'

'Mega yacht,' said Adam.

'And every dinghy in the county.' She slurped her wine, pinky up. 'He's very important.'

'We gave the driver a show in my car.' Anastasia winked. 'He is not important.'

The band started up again, playing something fast. She drained her drink and gave Adam the empty glass. 'Shall we dance?'

Liliana followed suit, leaving Adam holding two empty glasses. 'We shall! Come, Beatrice. Let's give these geezers a show!'

There was no point in protesting, so Bee did what she was told and followed the Anas to the middle of the dance floor.

She gave Adam an apologetic look on her way into the melee.

He popped a dimple and held up the wine glasses in salute.

'So,' Liliana cooed, grabbing Bee by the arm and spinning her around. 'Things are going good?'

Bee tossed her head back and groaned at the ceiling. 'I hate myself.'

Anastasia dipped Liliana low. 'Don't be so dramatic. You were dancing so close, how bad can it be?'

Bee swayed to the music, caught sight of Adam leaving the dance floor.

'Look at his shoulders! How, how are they so – so broad!' She wrapped her arms around Anastasia and spun. 'I want to climb him like a tree.'

'Hey, Bee,' Malika said, her voice muffled like she was chewing something. 'Comms are still on.'

Bee froze. 'What? No, they're not.'

'Yeah, they are,' said Adam.

Bee's mouth fell open, and her stomach hit the floor, right between her medium-height silver Jimmy Choos.

That was it. She was going to fling herself over the rail.

The Anas trailed after her.

'What is it?' Liliana asked. 'You look like you're gonna hurl, and that shade of green with that dress makes you look like Christmas.'

Bee pulled the earpiece out and handed it to her, picking her pace up to a light jog. There were benches by the rail that were the right height to crawl under and wish for a quick death.

'Hello?' Liliana held the earpiece in front of her mouth to speak, moved it to the side of her face to listen. 'Bee is busy right now attempting to curl into the fetal position. Might I take a message?'

'Give me that.' Anastasia plucked the comm with her index finger and thumb. 'Who is this?'

It was too much work to bend down under the bench. Instead, she collapsed on top of it and held her head in her hands. 'It's fine,' she said. 'I can take that back now. I am definitely not going to throw it into the ocean.'

Anastasia shook her head. 'This bossy girl says not to give it back to you yet.' She pushed the device into her own ear. 'You are bossy,' she said. 'Do not screech at me, Bossy Girl. I am helping you.'

The music stopped, and the crooner took the mic in hand. 'Thank you, thank you. We're going to keep playing for you all, but it's my pleasure to tell you that we've crossed the invisible line that opens up the gambling deck!'

The crowd applauded.

'I hope you all win big! Buy me a drink, eh, big spenders?'

The band started up again, and half of the dancers made their way to the elevators.

'See, there!' Liliana waved her hand around. 'Let's go gamble. I've almost got the blackjack thing down.'

Anastasia shook her head. 'It is too much math for me.'

Bee checked her wig. 'It's a hi-lo strategy. The math is very simp— OK, here, you sit next to me. We'll go over it again.'

They headed to the nearly empty stairs Adam had led her up earlier, and she pretended she didn't see the Anas' fist bump behind her back.

The trick to counting cards was to not look like you were counting cards. Bee ordered a vodka soda, tipped the dealer well and flirted with the older gentleman sitting at the end of the table.

From there, it was keeping an eye on the cards that were being dealt, as well as the cards that weren't. Lower cards were one, middle cards were zero, high cards were minus one. As long as she kept twirling her hair around her finger and giggling after each win, no one batted an eye when she raked in the chips.

'I don't get it,' Anastasia snapped. She stuck the comm back in Bee's ear. 'I am trying to listen to Bossy Girl, but she is more difficult than the math.'

'I am not bossy,' Malika said. 'Just smarter than everybody else.'

Bee smiled brightly and took a loud sip of her drink. 'Don't worry about it, darling.'

Liliana held her head up with an elbow propped on the black felt table. 'Are aces high or low?'

Bee cursed through clenched teeth then laughed. 'They're crazy,' she told the dealer, tipping him. 'Practical jokers.' She laughed again.

The dealer couldn't have been older than twenty-one. He had an unusually small face, made more apparent by his blond hair, which was spiked with industrial-strength glue. He glanced at his tip pile, shrugged and kept his pierced mouth shut.

Bee breathed out a sigh of relief.

'Can you go over it again?' Liliana asked. 'Is my goal to be at zero?'

'What about the other decks?' Anastasia pointed at the shoe. 'He keeps using new cards!'

Bee clutched her forehead. 'Flippin' rubes.'

The dealer sighed. 'You guys can't blatantly count cards. Like, I'm not an idiot.'

Liliana rose as high in her seat as her small frame could manage. 'I'm not counting the cards, sir. I'm keeping track of them. What, like it's illegal?'

Bee reached around Anastasia to squeeze Liliana's bicep. 'Stop. Talking.'

'No, this dude called me an idiot!'

'I called myself an idiot,' the dealer clarified. He shifted weight on his feet. 'Actually, I said I wasn't an idiot. You guys are being super obvious, and it doesn't matter how well you tip, that's not going to pay my rent.'

'Obvious? Super obvious? How dare you!'

'Calm down,' Bee begged. 'You're causing a scene, and I've got kind of a thing to do here.'

'*Oooooh*, you haven't seen a scene!' Liliana cracked her neck. 'Do you have any idea who my father is? Hmm? Do you?' She stood, somehow shorter than she had been sitting, and dug her bubblegum-pink acrylic nail into the table. 'I get to do what I want on your dumb little boat, and nobody is going to stop me!'

'Ladies, ladies,' a male voice said from behind them.

Bee relaxed. *OK*, she thought, *this'll work*.

'Mr DiMarco,' the dealer said, 'these women are counting cards.'

Robert DiMarco, the operator of the casino ship, approached the table with open arms, his gold H belt glistening in the light. 'Is this true?' He caught Liliana's eye first. 'Ms Delgado, it's good to see you again. But you know I can't allow cheating. How would I make any money?'

'Hold on a minute,' Malika said. 'Is our mark wearing white skinny jeans?'

Bee finished off her drink.

'I'm not cheating,' Liliana said. 'I am gambling with my girlfriends.' She gestured her whole arm at Anastasia and Bee. 'And keeping track of what I'm doing isn't illegal, last time I checked.'

'No, but—' He turned to look at the other woman and froze when he saw Bee's face.

She grinned, soft and slow. 'Hi, Banks.'

Robert 'Banks' DiMarco, Charlie's second, was a smarmy fellow. There really wasn't a better way to describe him. Average height, thin but toned, always dressed impeccably, a wealthy kid from New Jersey who'd befriended Charlie back when Charlie was the only child of a single mother who barely had two cents to rub together. Back when Charlie was the one taking orders, doing the grunt work. But then they'd grown up.

Then Bee had picked Charlie.

Now Charlie had the enterprise – criminal or legitimate depended on who you were asking – Charlie had the money; Charlie gave the orders. And Banks did his best to hide the fact that the jealousy drove him crazy, but Bee could see it in his false, easy smile.

It was the false, easy smile that he flashed her now. 'Bee. It's so good to see you.'

'Well, I hate him already,' Malika said.

'Yeah, join the club,' Adam groused.

Bee said, 'It's good to see you too. Been kind of an eventful few days.'

'You two know each other?' Anastasia asked.

But Banks ignored her. 'Kevin, let these ladies do whatever they want. Ms Delgado, tell Martin I said hi.' He offered Bee his arm. 'You, uh, you want to talk? In private?'

She nodded, ducked her head and looked up at him from beneath her lashes. 'Yeah, I'd like that.'

'Ugh,' came Malika's voice. 'This is hard to watch. Could you lay it on thicker?'

'Gotta set the hook,' said Adam. 'Let her work.'

Bee hopped off the chair and held Banks's arm tight. 'Keep an eye on this for me?' she asked the Anas, finally ridding herself of the empty clutch.

Banks led her through the gambling floor, barely taking his eyes off her, and patted her hand.

Then he left it there, on top of hers, uncomfortably clammy.

He ducked his head close to her ear. 'I was so worried about you,' he said. 'I've been keeping tabs on Oliver. Alvarez is taking good care of him because he's pretty confident he's getting his money back.'

That was why Bee couldn't risk a phone call. If Banks was keeping tabs on Alvarez, sure as the sun rises in the east, Alvarez was keeping tabs back.

Banks exhaled like he was in the middle of a yoga session, loud and mouthy. 'But you know Charlie.'

'Boy, do I.' She rolled her eyes. 'He hired a bodyguard to get me and Oliver out of the city. At least he had the sense to do that, I guess.'

He grimaced but said, 'Well, you're standing here, so I guess that means the bodyguard did at least half of his job right.'

She shrugged. 'He's a punch-up artist. Not much of a thinker.'

Adam said, 'Thanks.'

'But yeah, I'm here. And Oliver . . .' The words were heavy in her mouth. 'I'm going to get Oliver back.'

The hallway was empty except for a few security guards. Bee glanced over at them. They didn't look like Cardello men, but it wasn't like Charlie to not have his own guys near the money.

Why would Banks hire outside security?

'I'm so glad to see you, I really am.' Banks patted her hand with his clammy palm again. 'But why are you here?'

'Funny you should ask,' Bee said, even though it wasn't. It was kind of the whole point. 'I have a business opportunity for you. If you want to hear it?'

He smiled, face still too close, and stopped at the door at the end of the hall.

'After you,' he said.

Adam said, 'Reel him in.'

TWENTY-THREE

Bee grabbed the doorknob behind her back and smiled like she wasn't trying to make a break for it. Banks's office was simple but fully capable of spying on every gambling table on the ship. A small desk filled with incoming and outgoing paperwork, a comfortable chair and a wall built of monitors. She could see everything from here. Every hand held close to the chest, every dealer picking their wedgies between rounds.

Banks had listened to her plan with only minor interruptions, nodding along and asking the occasional question, all the while moving himself more and more into her personal space until there was nowhere else to go but in his arms. He twisted a string of red hair around his finger, drawing her attention to his smiling face, much too close to her own. 'This thing is ridiculous,' he said. 'Take it off for me?'

Screw you, Bee thought. But she needed him happy and willing. She meant what she'd told Malika. If Banks wasn't at her side tomorrow, there was no hope of swaying Alvarez. And if she couldn't sway Alvarez . . .

Bee could see her son like he was in the room with her, spying on the gamblers, his eyes shining with the thousands of jokes he couldn't wait to tell.

She released the doorknob, careful not to make a sound to indicate where her hands had been, and pulled out the pins keeping her Jessica Rabbit hair in place one by one.

Banks's eyes tracked her every move. She kept hers on his face while she pressed the pins into her palm. He'd always been like this. Watching her keenly, standing too close, always making her aware of just how aware of her he was. He never forgot a birthday, hers or Oliver's, and called every Christmas Eve. She'd wondered for a long time if he meant to be as obvious as he was, or if he was bad at hiding his intentions, but either way, it worked for her now.

There was no easier mark than one in love with you.

'Hey, Bee,' Malika said. 'Not to, like, disrupt the flow here, or whatever angle you're working, but Adam's kind of in trouble.'

'No,' Adam panted. 'Oof! I'm— Ahh! I'm fine.'

'He's super not fine. He's getting his ass handed to him by a WWE wrestler. Honestly, I feel a little guilty I didn't purchase pay per view.'

The wig came off easy into her free hand. Bee dropped it to the floor and shook out her real hair, letting it cascade down her shoulders in a mess of untamed waves.

'That's better.' Banks smiled, tucking a wayward strand behind her ear. 'You're so beautiful.'

Bee leaned into his touch the way he expected. 'Thank you.' Her eyes fluttered close, and she sighed softly before peering up at him under her lashes. 'I can count you in for tomorrow, right? Bright and early?'

'Yeah. You can count on me. Alvarez won't know which way's up when we're done with him.'

Malika said, 'Prepare yourself,' and a view of a seven-foot-tall hairy mammoth that had learned to walk on his hind legs appeared in her eye. With curly black hair to his shoulders and a spectacular bushy beard, he had watermelons smuggled under the shirt sleeves of his quick-dry athletic shirt, which read 'JUST DO IT' across his nipples. At any moment, he could pick up a folding chair and knock someone out with it.

He reared back his basketball-sized fist and nailed Adam right in the face.

She could hear the sound of flesh striking flesh, the loud groan he made, and then she could see the ceiling in some other room.

'You should totally hurry,' Malika said. 'We noticed he looked out of place amidst all the well-dressed gamblers, so Adam went to go have a chat with him. Sure looks like someone sent him to find you. Let him find you before Adam dies.'

'No,' Adam panted again. He scrambled to his feet and brought his fists in front of him like the professional he was. 'I got this.'

Mammoth Man furrowed his brow. 'Who are you talking to?' His unusually deep voice made the question sound more like a growl than English.

Adam swayed on his feet, fists still up, ready to strike. Ready to block. 'Myself. I benefit from pep talks.'

'You do not got this.'

'Yeah, probably.'

Adam swung and hit the other man's sternum. The only part of Mammoth that moved was one twitching eyebrow.

'Oh, this is gonna be bad,' Malika said. 'Do you think room service has movie-theater-style popcorn?'

Mammoth hoisted Adam above his head, spun him around and chucked him at the wall. His body left a dent in the plaster.

Swearing, Adam struggled to right himself, his breathing ragged. 'My jacket ripped.' He tore it off and pulled it taut in his hands. 'This'll work.'

He launched himself at Mammoth. His ruined suit jacket was the perfect strangling device.

Bee needed to get the hell out of the room, but she couldn't leave on anything less than stellar terms.

She needed Banks too much.

'I'm glad you're on my side,' she said. 'I owe you a cup of coffee.'

Banks curled his hand around her throat and moved in close, pushing her against the only exit in the room. He stroked her chin with his thumb.

He might as well have shoved a fistful of ice down the front of her dress. She shivered. Every hair on her forearm stood at attention, pointing to the door behind her, urging her to flee.

She held the doorknob tight behind her back. The pins from her wig bit at her palm, reminding her they were there if all else failed.

His hot exhale fanned across her face, the smell of orange Tic Tacs filling her nose. 'I've missed you, Bee. I think about you all the time. You know that, don't you?'

It took Bee several long moments to realize the hysterical laughter rolling around in her skull wasn't her own.

'Oh shit,' Malika gasped. 'Oh balls. That's the funniest thing I've ever heard.'

His dark eyes were watching her mouth. 'I tried finding someone else. Anyone else . . . a thousand other blonde-haired, blue-eyed girls. But none of them came close to you.'

'Does – does this make you the protagonist in an early 2000s YA novel?' Malika laughed again. 'Her only personality trait is clumsiness, and yet every man she comes across falls madly in love with her for no discernible reason!'

Bee knew this of course. He wasn't smooth or good at subterfuge.

She was using it to her advantage now but had dismissed him years earlier. He didn't have the potential she'd seen in Charlie. Comfortable in the status quo. When Pinkerton had investigated and brought her photos of all the worthy candidates in her Get a Mafia Guy to Marry Me So I Can Hide from Os scheme, she'd tossed Banks's picture out first.

Reel it in, dumbass.

'Thank you.' The pins knocked against the doorknob when she released it, a soft metallic sound reverberating around the office. She moved them over to one hand, grazed his pink shirt with her empty hand, touching each polished button until she reached the top. 'But I think it's best if we try to keep it professional.' Bee laid his collar flat, her face inches from his, and whispered, 'For now.'

Banks grinned, and the kiss on her cheek smelled like oranges.

'I'll see you in the morning, doll.'

'Oh yes, you will.'

'Go up the stairs and take a right,' Malika said. 'He's going to die if you don't get a move on.'

Adam said, 'I'm fine.' He struck his opponent in the mouth. 'I've got this.'

Bee's high heels clicked against the linoleum floor of the ship's hallway. 'How did this guy even find me anyway? We've been so careful!'

'Well, this is a Cardello-owned company,' Malika said. 'It literally has your name on the side of it. The *Bumble Bee*. Everything is decorated in yellow and black. For four and a half million dollars, why not check out something obvious?'

Bee could see the face of Mammoth, his lip bloody, standing above Adam like a bear defending her cubs. Bee yanked off her shoes at the base of the stairs and ran with bare feet as fast as she could, Jimmy Choos dangling from her fingertips. 'I'm coming! Just hold on!'

'It's like I'm watching two very different movies collide,' Malika said. 'Like an action-adventure rom-com. Has there been a buddy-cop movie where the two leads make out? Anyway, take the third door on the left.' She sighed, the chair she was sitting in creaking when she sat back in it. 'I could really use some popcorn.'

Bee crept to the indicated door.

She could hear the muffled punches, the growls, the cursing bouncing in the hall and in her head.

'Ugh, finally.' Malika's voice broke up the violence. 'Dude's face got recognized by the CIA's FRS. Adam, you're getting your ass handed to you by a Mr Jeremy Franks, who's been in and out of prison for the last two decades. He's a low-level knee breaker for a local bookie. I guess you were right about all the lower-level scum coming out and searching for an easy payday, Adam. But it looks like a lot of the people he, uh, encourages to settle their debts end up doing extensive time in the hospital, so you should probably hurry up, Bee.'

Adam jumped on Mammoth's back and wrapped his arms around the dude's tree trunk of a throat.

He squeaked out a particularly vile string of curses about Mammoth's mother's parentage when his back smacked the wall.

Bee cracked open the door. The room, obviously meant for storage, had been turned upside down by their fight. Shelves, tables, chairs and cleaning supplies littered the floor.

Though Adam was pinned between the wall and his opponent, blood pouring out of a wound on his forehead and running down his face, he was doing a good job of holding the man in place. Both men were turning a lovely shade of chartreuse. She tiptoed around the debris, holding her shoes in her fists.

Adam grunted and summoned up the last of his strength to hold Mammoth's head still.

She slammed the heel into the giant's eye.

He screamed. Well, it was more of a loud, frantic, gurgling noise than a scream. But it was guttural, awful, and it churned Bee's stomach. He fell to his knees, hands hovering in front of the silver shoe lodged into his eyeball.

Adam used his higher ground and squeezed on Mammoth's throat for all he was worth.

The gurgling noise stopped; the man's good eye rolled back into his head. Adam let go, and he fell to the floor.

Adam limped to her side. He held on to his knees, breathing heavy, then gave up, plopping down on to the ground. 'You all right?'

'Yeah.' She sat on her naked heels. 'He's – he's gonna be OK, right?'

He nodded, wiping the blood out of his eyes with his shirt sleeve. 'Yeah. Yeah, he'll go to the hospital and they'll, you know, they'll do something about . . .' He gestured to his own face, and Bee hid her head behind his shoulder.

'Yeah,' he said again. She could feel his torso rise and fall with each quick breath. 'I'm sure he'll be fine.'

Mammoth released his bowels.

'Oh no!' Bee pinched her nose shut, screwed her eyes closed. 'Did he crap himself?'

'Yeah.' This time it sounded like Adam wasn't breathing. 'Yeah, he did. He's definitely dead. He's dead.'

Malika crunched over the comms. 'Good news, guys – there was totally popcorn in the minibar.'

Bee dug her face further into Adam's shoulder blades.

Adam touched his cheek and hissed. 'Asshole got me good. We should get going before somebody wanders in here.'

She sat up, still holding her nose closed, and peeked at their incapacitated assailant through squinted eyes.

'You, uh' – he cleared his throat – 'you want me to get your shoes?'

Any color left in her face promptly drained away. 'I don't really want to wear them anymore.'

'Yeah, no, I get that.' He stood up and offered her his hand. 'C'mon.'

She let go of her nose long enough to accept his help. 'No way we get out of here like this without attracting attention.'

He looked first at her – shoeless, wigless, eyeball goop and blood splattered across her chest and forearm. And then looked at himself – his pants ripped, his shoes coming apart, a formerly white shirt that was now striped with scarlet, stained with sweat and random brown splotches the origin of which it was best not to wonder too hard about. Not to mention the things he couldn't see. Namely, his own busted face.

'What do you suggest?'

'Costume change?'

TWENTY-FOUR

'There's a service elevator, crew only, that'll take you below deck,' Malika said. 'Should have changes of clothes in the laundry room.'

Bee poked her head out of the room. The long, stark white hallway was empty. The recessed lights flickered overhead, and for a moment she held her breath and expected twin girls to appear. But she saw not a soul and eased herself out the door.

Adam dutifully followed after her but still asked, 'Where you goin'?'

She arched an eyebrow. 'The . . . service elevator?'

He pointed at his ear. 'I think my comm's busted.'

'I think his face is busted,' said Malika.

Adam didn't react.

That answered that.

'Yeah,' Bee said to both of them. 'It took a pretty good beating there. Is the contact still working?'

She saw herself from his point of view, following along the quiet hall of the ship.

'That's enough of that,' Bee said. 'Don't get me wrong, I like to look at myself, but wearing Givenchy and blood isn't my Who Wore It Best moment.'

'Don't forget the eyeball goo,' said Adam.

She shivered, gagged. 'Never. That'll haunt me in my dreams.'

Around the corner was the elevator. Adam pressed the down button, and it slid open right away.

The service elevator was no frills, no music, barely any lights, but when it opened, it had a terrific view of a security guard stationed outside an alarm-rigged door with a Glock on his hip.

Adam shoved Bee into the corner. They didn't so much as breathe until the doors slid closed again.

'OK,' Bee whispered into Adam's sweat-covered neck. She squeezed his shoulders. 'If he saw us, he would've approached.'

Adam moved back far enough that she didn't have to lean on the wall anymore.

'Maybe we can use him,' he said. 'The guy probably knows you.'

Bee scratched her forehead. 'What? What guy?'

'The guard outside. This ship is named after you, isn't it? The *Bumble Bee*? Won't the hired help do what you want?'

She set a fist on her hip. 'How would some random button man know who I am? Is it— I mean, do you think every lower-level suit studies a picture of their boss's ex-wife?' The other fist made its way to her other hip. 'Am I Mother Mary, my picture framed at all these houses, with them lighting candles underneath it?'

'You know what?' Adam tapped his index-finger knuckle against his broken mouth. 'I got shook around pretty good, and I don't like your attitude right now.'

Bee blanched. 'My attitude? *My attitude!*'

'Why don't you go out there and make him do what you want? Huh?' He pressed the door-open button, and the two of them snuck another look. The guard hadn't moved, his hands still behind his back, his gun still holstered at his side.

She frowned as the doors closed.

'You're the grifter in this team, so grift. I've done my part. I mean' – he waved at himself – 'I took a pretty big one for the team today.'

Bee touched the hollow of her throat and gasped. 'How *dare* you? You think I enjoy getting hit on by my ex's business partners? You think it's fun for me to flirt with men wearing white skinny jeans in their place of business?'

He sighed, looked at the wall. 'No.'

'No,' she repeated. 'No, it is not. So now I have to deal with the fact that Banks is looking to pursue a romantic relationship with me when this is over. That won't complicate things at all, I'm sure!'

Malika sobbed, 'So many men love me! Whatever shall I do?'

'You had to put on a pretty dress and wink at a dude,' Adam said. 'I got picked up and dead dropped from ten feet in the air.'

She held up her palms. 'Let's not make this a competition, Adam, because you will lose.'

He scoffed. 'Oh, really?'

'Really.'

'That's what you think?'

'I do!'

Malika moaned, so loud in the small space that Bee winced and

Adam could hear it. 'Would you two shut up and make out already? Gross. You're making me queasy.'

Bee hung her head. She stared at the red nail polish on her toes. 'I'm sorry I snapped at you.'

'I'm sorry I said you weren't pulling your weight. I didn't mean it.'

Bee decided to come clean. 'I do know that guy.'

Adam's eyes went as wide as an owl in an advertisement for glasses. 'What?' He snapped his fingers by his ear. 'Am I losing it? Because the whole time you knew you knew that guy and you still got all on me with the mother-of-Jesus stuff?'

'You wanna go down the whole who knew what and when thing, Mr Gage?' Bee licked her fingers and wiped the blood off her stabbing arm. 'Might I remind you, you were planning on double-crossing me up until an hour ago, and I knew about that and still let you come along on this adventure.'

He groaned.

'Besides, I didn't know I knew him the whole time. But I saw him the second time and then I'd already made such a fuss about it, I didn't want to admit I was wrong.' She licked her clean hand and started on the blood on her chest. 'But I was wrong. And I will do my thing. OK? I'll pull my weight.'

'Hey.' Adam wetted the back of his hand and rubbed off her leftover blood spots. 'I didn't mean it. I got clocked real good. Shook around.'

'Uh-huh. Sure.' She gave herself a quick, double-chinned once-over. 'You stay here and rest then, OK, Cookie?'

Adam sighed.

Bee stumbled into the hallway.

Luke, the guard, straightened when he saw her. 'Mrs Cardello,' he greeted. 'What are you doing down here?'

Bee walked into the wall, shoulder grinding along as she approached him. 'Down where? Where is this?' She got too close to him, nose hovering near his cheek. 'Do I know you? I never forget a handsome face.'

He blushed. 'I'm Luke Hunter. I've worked for Mr Cardello for a coupla years now.'

'Mmm, is that so?' Bee pushed herself against his hips, hands holding on to the wall for support. 'Maybe you'd wanna work for me for a little while.'

His blush spread to the tips of his ears. 'Mrs – Mrs Cardello' – he stepped back, arms held in surrender – 'I don't think—'

But his movement away from her caused her to lose her balance. Her hands slipped on the wall and pressed the button he was guarding.

The door popped open, revealing a short set of stairs to another room. 'Ooh, a romantic hidden passage!' She giggled. 'You're so thoughtful.'

'No, Mrs Cardello.' He reached out but hesitated, deciding instead not to touch her. 'You can't go down there.'

But down there she went. The second door opened after only the briefest of pounding knocks.

For a heartbeat, Bee forgot what she was doing.

She'd found the money room.

Six workers dutifully sorted the chips coming in from the gambling floor in those air tubes that drive-through banks utilized. They counted out the cash equivalent – *cash!* – put it in the canister and sent it up the tube.

She wiped the drool off her lips. Sure, she'd completed her mission, gotten Banks to agree to her plan. But why shouldn't she grab a little extra something for her trouble?

The disapproving face of Rosalie Waters flooded her memory and Bee grinned.

Maybe all the Cardellos were the same. Maybe she was a thief, a gutter rat, a snake and a serpent just as much as Charlie.

'Sorry, sorry, everyone,' Luke said. 'This is Mrs Cardello. She, uh' – he made a drinking gesture – 'she's the owner's wife. She's leaving now.'

'Leaving!' Bee slurred. She flung her arms out, nailing Luke in the stomach. He doubled over in pain, and she spun around. 'This place is Christmas!'

One of the tellers snorted.

Bee ignored her. 'Don't most people gamble on credit nowadays?'

'Yeah, but still a lot of people like to use cash.' Luke took in a sharp, ragged breath and righted himself. 'We offload it every night though. It never stays on the boat for long.'

Dizzy from her parade around the room, Bee tripped over her bare feet and fell on to a counting table. Chips and cash went flying.

Three different tellers popped up to organize it. Snorter called Bee a name under her breath.

Luke lifted her off the table. 'Are you OK?' He kept hold of her upper arm and led her to the door.

Bee grimaced. She caressed the sore spot in the middle of her forehead. 'I think so. Hurts a little.'

They went up the stairs together. 'Let's get you some ice, huh? Crew quarters are this way.' He nodded to the right. 'They got a kitchen.'

Bee rested her head on his shoulder. 'Thank you for being so nice to me, Duke.'

'It's Luke.'

'Oh.' She giggled. 'Right.'

Bee watched Luke fill a plastic bag full of ice from the crew's freezer.

The crew quarters were cozy. The kitchen had a full-sized refrigerator and stove, and there was even a dishwasher next to the sink. But it was clear the area was used almost exclusively for the coffee brewer and microwave, both of which were dirty at the end of the counter.

She held his hand when he gave her the ice and stared at him from underneath drooping eyelids. 'You think they got shoes around here? My toes are cold.'

He glanced at her feet and rubbed the back of his neck. 'The, uh, well the laundry room's down the hall. And they got changing rooms for the crew next to it. I'm sure you'll be able to find something there.'

'Perfect.' Bee kept the bag against her head and walked around him. 'Down this hall?'

'Yes, ma'am,' he said and annoyingly followed her.

The changing rooms looked like every changing room she'd ever seen in a hospital medical drama, with lockers along the walls and backless benches in the middle. The light was a harsh, overhead fluorescent flicker. They were too far below deck to warrant portholes.

Bee raked her fingers through her hair until half of it was in her face. 'Are you going to watch me change, Luke?' She kept only one eye open in a drunken impression of a wink.

His cheeks flushed. 'No, ma'am. Mr C would kill me.'

'Yeah.' She laughed. 'He would. OK. Bye-bye now.' She slammed the door.

* * *

Bee peeled the top half of her dress off first, let it dangle around her waist. The neckline was damp. The red fabric had hidden the blood so well she hadn't noticed it until now.

Hopefully, no one else noticed it either.

The locker she'd managed to break into belonged to someone who worked as a dealer during the day shift. Their ship uniform hung neatly, black and yellow, and she draped the slightly too large shirt over her shoulders.

The door opened and Adam walked in. She knew he'd been hiding, waiting for Luke to leave and a clear shot for where she'd led him. She smiled.

He nodded and moved to a locker across the room.

Her smile fell. He jimmied the lock, found clothes that didn't suit him and moved on to the next one.

'The laundry room's next door.' She finished her buttons and wiggled the dress past her hips. The uniform covered her until mid-thigh. 'Might have better luck.'

Not a single muscle twitched in her direction. He flung open another locker and shrugged. 'This'll work.'

Bee rolled her eyes. She took the stack of bills she'd jammed under her cleavage and dropped it on the nearest bench.

That got his attention.

He looked her way over his shoulder, fingers unbuttoning his ruined shirt.

'Ten thousand dollars.' She raised her eyebrows. 'What do you think about that?'

He raised his eyebrows back at her. 'This is a Cardello business, right? Aren't you stealing from yourself?'

Bee licked her teeth. 'Yep.'

Adam grinned and gingerly removed his shirt. Purple splotches covered old scars. 'Yeah. You're a real badass, Bee.'

She opened her mouth to say something super smart and quick-witted, but Malika interrupted the opportunity.

'Somebody's coming, Boss.'

Why would two people, half dressed like employees, be in the locker room in the middle of service?

'Adam!' Bee called out, climbing on to the bench between them.

He had a chef's jacket in his hands when he turned around.

She launched herself off the bench and landed on top of him. Arms around his neck, legs around his waist, mouth on his mouth.

Adam dropped the jacket and grabbed her rear. He didn't hesitate to return the kiss, his tongue sliding over hers, and he tasted like blood and champagne. The metal of the nearest locker was cold against her thighs.

His hands were everywhere. Up her legs, down her sides, tangled up in her hair. She clutched his shoulders for balance and whimpered against his lips.

There was a good chance he didn't realize this was fake.

He responded with a quiet, desperate little groan in the back of his throat and gripped her rear again.

The changing-room door was flung wide.

Adam froze. Bee sighed.

An older gentleman wearing a festive black fez with yellow trim coughed in disdain. She peeked at him from behind Adam. He shook his head so hard his hat fell off.

Adam must have realized what was happening, why she'd done what she'd done, because he put on his best crooked grin. 'Sorry, sir,' he said over his shoulder, careful to stay in the shadow of the crappy lighting so Fez Man wouldn't see his injuries. 'Couldn't wait till shift was over.'

He fixed his hat, his lips a sharp frown. 'This is what we get for hiring temps. I told Mr DiMarco we didn't need any outside help for the event. But fine.' He sniffled. 'I remember what it's like being young. But this is inappropriate. Get back to work or I'll have to dock your pay.'

'Yes, sir,' Adam said.

Bee hid her face in Adam's chest until Fez Man had left.

Dismounting was awkward. Neither of them could muster up the courage to look the other in the face. Bee hurried over to her borrowed pants and pulled them on. She could feel the embarrassment burn her cheeks, work its way down her neck, fill her chest. She rubbed her clavicle with her palm and tried to will away the redness.

But then she realized something vitally important – he *had* thought it was real. And he had kissed her like *that* . . .

Oh, the burn was back, spreading down to her stomach now. It tightened behind her belly button, a tingle jolting down her thighs, and Bee pressed a hand to her neck.

She practiced smiling. Once, twice, stretching out the muscles in her face, until it felt natural. She tossed her hair over her shoulder and smiled at him.

'You thought it was real,' she teased.

'What? Me?' Adam scoffed. 'Oh, I knew it was fake. But I thought I'd go ahead and give you the best kiss of your life.' He winked. 'You're welcome.'

Bee scoffed in return. 'Not my life, no way.' She stashed the money in her pocket. 'Maybe yours.'

Adam tightened his borrowed belt, his eyes sparkling. 'What? No. Definitely yours.'

Bee put on her stolen black flats – a size too big but less noticeable than walking the ship barefoot – and headed for the exit. 'No,' she said, hand on the doorknob. A real smile bloomed across her lips, and she snuck a coy glance in his direction. The burn in her cheeks and the tingle in her stomach came back in full force. 'The best kiss of my life was in front of a fountain in Ibiza.'

She watched the memory dawn on his face out of the corner of her eye.

'I'll meet you in the kitchen.' She wetted her lips. 'We gotta clean you up.'

TWENTY-FIVE

Bee focused on the water running over her hands, soaking the paper towel, and not on the tightness in her lungs. The crew's kitchen had shrunk since she'd been in it a few minutes ago. The microwave and coffee brewer, however, were dirty as ever.

Adam leaned on the counter next to the sink, so close to her she could feel his body heat rolling off him in waves. Like a boat speeding through a canal, she was caught in the wake of him.

The faucet squeaked when she shut off the water.

She looked him over to see where she needed to start. His knuckles were a bloody, torn mess. Red marks littered his forearms and throat. He had a black eye, bruises and cuts on both cheeks, dried blood in his nostrils. The wound on his forehead had stopped bleeding some time ago, leaving streaks down one side of his face that made him look a comic-book villain. Oliver was addicted to those Marvel movies, had a couple dozen Iron Man comics that he thumbed through regularly instead of doing his homework. It was always so hard to get him to do his homework.

Bee shook the thought of her son away. She started with Adam's face, concentrating on cleaning him up without causing harm, and not on how comfortably warm his skin felt beneath her fingertips. 'You think you broke anything?'

'Nah.' He tilted his head to give her better access to his throat. 'My ribs aren't too happy with me, but there's no grinding when I breathe, so I think I'll survive.'

She could feel his pulse beneath the soft skin of his neck. 'Spoken like someone with experience.'

'Too damn much.'

Bee tossed the paper towel in the bin. 'I've done all I can do.' There wasn't any hiding the bruises or lacerations.

Adam turned on the water and lathered the soap on his hands, up his arms then scrubbed his face.

Ah. He'd let her play nurse for funsies apparently.

'It'd be bad if that giant guy woke up and found us here now with all that soap in your eyes, wouldn't it?'

He flashed her a sudsy grin. 'Especially since your shoes won't work as weapons.'

Bee looked down at her stolen flats and considered that. 'I could always throw them at his junk.'

Adam chuckled as he dried off. At least the blood was gone. The lights were dim enough in the ship that he wouldn't draw too much attention, but she would've felt better with a guarantee.

Or a distraction.

'Hey, Malika,' Bee said. 'What are the Anas up to?'

'Hey, yeah, sorry.' Malika didn't sound sorry at all. 'I was busy closing my eyes and humming the national anthem. Let me Where's Waldo them.'

Bee raked her fingers through her hair. 'We gotta be careful getting out of here. You know what to do, right? Walk with purpose, look straight ahead, don't make eye contact.'

'Yeah, yeah.' He tugged his earlobe. 'Probably a good thing there ain't a mirror around here. Don't want to get self-conscious.'

She touched her laughing lips. 'Don't worry about it. Women love oozing, open wounds.'

'Well, I wish someone would've told me that sooner.'

'Woulda saved you a lot of trouble, huh?'

'Hey, listen. About what you said—'

Bee framed her face with her hands and groaned, 'Not what I said!'

'—about Ibiza,' he continued, undeterred, that look of straight-lipped, playful amusement lighting up his features, 'I just . . . I wanted to say . . . me too.'

Goosebumps prickled over her exposed skin.

She steadied herself. 'Adam—'

'Found 'em,' Malika cut in. 'They're eating in the sit-down restaurant.'

Bee sighed. 'On our way up. Keep an eye on them please.'

She left Adam at the dimmest corner of the bar they could find and strolled across the deck, passing the maître d' and into the restaurant without so much as a, 'Hey! What do you think you're doing?' It really was amazing the places you could get into if you walked with purpose in a stolen uniform.

'Excuse me, ladies,' she said when she reached their table, standing next to it like she was taking a drink order.

Anastasia managed to spit-take back into her Martini glass with a level of grace most people would never be able to achieve sober. 'What? What is this? This is trick or treat?'

'Yep,' Malika said. 'This is your own personal Halloween. She caught you, Bee. Time to turn it in.'

Bee held on to the back of the empty chair across from them. 'I need another favor.'

Liliana raised her champagne glass, pinky up. 'It's going to cost you more wine, Beatrice, whatever it is.'

'When the boat docks, how would you feel about causing a bit of a distraction?'

Liliana swallowed her drink and attempted to pucker her motionless brow. 'How much of a bit?'

'A big bit,' admitted Bee. 'A really big bit.'

Anastasia clinked her glass against Liliana's. 'It's what we were born to do.'

The Anas didn't waste any time. The moment the boat docked and people started gathering belongings to leave, Liliana threw a glass of champagne in Anastasia's face and screamed in Spanish.

Anastasia shoved the much smaller girl, shouting in Russian.

And then they were tumbling across the floor, knocking over tables and people, shoes and weave flying.

Adam took Bee by the hand and walked around the melee. They were among the first to disembark.

'Some friends,' he said when they were in the car.

'Yeah,' Bee agreed, beaming. 'And to think it used to be only our kids that bonded us.'

Their borrowed Mercedes merged into traffic.

'Now you've got crime.'

'It's a solid foundation to any friendship.' She patted his hand on the gear shift. He surprised her when he turned his palm around. 'Right?'

He squeezed her fingers and held on for the rest of the ride.

The hotel lobby was busy. The same nerds from the day before hung out by the grand piano, singing along with the poor musician who was working for every last cent of his tip. But no one was in a rush to get back up to their rooms, so Adam and Bee had the elevator all to themselves.

He stood next to her when the door closed, his arm brushing hers, and Bee could feel the connection tingle all the way down to her wrist. She clenched her hands into fists and released them again, breath quickening, and stared at the occupancy notice.

They'd been alone together for a solid hour and a half before this moment. They'd held hands in the car! Why was she getting so worked up now?

Bee giggled at nothing and stepped to the side. 'What a night,' she said in a voice not quite her own. 'What a night.'

'We got done what we needed.' He shrugged, hands in his pockets. 'Banks'll be there in the morning. Good work all around.'

'Yep.' She swallowed, her mouth dry. 'And thanks. Glad you, uh, came around on my skills.'

He hung his head, not quite able to hide his smile. 'I'm never going to hear the end of that.'

'Not for as long as I'm alive you're not.' She shuddered. 'I'm never going to get over what I had to do to that poor shoe.'

Adam stepped closer. She had to lean her head against the wall of the elevator to see his face. 'Your poor shoe,' he cooed, a teasing, happy lilt to his voice. 'You just got it today too.'

'That's right.' She stuck out her bottom lip in a pout. 'I never got to use it to its full potential.'

'I'm not so sure about that. I think it far exceeded its potential.'

Bee grinned, grazing her teeth over her lip. 'Saved your life.'

'Nah,' he said, his voice a low whisper, 'I had it handled.'

She relaxed against the wall as he moved closer. 'I don't think so.'

'It's like you said.' Two gentle fingers under her chin lifted her face towards his. He ran his thumb over her bottom lip, his hazel eyes tracking the motion, and Bee's heart thudded so hard against her ribcage, she lost her breath.

His forehead pressed against hers; his hand moved to the back of her head; his fingers combed through her hair.

'Chicks dig wounds.'

'I didn't say chi—'

His kiss cut off her sentence.

Oh God. He remembered the way she liked it. Her knees buckled, and he wrapped an arm around her waist, holding her close. She clutched his back, feeling every defined muscle along the way, trying to remember exactly how he'd felt all those years ago. What was the same. What was different.

It felt like the first time again.

It felt like they'd never stopped.

Bee moved her hands to the back of his neck, locking her fingers together to hold him in place. She pushed her thumbs lightly against his head, and he responded immediately, changing the angle of the kiss to deepen it, and she gasped out an appreciative little mewl.

Adam's arms surrounded her and lifted her to her tiptoes, pulling her flush against him. Heat spread through her body, warming her cheeks, pooling in her gut.

Every thought in her head slipped away until the only things she was aware of were Adam's lips and Adam's hands and her own thundering heart.

Someone coughed.

The elevator had been called back to the lobby. The doors were open, and Adam and Bee found themselves with an audience of three.

Bee disentangled herself as quickly as possible, not making eye contact with Adam or anyone else entering the elevator.

'Don't have to stop on my account,' a bespectacled woman said. 'See, Harold. That's how you treat a lady.'

Harold, who was even balder than Adam, groused unintelligibly and pressed his floor button.

Bee covered her face with her hand. Her cheeks burned. She had to clamp her lips shut to keep from laughing.

Adam wasn't embarrassed about being caught in public. He held the small of her back and kissed her hair. 'It was a good night.'

'Not as good as it will be, right?' The third person in their audience – a thirty-something, stringy-haired man – raised his hand for a high five.

Adam glared at him until he lowered it.

String Hair high-fived himself. 'All right.'

TWENTY-SIX

Malika had powered down the comm system, showered and claimed the king-sized bed for herself.

'You owe me!' she called from the bedroom. 'You're like my mom and' – she faked throwing up – 'I need therapy.'

Bee frowned at that. 'I always thought of myself as more of a big sister.'

'Well, you were wrong.' She got up from the bed and stomped to the door. 'I'm going to sleep. And I'm going to put on my headphones and blast Britney Spears at full volume all night because I don't need to know. OK? I do not need to know.'

'Jeez, OK,' said Bee. 'Can we at least get ready for bed first?'

Malika narrowed her eyes and assessed the two of them, standing in the middle of the living room looking like teenagers who'd been caught by an angry dad with a rifle.

'Fine. One at a time.' She held up a finger. 'I mean it, mister.'

Adam held his arms up and looked around the room. 'What? What did I do?'

'Oh, you know what you did.'

Bee walked into the bedroom, and Malika left a crack in the doorway to glare once more at Adam. 'You know what you did,' she said again before locking the doorknob.

'He knows what he did,' she said to Bee. 'And so do you.'

Bee grabbed a pair of black pajama pants, a matching long-sleeved shirt and rolled her eyes.

The twenty-four-hour news stations were reporting the same stories about the terrible state of the world on repeat. Bee changed it to cartoons and laid her head down on the armrest.

This one, about a family who owned a restaurant, was one of Oliver's favorites. Guilt crept up the back of her neck and settled into the base of her skull. She curled her knees closer to her chest. Her baby was being held captive, and here she was, in a swanky hotel, kissing the dude she had a crush on. But, she reminded herself, it wasn't like she was out for a night on the town for fun. She was working, and her work would keep Oliver alive. That was the only thing that mattered.

Adam came out of the master bedroom in nothing but a pair of dark sweatpants.

Bee pretended she didn't notice the particular ticking motion behind the middle seam.

'Cartoons?' she squeaked. 'The, uh, the news was too newsy.'

He sat down by her feet. 'This is fine. I tried to find something earlier when you were in the shower, but I couldn't get it to work.'

Bee laughed and pushed his thigh with her toes. 'You can't work a cable box?'

He pulled her foot into his lap and massaged his thumb in the arch of her sole.

She *mmm*ed in appreciation. It was possible he was still lying to her. It was possible he still was planning on getting her to lead him to the money and then leaving her penniless.

But, honestly, she wasn't sure she'd like him half as much as she did if that wasn't a possibility.

Adam said, 'I'm not a big computer guy.'

'It's not a computer,' she said, eyelids heavy.

He took hold of her other foot and set them both in his lap, working his fingers in circles from her heels to her toes. 'If it's got buttons, it's a computer.'

'I don't' – Bee yawned – 'know enough about computers to argue that.'

The cartoon children rode their bicycles alongside grown ups in leather vests riding Harleys and Bee giggled.

'Remind you of something?' Adam asked.

'Kinda, yeah.' She bit her smiling lip. 'Did I ever tell you about my dad's old Harley?'

'Your dad rode motorcycles?'

'Only long enough to knock up my mom, Happy Valley's prettiest motorcycle groupie.' She swung her legs off Adam's lap and sat up, her shoulder on his arm. 'I guess you could say he was the original grifter of the family. He kept the bike though. This beautiful 1980 Wide Glide. You know, with the orange flames? Left it in the garage to rot. I'd catch Mom staring at it when she'd go outside to smoke. And I swear I could see her thinking about hopping on and leaving. Even after the cancer, when she swapped the cigarettes for gum, she'd stand in the garage and daydream.'

Her nose stung. Bee blinked at the light of the lamp on Malika's workstation. 'Happy Valley was her dream, Adam. And Os sent me to ruin it. My mom was dead, and he sent me to clean up that ugly little town, the only home she ever loved, so he could have a place to launder money. I hurt people who loved me my whole life just because Os told me to.'

'Hey. Hey, listen.' Adam put a reassuring hand on her back. 'Os is a manipulative little shit. What happened in Arizona wasn't your fault.'

She huffed.

'It wasn't, Bee.' He touched her chin. 'It wasn't your fault.'

Pinpricks poked the back of her eyes. 'He sent me to do a job, yes. But what I did what I chose to do, that's all on me.'

Adam shook his head. 'No. You did what you thought was right. You made a call.'

'I made the wrong call,' she said. 'A couple of 'em.'

Adam took her hand in his, holding tight. 'Everybody . . . Look, in this business, in just life, everybody feels like that about something in their past. But there's nothing any of us can do about it. All we can do is try to make the right call the next time.' He flashed her a self-deprecating grimace. 'Whatever the hell that is.'

Bee faced the television. A tear rolled down the tip of her nose and she wiped it away, hoped he didn't see.

'You know, I got a couple nieces and nephews now,' he said.

Bee sniffed and looked at him with her brow furrowed. 'You do?'

'Yeah.' He grinned. 'They're great. I don't get to spend as much time with them as I'd like.'

'Do you have any pictures?'

With his free hand, he gestured at his lack of clothing and therefore lack of places to keep photos, and Bee smiled to hide the way her cheeks blushed. 'Later then,' she said. 'We'll look at them when all this is over.'

'Yeah?' His fingers squeezed hers. 'You still wanna make plans for after?'

Bee thought about it. Did she? 'It's a tentative yes, for now.'

His dimples popped. 'I thought for sure you'd kick me out after I told you about the, well . . .' He didn't speak again, but he didn't have to. After he'd told her about the betrayal, the fact he was a lying liar, the way he was using her to steal already stolen money.

She supposed she didn't have to tell him exactly how that made her feel about him because she didn't know exactly herself. That was complicated. Sure, she liked it. But she hated herself for liking it, so she supposed that showed growth as a person. Didn't it? Didn't self-indulgent self-hatred show personal growth?

'What are you gonna do?' he asked. 'With your share?'

'Open a bookstore,' Bee answered immediately. 'Open a bookstore somewhere Oliver won't ever have to deal with this crap again. You?'

'Would you believe me if I said retire?'

'Not for a second.'

Adam chuckled. 'I wanna spend time with my sisters' families. And then, we'll see.'

Bee toyed with her lip between her thumb and index finger as the credits on the cartoon rolled and faded to commercial. She still didn't trust him, not really, but she wanted to. Oh, how she wanted to.

'I don't know if I believe your bookstore gig, to be honest,' Adam said. 'Since we're being honest now.'

She tucked her leg underneath her, her knee on his thigh, and watched his profile. 'What do you mean?'

'Your nanny is a hacker for the CIA.' Adam turned his head on the couch until his face was only a breath away. 'Your best friends are both mobbed up.'

Her face flushed, and she tried to hide it in the couch cushion. '*Different* mobs.'

'Yeah, yeah, I got that.'

She stared at the hand that held hers and traced the pad of her index finger around his bruised knuckles, careful not to hurt. 'I guess . . . I like having options. I don't ever want to be stuck again. So I'll use the stolen money to open a legitimate business. And then we'll see.'

'And then we'll see.' He smiled. 'I like that.'

Bee wetted her lips. Did she need to trust him? Did she need for this to be real?

What difference did it make really?

She kissed him. His broken lips were soft and yielded to hers. Her palm on his throat felt his pulse jump and race. Adam held her face with his free hand then wrapped his fingers around her hair. He pulled away but let his forehead rest against hers.

'Sorry,' he whispered, 'but my face hurts too much to kiss you properly.'

Bee hadn't expected that. She giggled. 'Is that so? Your face hurts?'

'Don't, Bee. So lame.'

'Because it's killing me!'

'Yeah, yeah.' He popped a dimple. 'Good one.' He stretched out on the couch and opened his arms.

She lay down at his side, her head on his shoulder and her back against the couch. Normally Bee had trouble going to bed without a nightcap. But the thrum of his heart and the warmth of his chest lulled her to sleep.

Her alarm went off before the sun was up. Bee wiped her eyes and struggled to blink them open. Yawning, she tried to sit up but found herself comfortably stuck between Adam and the back of the couch, her legs tangled in his, her head on his shoulder.

She nestled back down, determined to enjoy the snuggle, even if only for a minute more.

Malika opened the bedroom door and strode out like a newborn gazelle. She froze, eyes wide, at the sight of them on the couch. Bee could see the wheels turning in her tired mind.

'Huh?' She wiggled her eyebrows. 'Huuuuuh?'

'No,' Bee said, her voice covered in sleep. 'Come on, Adam.' She tapped his pecs to wake him up. And then again a few more times because they were really nice. 'We got work to do.'

'Speaking of,' Malika said with a grin, 'I got something to show you, boss.'

TWENTY-SEVEN

The drive to the hangar went faster than they'd anticipated. Not wanting to be early, they drove through a coffee shop and grabbed drinks for everyone.

Banks was happy to see them when they made it to the helicopter. Bee specifically. The hug he subjected her to was hippy. A hippy, pelvis-thrusting hug. She laughed out of it and shoved his drink between them.

'Everybody ready?'

The pilot waved.

Banks's bodyguard, and the only suit from his crew that he was opting to take, was a man who'd earned the name Joey Triggerman back when Cardello Industries operated out of New Jersey. He hadn't earned it from doing anything particularly heroic, but because he had a reputation for firing first and asking questions later.

The four of them slid into the seats in the back, two by two, facing each other. Banks positioned himself next to her. And Joey Triggerman sat across from her.

She smiled politely, put on her headphones and watched the window.

The sightseeing was spectacular when they moved out of the mainland's airspace. Bee loved the Florida Keys. A skinny strip of land between two bodies of water, defiantly connected by dozens and dozens of bridges.

They soared above the Seven Mile Bridge, a two-lane stretch of man-made ingenuity that connected the middle keys with the lower keys. The Seven Mile Bridge was her favorite bridge for both being the most famous of the forty-two bridges in the Keys – it's the one in all the car commercials – and for being a liar, running between islands at around 6.75 miles.

'One way in,' Banks said, and she could hear him in her headphones, 'means one way out.'

Bee knocked her knuckles on the side of the chopper. 'Not for us.'

'Not this time.'

She decided not to respond to that rather ominous sentence and turned her attention to the sparkling blue waters below.

Alvarez's home was on a private island, only accessible by boat or helicopter. Two-story, solid concrete – even the roof. The helicopter landed on the designated pad behind the house, and men wearing flip-flops, linen pants and loose-fitting Tommy Bahama shirts welcomed them.

If it weren't for the Uzis at their sides, Bee would've thought they'd landed on the wrong island.

Joey Triggerman hopped out of the helicopter when the blades were still running. He helped Bee slide out. The wind from the blades whipped the few loose strands of hair she'd kept out of her topknot to frame her face into her eyes.

The blades didn't stop until Adam and Banks were standing next to them.

'Wait here,' Banks told the pilot. 'Shouldn't take long.'

Bee smiled. 'It's a lunch. We'll bring you something back, OK?'

'I don't eat gluten,' the pilot said.

Bee kept the smile on her face. 'All right. I'll do my best.'

Adam set his hand on the small of her back as they walked behind Banks and Joey Triggerman to the gangster fishermen.

One of them used their non-Uzi hand to shake Adam's. 'How's it going, man? Boss said you were coming.'

'Good to see you, Johnathon,' Adam said. 'How's Martha?'

'Doing good, yeah.' Johnathon led the way to the stairs. 'I'll tell her I saw you. She'll be sad she didn't make some of her banana bread for you.'

'She'll be sad? I'm sad just hearing about it. Love that stuff.'

OK, Bee thought, *this is weirder than I anticipated.*

'If you act nervous, he'll sense it,' Banks warned. 'Keep your shoulders back. Keep your chin up. Don't let him see you sweat.'

'Wow,' Malika said, 'he fit a whole lotta cliches in one condescending pep talk.'

Bee walked past Banks, throwing, 'Do I look nervous?' over her shoulder as she went.

'Seriously,' she whispered to Adam. 'Do I?'

He took his hand off her back. 'Nah.' His face brightened without smiling. 'You look like you own the joint.'

* * *

The second floor of Alvarez's island home looked like it had been decorated solely with the summer seasonal section of Home Goods. White wicker furniture with pops of teal and light brown sat on the sand-colored tile floors. The dining-room table was a large, glass circle, surrounded by more white wicker chairs. And of course, as is necessary for every drug dealer, on the wall next to the dining-room table was a giant fish tank. However, there didn't appear to be many fish in it.

Or any fish in it.

A large oil painting of waves crashing on to the shore hung above the empty tank.

Two more men, in the same relaxed, going-fishing outfits, hung out on the couch. The older one stood and made a beeline for Adam. He was a few inches shorter than Adam, his hair a dark grey, deep lines on his tan face from too many hours spent in the sun without protection.

'Martin,' Adam greeted, shaking his hand and bringing him into a brief hug. 'Good to see you, old man.'

'I'll go get the boss,' Johnathon said and disappeared down a hallway.

Martin held Adam at arm's length and patted his shoulders. His brown eyes sparkled with an unspoken joke. 'It's been too long.'

Adam chuckled. 'Yeah? Seems like just yesterday since we were together.'

Bee wandered over to the painting.

It was an original, not a reproduction. The artist had done an exceptional job of making it look more like a photograph than a painting.

'Such a shame,' said a man's deep voice from behind her.

Bee pressed her lips together and didn't startle, didn't react. Alvarez stood at her side, his arm brushing hers as he moved to hold them behind his back.

Alvarez stood a head taller than her, with salt-and-pepper hair and a clean-shaven, square jaw. His shoulders were broad, his chest barreled, and his white linen shirt both complemented his brown skin and tucked into his khaki pants with ease.

He was a decorated general on a well-earned vacation.

Malika whistled in her ear. 'That is an attractive man.'

Alvarez tsked. 'I had collected so many beautiful tropicals. My kids, you know, they are still small. I had gotten them clownfish and the blue ones. And Bill—' He sighed and motioned at the sliding glass door next to the fish tank. A slightly overweight white man struggled to climb on to a pink hammock in the middle of a concrete patio. 'Bill forgot to feed them. Or clean them. Or something, I don't know. He left the details hazy.'

'Bill is your' – Bee grimaced – 'fish guy?'

'Brother-in-law,' he corrected. 'I love my wife. But her family?' He sighed again, heavier this time.

She smiled. 'Yeah, I understand. My mother-in-law is an old-school Italian woman who hasn't left her neighborhood in Brooklyn in twenty years. She still hates me.'

'Oh? Why do you think?' He looked back at his brother-in-law, who'd fallen off the hammock and was lying prone on his back like a turtle who couldn't get back up again. 'You do not seem to be as big of an idiot as Bill here.'

'Thanks for that. But you know, I'm not Italian. Or Catholic. I don't cook. I'm everything she didn't want for her son. But she loves her grandson, so what can I do?'

He nodded. 'Family is important. I do what I can to keep my wife happy.'

'Happy wife and all that.'

'Yes, and all that.'

'But I was actually admiring your painting.'

He smiled, lips parting to reveal perfectly straight, shining white teeth.

'I mean,' said Malika, 'I'm literally not one to dick around. But this guy could've been in the movies. He could've played a drug dealer.'

Alvarez said, 'It's from a local artist. I like to support the locals when I can, from the artists to the shop owners. Even the police.'

Bee turned to face him head-on. 'Smart. They leave you alone here?'

'We do not invite attention,' he admitted. 'We don't screw up traffic. We obey the fishing laws, even the stupid ones. The locals leave us alone.' He smiled his movie-star smile again. 'It is more of a vacation home.'

Malika said, 'That's a – that's a man who would ride in on a horse and take out an entire gang with one round of bullets in the Old West.'

'Is your wife here?' Bee asked. 'I'd love to meet her.'

'Oh, no. I wanted to meet you in a peaceful place.' He lifted his chin in Adam's direction. 'As a favor to old friends. But I do not conduct business with my wife around.'

'Shall we get down to business then?'

Alvarez knocked on the glass door, startling the man who'd just managed to climb into the hammock. 'Bill! Lunch. Now.'

Bill wore a Kiss the Cook apron when he served them overcooked local lobster that even melted butter couldn't save. Bee lost count after a hundred chews without a swallow and delicately raised her napkin to spit it out. The open patio doors let in the humid ocean breeze, wafting in nosefuls of sulfuric sargassum.

She gagged behind her napkin and chugged her glass of Perrier.

Alvarez set his fork down with a sigh. 'Adam, maybe you could teach Bill how not to murder my lobsters for a second time.'

Adam wiped his face with his napkin and glanced at Bee.

She pretended not to notice.

Banks noticed. He raised an eyebrow and pushed his chewy lobster around with the back of his fork.

'Come on, Bill,' said Adam and led him into the kitchen. 'You got any more of these tails we can work with?'

Alvarez watched the two of them move about the kitchen, his gaze sliding off them and over to her once Adam had donned a similar apron. 'I must say, Mrs Cardello,' he said, his voice quiet, 'I find you to be a truly perplexing woman.'

'Why do you say that?'

'You come here, on your own, to my island fortress?' He sat back in his seat. 'You eat lunch surrounded by my armed guards. It is simply not the action of a woman concerned with self-preservation.'

She chuckled. 'You have four men in flip-flops. I have Adam.'

Adam ran a chef's knife over a sharpening stick. The metallic tang sounded like a sword being drawn.

'That's fair,' Alvarez admitted. 'I know what he can do. I know what you can do too.'

He raised two fingers and bent them forward. One of his going-fishing guards set a thin stack of pictures printed on legal-size paper. Bee stiffly drew her head back at the sight of them.

'Here we go,' Malika said. 'Hold on to your butt cheeks.'

The topmost paper on the stack had a picture of twenty-year-old

Bee sitting on the back of a motorcycle, arms wrapped around her uncle. His arms were covered in tattoos, most noticeably the American flag design on his bicep – it looked like he'd been mauled by a bear, skin slashed, to reveal he didn't bleed anything but red, white and blue.

'Your uncle died only three months after this picture was taken.'

After her mom died, he'd been the only part of her family worth her time. Her father, though alive and still gambling, only ever wanted money. Bee still didn't know if Os's interest in Happy Valley had been sparked before or after she'd joined his team, but he'd seen the small town, its only source of income either dealing meth or taking shifts at the canning factory, as a perfect place to develop, to gentrify, to clean his money.

Alvarez slid the next paper across the glass table. 'Maybe you'll recognize this one.'

Bee looked at it from the corner of her eye.

She couldn't have been older than nineteen. Her blonde hair had been done in a dramatic updo, a few select curls framing her heavily made-up face, her smiling lips cherry red. Her tight black gown had been picked out and purchased by the man standing next to her specifically for their trip to the club in Italy.

Os, forty-something, short and round around the middle, wore his lucky suit – he thought the pinstripes made him look taller – and grinned brightly with his arm wrapped around her waist.

That trip hadn't been a job. He'd wanted arm candy.

She'd been the most delighted she'd ever been to provide him that service. Little Shelby Lynn had gone a long way, from the double-wide trailer outside of Vegas to being on the arm of a billionaire in a guest-list-only casino.

'Thomas Osbourn was one of the richest men in the world,' Alvarez said. 'He solved a lot of problems for men like me. His brother, of course, ran their family business and still does. But Thomas, who had always been more comfortable away from the spotlight, found himself in the middle of a major racketeering case.'

He set a third paper, this one a printout of the front page of *The Washington Journal*, on top of the other two.

Os was being led away from a courthouse in handcuffs. His attention wasn't on the cops who manhandled him, or the press having a field day, but on someone specific towards the edge of the sizable crowd.

Someone had drawn a bright red circle around the object of Os's attention: Bee herself, wearing jeans and a sweater, with a two-year-old Oliver on her hip.

'Oh good, he found that,' Malika said. 'I worried he wouldn't. I had to set up accounts on this Illuminati conspiracy theory forum and talk about how he's looking at someone in the crowd. Who in all caps followed by a series of question marks.'

'He's still in jail,' Alvarez said. 'This is surprising to me, given the amount of money he has. But I suppose sometimes the justice system does the bare minimum.'

Bee checked her nails. She pushed back a cuticle and, in the background, could see Adam finishing up the second round of lobster tails.

'And what exactly is your point, Mr Alvarez?' Bee covered her question in boredom and annoyance.

'I'm getting there, Mrs Cardello.' He smiled. 'Only one more left.'

The final picture stole Bee's breath. Her mouth fell open, her lungs groaning in protest.

'You got this, Bee,' Malika said.

It was a crime-scene photo. Pinkerton, dead on the street, shot with a .45 through the chest. It had ripped a hole in his body. His eyes were still open, looking like maybe he was playing a prank, except for the awkward angle, the way half his body was on the sidewalk, his head on the asphalt of the road . . . the life gone from his dark eyes.

Bee was on the sidewalk. The police had moved her away from the body, but she hadn't been able to stand. On her knees, wrapped in a blanket from the paramedics, her hands covered in Pinky's blood.

Her hair obscured her eyes in the photo, but Bee could remember the tears that fell, the hysterical sobbing, the paramedic who'd hugged her until she could breathe again. Oliver, in his stroller, sound asleep.

She blinked rapidly, eyes stinging.

She wouldn't destroy her uncle's motorcycle gang. She wouldn't follow orders. She refused to remain under his control. So Os had lashed out and killed the only person in her life she'd been able to rely on every single time she'd needed him. Pinkerton might not have been her actual blood, but he was her family, through and through.

'This man, I found, was wanted in multiple countries for grand theft and fraud before it seems his choices caught up to him.' Alvarez leaned towards her. 'The question is, what were you doing with him at all, much less when he died?'

'Shit,' Banks said, half a laugh. He grabbed the crime-scene photo. 'You said this guy was your brother.' He flicked the picture. 'He walked you down the aisle!'

Bee wondered if he was regretting his time spent pining after her.

Adam and Bill set the new lobsters down in front of them.

'Take a bite,' Malika said. 'Relax. You got this.'

She picked up her utensils and cut a small bite. It melted in her mouth, and she moaned in appreciation. 'So good, Adam.'

He sat down across from her and winked.

'My point, Mrs Cardello' – Alvarez picked up his fork – 'is that you have quite a reputation for being nothing short of a black widow.'

Bee huffed. 'Please. A man isn't in danger around me until he's no longer useful.

'That's why I've come to you.' Bee crossed her legs, her short dress riding up her thighs. 'Charlie has proven that he's outlived his usefulness.'

TWENTY-EIGHT

Alvarez openly stared at her. He shifted in his seat, palms sliding across the glass top. They squeaked and left a smudge behind, but no one dared interrupt his stunned silence to comment.

Bill sneezed in the kitchen. 'Sorry.' He wiped his nose on his apron. 'Sorry, everyone.'

Alvarez blinked, twisting his expression into one that suggested he was vaguely impressed, and Bee relaxed.

She had a bite. Time to set the hook.

'Why don't you explain to me what you mean by that, Mrs Cardello,' Alvarez said. 'I will listen and make up my mind about your fate, and the fate of your son, when you are finished.'

'Thank you,' said Bee, meaning it. Alvarez promising to wait until you'd finished to decide whether or not you lived or died was practically on par with being knighted.

Or . . . damed? What happened for women?

Anyway. 'Please, it's Ms, but I prefer Bee. It's true, I do have a history of . . . let's call it, creative entrepreneurship. But I'm smart enough to realize a man like you shouldn't be the target of such an endeavor.'

'And yet' – Alvarez crossed his arms – 'your husband—'

'My ex-husband is an idiot,' Bee snapped. She rolled her shoulders back and dared anyone at the table to argue with a glare. 'That's why I divorced him and took half his stuff. And I would have been happy to leave it at that if he hadn't put my son's life in danger.'

Alvarez looked at Adam. Her bodyguard kept eating his lobster like nothing was amiss.

'Well, Ms Bee,' Alvarez said, 'what is it you are proposing?'

'I can get you the money.' Bee held up her glass for a refill. 'He hasn't spent a dime. I know where it is, and I will happily retrieve it for you. On four conditions.'

He stroked the stubble on his jaw.

'First, I want Oliver back, and I want you to call the hit off. I don't want anyone else coming after my son or me again.'

He considered her for a long moment. 'As far as the hit goes, I can put the word out. That doesn't mean everyone will hear it. Your son is safe, unharmed and happy. For now.'

He waved two fingers, and a go-fishing guard handed him an iPad. 'So you know I am an honest man.'

He let Bee look at the screen. Oliver was on a couch in someone's living room, playing video games with two grown men at either side of him, a giant smile on his face.

Her heart fluttered in her chest at the sight of her son. 'How do I know this is live?'

Alvarez nodded at the guard, who in turn waited for Bee's order.

'Three,' she said.

The man pulled a phone out of his pocket and typed something.

Seconds later, the man sitting on Oliver's left held up three fingers at the camera.

Bee took a bite and chewed, trying to get her thoughts in order before she spoke again. Oliver wasn't here, and she wouldn't be walking away with him until Alvarez had the money in his sights. She swallowed her mouthful. 'Second, I want the twelve percent.'

Alvarez grinned. 'You want the finder's fee. I can do that. What else?'

'I want you to kill Charlie.'

His grin stayed the same even though the smile fell off the rest of his face. 'Do you now?'

'Yes. He's proven himself unworthy as a father.' Bee took another bite of lobster. 'I realize that killing Charlie causes a . . . hmm, territory issue. That's why Mr DiMarco is here. I take it you two know each other.'

'We've met,' Alvarez said.

Banks nodded.

She wiped her mouth and set her napkin on the table. 'Cardello Industries is, of course, the largest manufacturer and distributor of ketamine in the south-east. I'm sure this is why you've been able to work with Charlie amicably until now since ketamine isn't in your – nothing short of impressive – inventory.

'Banks will be taking over Cardello Industries with your full support.'

Alvarez barked out a laugh. 'And why would I do that?'

'I was hoping you'd ask.' She smiled. 'You're not the only one who does their research, Mr Alvarez. I know that your guys still do some good old-fashioned cargo stealing. And I know that a large quantity of hospital-grade propofol was stolen on one of your preferred spots along the border.' She clicked her tongue. 'That's a hard drug to move, even with your vast connections. Your average junkie isn't really looking for a good nap, is he? Especially now that the King of Pop has been dead for quite some time, anyone looking to try it out has already done so and gone back to their staples.'

He tapped his finger against his lips, twice, three times, and shrugged. 'Let's say I do have a windfall of such a drug. What can you do to move it? Hmm?'

She touched her chest. 'Not me, oh no. But Banks here, he can move it. Cardello Industries already has the routes and buyers in place. Most legitimate, some less so. But we don't sell it on street corners, Mr Alvarez. We have a team of young women, all recruited from their recent state fair pageant win or high school cheerleading squad, with Special K stored in rolling suitcases who march into doctor's offices and hospitals and fraternities all across the country and sell it for us at a much more reasonable price than our competitors.'

Banks said, 'It's true. A lot of places buy from us to give their patients who might not have insurance a break. Others buy it from us to make a bigger profit. And we do have the occasional, you know, on-the-street wholesaler who can move it with marijuana.' He shrugged. 'It's turned into a popular party drug over the years. Effective and quick.'

Bee leaned across the table and dropped her voice down to a whisper. 'You know who never gets stopped at the border? Who's never held by the TSA? Pretty little twenty-somethings in pencil skirts.'

'You know a lot about your ex-husband's business model.'

'She should,' said Banks. 'She set it up.'

She languidly sat back in her chair, reaching for her glass and watching the bubbles pop. 'We'll use our team, our system, our contacts, to move your propofol for you. At, let's say' – she winked at Banks – 'twelve percent of the profit.'

His lips disappeared, but he didn't argue.

She took that as a good sign and sipped at her drink as she turned back to Alvarez.

He knocked his knuckles against the glass. 'You are a brave woman. Crazy, yes. But brave.'

She smiled. 'Sounds like we have a deal then. You call off the hit, you kill Charlie, you give me the finder's fee, and you support Banks in his takeover of Charlie's company.'

'And you get me the money and you sell this damned propofol. But.' He exhaled through his nostrils. 'I have a condition for you.'

'Oh?'

'My niece, Cassie.' Alvarez shook his head. 'She got caught up in this. She is too good of a girl for the world she has found herself in. I want her back, safely, with me and my wife.'

'I can do that,' Bee said. 'I can get you Charlie, the money and Cassie all in one go. But I want Oliver in the trade.'

'Can you do it in forty-eight hours?' he asked, and she understood that it wasn't a question at all but a hard deadline. If she went past it, the deal was off the table, and she'd find herself without a face fairly quickly thereafter. She didn't want Oliver subjected to her muscular system.

She held out her hand and arched her eyebrow, still smiling. 'What do you say?'

Alvarez sent one last look in Adam's direction before shaking her hand. 'You have a deal, Ms Bee. Don't let me down.'

'I wouldn't dream of it, Mr Alvarez.'

Joey Triggerman held her hand when she super gracefully climbed back into the helicopter.

'Here you go.' She handed the pilot a tinfoil-wrapped paper plate. 'Gluten-free lobster, I'm pretty sure.'

He frowned and started up the blades. 'I'm allergic to shellfish.'

'All right.' Bee buckled herself in and set the plate on her lap. 'That's totally fine. Not annoying at all. Had to borrow a notorious kingpin's tinfoil, but whatever.'

Malika said, 'Well, I'm starving.'

'It won't be any good by the time we get back. Will it? I mean, it is lobster.'

She sighed. 'I'll just order room service on Mr Lynch's dime again.'

Joey Triggerman and Banks got in next. Adam and Alvarez stood on the grass, still talking, but the blades were so loud she couldn't hear what they were saying.

Banks chose to sit kitty-corner from her – apparently he was regretting last night – and put his headphones on. 'They're chummy,' he groused, frowning out the window.

Bee shrugged and kept her mouth shut.

They *were* chummy.

Adam and Alvarez parted ways with a brief hug. He shook Martin's hand and boarded the helicopter, blessedly taking the seat across from her.

Banks waited until they were well on their way before speaking again. 'You know where the money is?'

'Oh, no.' She fiddled with the tinfoil. 'I have no idea where he put it or if he even still has it.'

Banks's jaw went slack. He licked his lips and got them moving again. 'At least you'll be able to get Charlie down here pretty easy.'

'Yeah.' She tore a hole in the foil. 'Oops. Actually, um, we parted on not-so-great terms, so . . . might be a little harder to get him to come down here, you know, where everyone is trying to capture him.'

He touched his forehead. 'What are we gonna do? We're screwed!'

'Calm down,' Bee said. 'It's fine. I got this. Besides, your job is done. You sat there and you supported me, and that's all I needed. You let me handle the rest, OK?'

'Do you *at least* have a plan?'

'I have parts of a plan,' she said. 'Don't worry about it.'

He bent forward at the waist and put his head between his knees.

Adam reached over and smacked him on the back. 'Buck up, buttercup,' he said. 'We got this.'

Banks sat up to stretch the pain out of his back, his lips a tight grimace.

'That's better,' Adam said.

'What is the play, Bee?' Malika asked.

Bee pretended to cough and clapped a hand around her microphone. 'Expand the team.'

'I need to speak to your CIA contact.' Bee wasted no time getting to business; the moment the coupé's door closed, she fished out her phone. 'Patch me in, do what you gotta do, but I need to speak to her now.'

Malika yawned. 'OK, OK. Let me give her a heads-up. We'll do a conference call, OK?'

'Works for me.'

Adam pointed at the plate of food on the backseat of the car. 'What are you gonna do with that, Bee?'

'I only got it for that pilot, but he was super picky.'

They stopped at the next intersection and Adam waved over the nearest panhandler. 'Here,' he said, handing him the plate. 'Fresh Florida Keys lobster. Cooked it myself today.'

The man took it with a perplexed smile. 'Aww, thanks a lot, sir.'

'Yeah, no problem.' The light turned green. 'Have a good day.'

He drove on, rolling up the window.

'Are you done?' Bee asked. 'Robin Hood, have you done your good deed for the day?'

He grinned. 'That guy did me the favor.'

Bee's phone rang in her hand. She jumped.

Adam chuckled. 'Calm down. You're as bad as that jerkoff on the helicopter.'

She fixed her hair before answering with a cheerful, 'Hello!'

Malika said, 'Bee, this is Agent Cardova. Cardova, this is Bee. I've given her a rundown of what we're looking for, Bee.'

'Hey, yeah,' Cardova said. 'I've heard a lot about you.'

'I can't say the same.'

'No, you better not,' Cardova replied, her tone light. 'Listen, uh, what you're asking for isn't completely legal. Um, at all. Plus, it's super out of my jurisdiction. But Malika is a huge asset to me, so I'm going to call in a favor, OK? I'm going to send you to this guy I know in the FBI. He's the worst, truly. He's a ferret in a suit. But he's promotion-minded and will help you for his own personal glory. And when you meet him, you tell him that to his face.'

Bee laughed. 'Yeah, sure.'

'I'm serious.'

Bee stopped laughing. 'Oh.'

'I'll set up the meeting, and I'll give Malika the time, OK?'

'Thank you so much,' said Bee. 'We owe you.'

'Maybe you do,' Cardova said in that light tone of voice. 'But I'm doing this for Malika.'

'Aww, shucks,' Malika said. 'I love you too, Cardova.'

TWENTY-NINE

'Where's my lobster?' Malika glared at them when they stepped into the suite. 'Seriously? I save your butt today and you throw my lobster away?'

'Adam gave it to a homeless guy,' Bee said, kicking off her shoes. 'Besides, I thought you settled on room service.'

Her facade cracked, the smallest of smiles breaking through. 'I totally did. I got us all a round of cheeseburgers. Just felt like messing with you.'

Bee's stomach growled. Obviously, it had both heard and understood the word 'cheeseburger'.

'Sounds perfect.' She collapsed on to the couch. 'That lobster was good but not super filling.'

Adam wiped his face with his palm. 'I could use a beer.'

'Order one,' Bee said. 'Order two.'

'Order three!' Malika said. 'Just kidding. I know I'm not old enough to drink. Old enough to save the world from terrorists, sure, but not old enough to drink.'

There was a knock on the door.

'Oh, too late.' Malika went to answer it. 'Cheeseburgers have arrived.'

'Just tell the guy you want a beer,' Bee said. 'He'll go get it.'

Adam moved to the door when Malika opened it. Two bell boys came in, dressed in employee uniforms. One had a tattoo covering half his face.

They flung the cart at Adam, knocking him off his feet, and slammed the door shut.

One boy grabbed Malika and put a knife to her throat.

'We know who you are, lady,' he said to Bee. 'You're gonna come with us or she's gonna die.'

Bee raised her hands in surrender. 'OK, OK, I'll come with you. Put the knife down.' She rose to her feet, maintaining eye contact with the one who held Malika.

She didn't look at Malika but could see her panicked face all the same.

Adam sat up, and the second young man, who was definitely not a bellhop, pulled out a silver .357 Colt Trooper. 'Stay down, old man.'

'I don't understand,' Bee said. 'Why go through all the trouble with the bellhop outfits? I mean, you probably had to knock a couple guys out or whatever, right?'

'Whatever,' the guy holding Malika said. 'What's your point?'

'I just . . . you know.' She grimaced. 'The, um, outfits don't hide, you know, your . . . tattoos. Any witnesses will be able to identify you easily. So, like, why bother changing?'

He squeezed Malika tighter. 'You talking about my face tattoo?'

Bee nodded, wetted her lips. 'What – what is it?'

'It's a spider web,' he snapped. 'I'm a big fan of Spider-Man.'

Malika clutched the forearm wrapped around her neck with both hands. 'This doesn't seem like a Peter Parker-approved activity!'

'Yeah, what would his aunt say?' Bee added. 'She'd be so disappointed in him for doing something like this.'

'Not if he was doing it to save her,' he said. 'Now shut up and come here.'

Bee took a step and looked over at Adam. He was sitting up, still half under the cart, covered in cheeseburgers and French fries. And he was pissed off.

'Don't look at him,' Spider Fan said. 'Look at me. That's right. Now, come here.'

'I don't know what you think is gonna happen, but Alvarez called this all off.' She stood so close she could feel Malika's shallow, frantic breathing on her arm. 'I had lunch with him today. I just got back. We're working together now.'

He snarled. 'That ain't true. You had lunch today, but now you're eating cheeseburgers? It's barely three.'

'OK, Peter Parker, I don't need your judgment.' Bee kept her hands up in surrender but waved them in such a way to display her objection. 'I'm allowed to eat.'

'You're a surfboard, lady,' he said. 'Like I'm gonna buy that. Where's your ass?'

Bee's mouth fell open, and a loud gasp escaped. 'How. Dare. You!'

Adam launched a cloche. It spun through the air like a flying saucer and knocked the revolver out of Bell Boy #2's hand.

Bell Boy #2 shouted and jumped for the gun. Adam tossed the cart on him.

Spider Fan said, 'What the—'

But Malika elbowed him in the gut.

His grip faltered with an 'Oof!' and she ducked away.

Bee kicked him in the groin with the top of her foot.

He dropped the knife and grabbed himself, tears pooling in the corners of his eyes.

Adam pressed the cart down on #2's throat. 'Get the gun,' he ordered. 'Get it now!'

Malika scrambled to grab the gun and immediately dropped it like it was a bar of soap in a shower, sending it near Spider Fan's feet. She swore and followed after it. 'Sorry, I'm sorry! My hands are shaking!'

Spider Fan grabbed his knife off the floor.

'Malika!' Bee shouted. 'No!' She tackled Malika out of the way.

The blade tore into Bee's side, white-hot pain searing through her. Her mouth closed, opened, but she couldn't scream. She looked down at herself, at the knife handle jutting out above her hip, and touched the blood staining her green dress.

Adam jumped off the cart and punched Spider Fan. The crunch of his nose breaking echoed in the room. He raised both hands in a fist above him and brought them down on the back of Fan's head.

He fell to the carpet, unconscious.

Bee looked at her palms. They were sticky and wet and covered in red.

Her thoughts slid out of her head.

'Bee,' Malika cried. 'Oh my God, Bee. You saved my life.' She held her face. 'Look at me. Bee! Don't you dare faint.'

She swallowed hard, her throat dry. 'I'm – I'm fine.'

Adam fell to his knees next to her. His hands hovered above her wound, careful not to touch.

Malika shoved him. 'Take the knife out!'

He shook his head. 'No, she needs stitches. I'm not taking it out until then.'

'Then let's take her to a hospital!'

'If they found us here, they'd find her there.' Adam touched the side of her head, his thumb on her cheek. 'We need somewhere safe.'

Bee nodded against his hand. 'He's right. I know where to go.'

Malika tossed her arms up. '*Where?*'

'Church.'

Malika tugged on her own hair. 'Oh, please don't make me go back to Rosalie Waters' church. All their matching T-shirts and veneers really freak me out.'

'No, not her church. Mine.' Bee forced a smile. 'Help me up?'

Adam held her in his arms.

'You two are crazy,' Malika said. 'Insane. She needs a hospital. What the hell is the church gonna do? Pray the knife away?'

'This isn't going to work through the lobby,' Bee said. 'Draw more attention.'

Adam looked around the room. 'Grab a sweater,' he told Malika. 'And my gun – get the gun.'

'Get the gun, Malika, he says,' Malika groused. 'Always get the gun, get the gun, can't not have a gun now, can we?'

'My shoulder holster's by the couch,' Adam said, bringing Bee to the door. 'Get that too.'

'Jeez, fine, fine.' Malika grabbed Bee's cardigan out of her suitcase and the loaded shoulder holster off the couch. She walked away and then doubled back, grabbing Bee's purse and her own duffle bag. With one hand, she swept her gear off the desk and into the duffle, leaving plugs and wires behind. 'Just a normal church service, right? This is what church is like?'

Bee rested her head against Adam's shoulder and fiddled with his shirt collar. 'Hurts a little.'

He kissed the top of her head. 'Let's go.' He stood back so Malika could open the door. 'We'll get set up in the elevator.'

Adrenaline faded and left pain behind. Bee gritted her teeth and forced the cardigan on.

'Oh, yeah, that totally hides the knife in your side,' Malika squawked. 'Should I create a distraction? This lobby is so filled with nerds, all I'd have to do is shout, "*Firefly* is overrated!" and there would be a stampede.'

Bee leaned heavily on Adam, wincing through every breath. 'Just – just stay at my side, OK?'

The elevator doors opened, and the three of them walked out; Adam with an arm under Bee's shoulders, Malika strolling oh so casually next to them. 'You two are crazy,' she stage-whispered. 'Have I said that already? It bears repeating. Those guys are gonna wake up and— Are those guys gonna wake up, Adam?'

He made an 'I don't know' sound in his throat. 'I hit that one guy pretty hard on the head.'

'Right, so he's unconscious and then he'll wake up. Do you think he heard where we're going?'

'He ain't just gonna wake up,' Adam said. 'It's called a traumatic brain injury for a reason. Best case scenario he wakes up with a major headache and a minor concussion. He won't be bothering anybody.'

Every step sent shockwaves through Bee's body. She clenched her jaw and tried to even her breathing. Tears choked her throat.

'Malika, I need my,' she gasped, 'sunglasses. Please.'

Malika dug them out of Bee's purse and set them on her nose.

Another step. She closed her eyes and the tears fell.

'You can do this,' Adam said. 'We're almost out the door. But we're being followed.'

'What?' Bee put her head against his chest. 'By who?'

'Gotta be friends of our guys upstairs.' He sounded impressed. 'They got costumes and came with backup. Not bad for amateurs.'

Malika chewed so hard on her bottom lip she could've torn it off. 'What about the other guy? The guy you choked out? You think he heard where we were going?'

'I choked him out with a metal cart, Malika,' Adam said. 'He's gonna be more worried about his crushed windpipe than tracking down what church we're going to.'

'Crap, Adam,' Malika snapped, keeping her voice low. 'Why didn't you shoot the poor guys?'

'Didn't have a suppressor. Woulda been too loud.'

The hotel doors opened automatically, and a valet came up to get their ticket.

'Not that I don't enjoy this totally not disgusting conversation,' Bee ground out, 'but knock it the hell off.'

'I'm sorry, sorry.' Malika grabbed on to her elbow. 'I love you. Are you OK? What can I do? I'm sorry.'

Bee squinted her eyes open and sought out Malika's blurry face. 'Am I leaving a trail of blood behind me?'

'What?' She looked. 'No! No. You're— It's fine. It's not a lot. It's a normal . . . No one will notice, I'm sure.'

Their car pulled up. Adam helped Bee in and tipped the valet.

She lay down on the backseat, head in Malika's lap, and tried very hard not to look at the knife handle in her waist.

Adam peeled out of the hotel parking lot, cutting off multiple cars to get across the lanes of traffic, and ran a yellow light to make a U-turn.

'Watch it!' Malika buried her hand in Bee's hair.

'Got a tail to shake,' Adam said. He made a hard left turn, and Bee cried out. 'Sorry,' he said. 'But this is better than bullets firing.'

'He's right.' She buried her face in Malika's thigh, grazed her fingertips across her wound. 'Broken glass is a pain in the ass.'

'Tell me about it.'

Adam cut through the back lot of a grocery store and sped down a quiet neighborhood street. The gravel jolted underneath the car tires and Bee groaned.

Malika wrapped her arms around Bee's face. 'Easy, easy!'

Bee tapped her wrists. 'Can't breathe. Can't—'

'Sorry!'

Adam made a hard right, flying between two houses. He cut through a backyard, ran over a line of magnolias and popped out on a different block. 'OK.' He slowed down, turned on his blinker and headed for the freeway. 'They crashed into a pool, so I think we're good.'

Bee said, 'Malika. FaceTime Charlie. Tell him I've been stabbed.'

'All right.' She shifted on the seat to pull her phone out.

'Be frantic about it,' Bee said. 'Really panicked, OK?'

Bee pressed her hand down on her side until the searing pain had her crying out in anguish. Tears fell fresh and hot down her cold cheeks, and she tossed her sunglasses to the car floor.

Malika held the phone above her.

'Bee!' Charlie exclaimed, his worried face filling the screen. 'What happened?'

Malika scanned the phone over the knife in her side, the fresh blood soaking her dress, then moved it back to Bee's face.

'It hurts, Charlie,' she sobbed. 'Oh, I'm so sorry for what I said. I didn't mean it. Please believe me.'

He sniffed loudly, his dark eyes watering, and he grabbed on to his forehead. 'I believe you, Bee. I believe you.'

'I need you here.' Her lips trembled. 'I need you, Charlie. You and Cassie. I can't get through this without you. Please, Charlie.'

'Anything, Bee.' He rubbed circles over his eyelids and sniffed again. 'We'll be there. I'll get on a plane as soon as I can.'

She closed her eyes and arched her back, a shuddering cry escaping.

'I'm on my way, Beebee,' Charlie said. 'I'm on my way. I love you. I love you so much.'

Bee cracked her eyes open and looked at his face, splotchy from crying, and swallowed down shallow breaths. 'Hurry,' she begged. 'Hurry, Charlie. Bring my family to me.'

'We're on our way.' He kissed his fingers and hung up.

Bee relaxed against Malika, grunting as she shifted to what she thought would be a more comfortable position. Turns out it was mighty hard to get comfortable with a knife stuck in you. 'Well, that was fortuitous,' she gritted out. 'Did not know how I was gonna get Cassie down here.'

Malika hummed. 'Laid it on a little thick.'

'We're almost at the church,' Adam said. 'You sure this place is safe?'

'Yeah.' She wiped the sweat off her forehead. 'Nobody's ever there.'

THIRTY

Adam carried her up the stairs to the church above the shoe shop. It didn't look like a church at all from the outside – most people only noticed the discount shoe store on the bottom floor of the deteriorating Art Deco building. Very few ever ventured upstairs to the cozy chapel.

Malika opened the door into the foyer. The seats there were empty, the sign-in table barren, and she hurried to the swinging doors that led to the sanctuary.

She swung them open and froze.

Six women, all over fifty, turned round to see who was joining their Bible study.

They froze, mouths hanging agape, eyes sliding from the stunned young woman to the man holding a bleeding Bee in his arms.

The woman Bee recognized as the church secretary, Linda, stood up. She was a curvy Black woman, with dark hair pulled back into a bun, piercing brown eyes and tropical-colored glasses. 'Get Pastor Foster,' she told the woman closest to her.

'No police,' Bee said.

Linda smiled. 'Whatever you say. His office has a table we can lie you down on. Will that work?'

'Thanks,' Adam said. 'That'll be fine.'

Pastor Foster's office was back by the foyer. Malika pushed a variety of Bibles and children's craft supplies off the table in the middle of the room. Glue sticks rolled across the carpet; coloring books and Greek dictionaries splayed open.

'Hurry!' Malika jumped up and down, flapping her arms at her sides. 'What do we do? What do we do?'

'We don't do anything,' Adam said. He laid Bee gently down and leaned in close. He brushed her hair out of her eyes and kept his palm on her cheek. 'I'm gonna look you over, OK? How attached are you to this dress? Figuratively, I mean, because you are literally attached to it right now.'

Bee's face hurt when she smiled. Her skin was slick with sweat, and every muscle felt tight, coiled, about to snap.

Linda marched a rather green Pastor Foster into the room. A short British man well into his forties, he had patches of grey on his temples and eyes so light they were almost see-through.

'Beatrice,' he gasped. 'What happened?'

'You should see the other guy.'

Adam grabbed the chair behind the desk and dragged it over to Bee's side. 'Ma'am,' he said, 'she's at least going to need stitches. Do you or any of the other ladies have anything . . . a sewing kit, fishing line?'

Bee groaned, 'Fishing line!'

'I have a bag packed with a lot of medical supplies,' Linda replied nonchalantly. 'Basic first aid, sutures, needles, gauze, pain meds. Would that work?'

'Yeah.' Adam blinked. 'All right. Yeah, that'll work.'

Linda went to fetch her bag. She left the door open, and the five other women peeked inside.

'Is Bee in trouble?' one lady with a particularly round head and even rounder glasses asked.

Adam studied the group. 'She's gonna be OK.'

'I mean,' the lady said, 'is somebody after her? We could help. Be lookouts.'

'Yeah,' he said. 'Keep an eye out the windows, but don't look like you're keeping an eye out. Tell me if you see anybody coming in.'

'Here.' The shortest woman Bee had ever seen pulled out two glass bottles from her purse. 'I have peach schnapps.'

Pastor Foster took them. 'Thank you. Thank you, ladies.' He'd been in the States for years but sounded like he was on holiday, a short trip from London. 'We have this under control now, I believe.'

They left as a group to their posts. Pastor Foster popped open one of the bottles and chugged until it was empty.

He burped. 'Ugh, that's terrible.'

Bee said, 'I think that was meant for me.'

'Oh, of course. Here.' He opened the other bottle for her and handed it over.

She sat up on one elbow and shut her mouth down around a moan. 'Thank you.' She took a big gulp of the drink and cringed. 'Oh, that is terrible.'

'Yes, sorry.' He took the bottle from her. 'What happened? Are you in trouble?'

'Yeah.' She lay back down again, wincing the whole way. 'I'm sorry, Pastor Foster. I'm sorry I brought this here. I didn't know where else to go.'

'Well, a hospital might've been a better choice.'

Adam said, 'They'll be looking for her at the hospital. They won't look here.'

'I'm a preacher, not a doctor.' He tossed the bottle from one hand to another. 'I can't help.'

'Look, Father.' Adam stood up and grabbed Foster's shoulders. 'People can be two things nowadays – don't be so hard on yourself. But she doesn't need a doctor. She needs stitches and clean clothes. I can do the stitches. You go get the clean clothes.'

He chugged the rest of the schnapps. 'All right. I'll go see what the ladies can gather together.'

Linda strolled into the room, a giant red duffle bag over her shoulder. She dropped it next to Adam with a resounding thump. Malika had to jump to keep it from squashing her toes.

'Sorry about that,' Linda said. 'I've been packing it for quite a while. I guess it's gotten a little out of hand.'

Adam unzipped it and shuffled through. He pulled out a pair of scissors and offered Bee a small smile. 'Let's see what we're working with.'

He started cutting from the hemline up to the knife handle.

'Linda, what is this?' Pastor Foster demanded. 'What— Where have you been keeping this?'

She kneeled next to it and pulled out a pill bottle. 'You feel like some Percocet, Bee?'

'Yes. Please.'

'Percocet,' Foster repeated, high-pitched and disbelieving. 'What are you doing with narcotics in my church?'

'Not using them,' Linda said. 'But you never know when someone might need pain relief. Here, take two.' She stuck them in Bee's mouth and grabbed a bottle of water from the bag. 'You want three?'

Bee swallowed. 'Let's keep it at two for now.'

Foster sputtered and squeezed the empty bottle. 'You can't possibly be preparing for someone walking in here with a stab wound!'

'No, of course not.' Linda grabbed a thick blanket. 'This is for the zombie apocalypse.'

Malika offered her a fist bump. 'Nice.'

Adam cut Bee's dress off to her chest. Linda covered up her more sensitive parts with the blanket.

His fingers were light along her side, but every touch felt like fire.

'Zombies!' Foster exclaimed. 'There are never going to be zombies, Linda.'

'Well, the world could end in another way.'

'We're Christians, Linda! If the world ends, we get raptured!'

She shrugged. 'Maybe.'

Foster collapsed against his desk. 'Maybe. Really, Linda? Right now, you're doing this to me? Right now?'

Adam pressed gently on her hip bone, and Bee hissed.

'I think we got lucky, Bee,' he whispered. 'It's nicking your ilium, your big hip bone here. But it's missed your internal organs. He hit your, uh . . .'

Bee clenched her jaw. 'If you say muffin top, I swear to God . . .'

He shook his head and set the scissors down. 'Never. Linda, do you have any gauze? You think you can apply pressure on the back side of the wound when I pull out the knife?'

Bee covered her eyes with her forearm and tried not to cry. 'You're gonna pull it out? Can't I keep it forever?'

Linda gathered the supplies they'd need from the bag – lots of gauze, some sutures, needles, gloves.

Pastor Foster swallowed hard. 'How about I go round up the clean clothes?' He didn't wait for a reply, quickly ducking out of the office and shutting the door behind him.

Linda snapped on a pair of latex gloves. 'You a doctor or something?'

'Or something.' Adam riffled through the bag. 'You got any lidocaine?'

'Sorry. I only had the Percocet because I promised my in-recovery cousin I'd get rid of it.' She eyed him studiously. 'You have done this before, haven't you? What did you say your name was?'

'Not this exactly. And I didn't.' He stood up and touched Bee's arm. 'I'm sorry about this.'

Bee took in a shuddering breath. 'Not as sorry as me.'

Malika jumped forward. 'Hold my hand. Hold my hand!'

Bee grabbed hold of two fingers.

'Ready?' Adam asked, his voice that low, comforting tone that she loved.

She swallowed; nodded once. 'Do it quick.'

He wrenched the knife out of her side. Bee screamed as pain ripped through her body, leaving her taut on the table, pinpricks of sweat on her skin.

'It's out,' Adam said. 'It's out.'

She bit her lips between her teeth. Her stomach rolled, and she closed her eyes to block out the sight of the spinning room.

'There are washcloths in the bag.' Linda put pressure on the top and the bottom of the freely bleeding wound. 'Wet one for her?'

Malika poured a water bottle over a washcloth. She dotted it along Bee's forehead then wiped her cheeks. 'You OK?'

'There's a good chance I throw up.'

'Get the trash can behind the desk,' Linda told Malika. 'You're doing great, Bee.'

She moved the washcloth to her throat. The first stitch pierced her skin, and she clamped her eyelids tighter. 'You – you know what this reminds me of?'

'The nuns?' Adam tugged another stitch through. 'Pinky wouldn't stop leading them in rounds of show tunes.'

Her breathing was shallow, every exhale a struggle. 'He had a surprisingly beautiful singing voice.'

They'd hidden out in a parish on the border between Mexico and Texas for a few days after robbing a state fair blind without firing a single shot, thank you very much. Pinkerton had flourished among the sisters.

The tears burned when they wormed their way past her eyelashes. Her whole body shook, shivered, but she felt sweltering hot. She tried to hold back the sob that rose in her throat, but it squeaked its way out. She held her face in her hands and wished the table would break, that the floor would open, that she could disappear into the concrete beneath the building.

'It's my fault he's dead,' Bee cried, lips trembling.

Malika shushed softly and rewetted the washcloth. 'It's not your fault. You couldn't have known.'

She shook her head. 'He tried to tell me. He tried to tell me that I wasn't thinking clearly, but I didn't listen. And so he helped me. He helped me find Charlie. He helped me with my stupid plan that somehow marrying into the freaking mafia would keep me safe. And when I realized, years later, that he was right, that I'd made a mistake, that I'd lost myself . . . When the fog lifted and I realized what I'd let myself become . . . he was still there. He was trying to help me get out.

'I told Charlie I was visiting my brother, and I even asked him to come with me and Oliver, knowing he wouldn't. We were gonna crash and burn a car with a male and female corpse, and a toddler corpse. Sorry, Linda. Don't, uh, don't tell anybody.'

'Don't mind me,' Linda said. 'This is giving me a good idea for the *X-Files* fan fiction I'm working on. I would never snitch.'

Bee wiped her nose again. 'But it's not like unclaimed corpses grow on trees so we had time. I don't know if it was because I went to Pinky's and someone had been watching me or because we were out and about, having a good time. He was always so careful, you know. But I wasn't.'

She took the washcloth from Malika and dampened her hair with it. 'I don't know how Os found us. But he did. Pinky was pushing my little Oliver in a stroller when that shooter came up and killed him.'

The office door opened, and Pastor Foster poked his head inside. 'How are things going?'

'Halfway done,' Adam said. 'I need you to roll over, Bee.'

Malika helped her sit up. 'Easy, easy,' she urged.

Bee grimaced as she moved but made it to her stomach. She folded her arms underneath her head and told herself she was comfortable, even as another suture dug into her tender flesh.

'I'll leave you to it then,' Foster said and shut the door behind him.

Linda glared above her glasses at the door. 'He better not forget he's in charge of your change of clothes.'

'I got this,' Adam said. 'Why don't you go see what he's found?'

The latex gloves snapped as she pulled them off and tossed them into the garbage can. 'Holler if you need me.'

When she was gone, Adam cleared his throat. 'Listen, Bee.'

The Percocet had started to set in, lulling her to sleep, and she struggled to open her eyes. He'd followed her injury to the other side of the table and was closer to her face now. She could see the beads of sweat on his brow, the redness in his eyes.

'Pinkerton was a weird guy. Don't get me wrong, he was a great thief and the best fixer I ever saw. But he was always twitching. And he had a ton of quirks.' He tied off another stitch. 'I'm pretty sure you're the only friend he ever had, Bee. For a guy like Pinky

– he made a choice to stand by you. He made a call. He chose his team. And to die for your friend? Well, people have died for a lot less.'

'Everyone I've ever loved has died.' A tear rolled off the tip of her nose; stung her chapped lips. Bee wiped her face on her forearm and swallowed down the urge to vomit. 'My mom. Pinkerton. My uncle. He was the only connection to Mom I still had, and I couldn't save him from Os. I've lost all these parts, these big pieces of my life, and it's like I don't remember. I don't know who I am without them.' She settled her head against her arms and pressed her nose into the table. 'What if I can't get Oliver back? What if something happens to Malika? Or to you?'

Malika petted her damp hair. 'Nothing's gonna happen, Bee. That's what this is for. We're gonna fix it.'

Her thoughts started to fuzz around the edges, but even the Percocet couldn't shake loose the guilt that had taken root in her chest.

Pinkerton had died for her. Her uncle had died because of her. Oliver was in danger because of the man she'd chosen to be his father. Her sweet Oliver. He was in danger, and she was playing dress-up and kissing men in elevators. What kind of monster was she?

'It's almost over, Bee,' Malika said. 'Sleep.'

THIRTY-ONE

IBIZA, SPAIN
A LITTLE OVER TWELVE YEARS AGO

Bee sipped loudly at her cappuccino. The waitress had suggested a red wine to go with the Ibiza sunset, but she was already dragging her feet and needed the pick-me-up.

Her thick black sunglasses made it hard to see where the cup was exactly, but the fence was focused on Adam at her side.

'I think I got a buyer,' Scott Mott said. 'I'd like to verify the artwork myself first.'

'No.' Bee set her cup down. The table was closer than she'd expected, and some cappuccino sloshed over the side. 'We'll pick a neutral appraiser.'

He sighed, looking from her to Adam and back again. 'All right. Make a list. I'll pick from that.'

Adam nodded once, crossed his arms over the zipper of his leather jacket and turned to watch the sunset over the water.

Bee mimicked him, crossing her arms over her own leather jacket and trying hard to locate the sunset from behind her thick shades.

Scott Mott dropped a couple bucks on the table and left without a word.

Bee counted to thirty before she slipped her sunglasses off. The light was too bright. She winced and rubbed her eyes.

'You think we're being obvious enough?'

Adam moved his sunglasses to the top of his head and rubbed the bridge of his nose. 'Scott Mott has the biggest mouth of any fence I've ever known. If this doesn't work, I'll retire.'

Bee grinned 'What a name. Can we go to the hotel now? Please? Pretty please?'

He reached for the rest of her coffee. 'You don't want to grab something to eat first?'

'Room service?' she suggested, hopeful. 'I'd like a few hours to enjoy myself before becoming the damsel in distress.'

He drained the cappuccino and set a few more bills on the table.

'I bet that's the most money this waitress has ever made for one cup of joe,' Bee said.

The metal legs of his chair screeched across the brick of the café patio. The patrons closest to them looked their way. Adam grabbed her hand and kissed the tip of her ear.

'It's good,' Bee said. 'Super natural.'

He tugged her out of the café, and they walked hand in hand down the street.

'I'm trying,' he said. 'I'm not Mr Romance guy. I'm not the grifter.'

Bee stopped walking and pulled him close. 'You just have to act like you're desperately in love with me and we're running away to be art thieves together for all eternity.'

He stuck his free hand in his jacket pocket and almost rolled his eyes before looking down at her upturned face.

Bee wetted her bottom lip. She smiled, slow and wide, a Cheshire cat telling a joke, and kept her eyes locked on his.

He exhaled gutturally when he realized what she was doing.

'Yeah, yeah, I get it.' He let go of her hand to wrap an arm around her waist, fingers grazing the back pocket of her jeans. 'You're easy to love.'

'I make it easy to love me,' Bee corrected, preening. 'And now, beach please.'

'*Beach please*.'

She tucked her face against his chest and laughed. 'You're such a dork.'

'Don't tell nobody. I got a reputation to protect after all.'

Their hotel room was a ground-level suite, with a full kitchen and a queen-sized bed directly across from the sliding glass doors that led to their own private beach. The artwork was of purple and pink flowers that were strangely feminine, in cheap frames, and the walls were an eggshell white that was so bright it burned her eyes. But the bed was comfortable, the view was superb, and the grey carpet was lush and clean.

She dropped the leather jacket to the floor and kicked off her shoes. Her bikini was the first article of clothing in her suitcase. She grabbed it and darted into the bathroom, not bothering to shut the door before changing.

Adam kept his back to her and slid open the door to their private beach.

'Say what you want about Os.' Bee stepped out of the bathroom, tying the string behind her neck. 'He spares no expense on stuff like this.'

Adam turned around and looked at her. If he liked what he saw, his poker face didn't betray him.

But his mouth did. He said, 'Sharks are more likely to attack at dusk.'

'Oh, don't be scared.' She grabbed hold of his jacket zipper and pulled it down. 'I'll protect you.'

He sighed and undressed the rest of the way.

Bee giggled and hightailed it for the sand outside their room.

'Aren't you gonna put on sunscreen?'

'Later, Mom!'

She froze as soon as she stepped off the artificial flooring. Bee smushed her toes into the damp sand, watching the blue-green waves cap white on top and crash into the shoreline. With no land past what she stood on, the line where the ocean stilled and touched the sky filled the world before her.

Bee spread her arms out and ran. When the water hit her ankles, she raised her hands above her head and dove in.

Her blood screamed in her veins, a million goosebumps covered her flesh and she would've gasped from the shock of the cold water if it wouldn't have drowned her.

She resurfaced with a nose full of salt water and hair in her eyes.

Bee wiped her face clean, pushed her hair out of the way and saw Adam standing on the shore.

'You coming in? Water's totally the perfect temperature.'

'Naw, I'm good.' He pulled a foot out of the wake and shook it off. 'A little cold for my taste.'

Bee recognized a challenge when she heard one.

'Don't even think about it,' he warned, taking a step back. 'Shelby Lynn—'

Her splash only served in getting his shorts wet, but it was enough to make her laugh so hard she snorted.

'All right. So that's how it's gonna be, huh?'

She blew a raspberry. 'I'm already soaked.'

'Yeah, but you ain't sandy.'

'Don't you dare! Adam!'

He grabbed a handful of sand. Bee ran for the safety of the chilly waters, arms over her head to protect her hair. She kicked as much water his way as she could, but the splash to his torso didn't deter him.

He grabbed her elbow with his free arm, and she shrieked, spinning them both around in the knee-deep water.

Adam laughed, friendly and warm, and it surprised her how much she liked to hear it.

Not as surprised as he was when she tackled him.

They collapsed into the water, the waves crashing over them. He was still laughing when they crawled back up on to dry land.

So was she.

Bee plopped down on the sand and pushed her hair out of her face. 'It's my first time in the ocean.'

Adam sat down next to her, extending his legs out into the oncoming waves. 'Really? How old are you?'

She stuck her tongue out at him.

'You aren't doing yourself any favors here.'

'We didn't exactly have a lot of money for vacations. I didn't leave Arizona until Os scouted me. Small town called Happy Valley.'

'Never heard of it,' Adam said.

'No one has.' Bee leaned back on her elbows and studied the place on the horizon where the ocean kissed the sky. 'It's beautiful here.'

Adam copied her posture. 'Water's a little cold.'

'Yeah.' She grinned. 'A little chillier than I expected.'

'Listen.' He cleared his throat. 'Why don't we go out on the town for dinner? We're supposed to be obvious and all that. Ocean'll still be here tomorrow.'

Bee frowned. Sure, the ocean would still be there, but she might not be. He had a point though. The mission was to be obvious in their over-the-top love for one another, and even though staying locked up in a hotel room was a good way to be obvious about that, it only worked if the interested party knew where to look.

'Yeah, OK.' She stood up and dusted the sand off her legs.

The sand remained on her legs.

'I get first dibs on the shower though, and I get to take as long as I want dressing up, and all you get to say is' – she dropped her voice low – 'worth it.'

He smiled so bright his eyes wrinkled and his dimple popped. 'Deal.'

Bee washed her makeup off in the bathroom sink. She worked the soap into her cheeks, over her lips, but her face stayed flushed.

It was fake, she told herself. It was for show. Just because it had to look real didn't mean it was real.

Just because it had felt real didn't mean it was real.

And just because she'd only ever kissed one other man in her entire life didn't make Adam special. Sure, he was a good kisser. One might even call him a great kisser.

But it was a con. A play. And even though he'd pulled her in close when they'd danced under the stars to the man playing guitar and softly singing in Spanish in front of an illuminated fountain . . . even though his lips had grazed her cheek before finding her own, hesitant and growing bolder when she'd responded . . .

Fake.

It was fake.

This was all fake.

Bee unrolled a fluffy towel and dabbed the water off her face.

The kisses that had followed, when he'd picked her off her feet and spun her round and kissed her hard in front of the hotel, or when he'd taken her face in both hands and kissed her soft outside the restaurant . . .

Those were even faker.

She held on to the countertop and ducked her head, trying to summon her courage from where it had burrowed deep inside of her. Now that they were back in their hotel room, away from prying eyes, things would go back to normal.

They'd be friends. Friends who didn't kiss each other.

Friends who slept next to each other platonically in the only bed in the room.

This was fake. She didn't need to be nervous.

She could go out there and sleep next to him and not worry about her experience level or how detailed her most recent shave was because the sparks between them weren't real.

'OK, pull it together.'

She pumped a small amount of lotion into her palm and walked out of the bathroom moisturizing her hands, lest he think she was using the facilities for more unappealing purposes.

Not that she cared what he thought because they were just friends.

Colleagues mostly. They were colleagues who were friendly.

Adam was already in bed, reading a biography of Alexander Hamilton, the covers pulled up to his belly button.

He wasn't wearing a shirt.

That was fine. He could sleep in whatever he wanted to sleep in. Or not. She didn't care.

Bee pulled back the comforter and lay down next to him, feeling self-conscious in her simple yellow nightgown.

Maybe she should have packed a robe. Did the hotel have one? They probably did. Should she get up and check the closet?

'You ready for bed?' Adam asked over the book cover.

Bee clutched the covers to her chin. 'Yeah, I'm beat. Could be a busy day for me tomorrow.'

He grinned and set the book on his end table. 'Could be. Could not be. Depends how far off the mark is.'

She rolled to her side so she could see him. 'Clever. You have quite a way with words.'

Adam turned off the light and settled into his spot. 'It's good cause it works on two levels.'

'Yeah, that's why I was praising you.' Bee smiled. 'Don't make me take it back now.'

She could see his profile in the moonlight; watched his lashes move each time he blinked. The overwhelming desire to run her finger over the bridge of his nose filled her. Instead, she tucked both hands under her head.

'You think he's far off?'

Adam exhaled through that nose of his. 'I don't know. Os seemed to think he'd be nearby. But nothing's gonna happen tonight, Bee.'

Her heart sank at his words before she realized what he meant.

'Get some rest. I'm here. I got you.'

Her heart flew back up to her chest so hard it overshot its proper location, ending up somewhere in the vicinity of her throat.

Her cheeks warmed, and she thought about the kiss in front of the fountain. Her lips tingled at the memory, her stomach coiling tight.

It wasn't real, she told herself. *None of this is real.*

So . . . why should it matter?

Bee swallowed and eased one hand out from under her head. Her fingers found his under the sheets.

Adam laced his fingers through hers, and the coil in her stomach pulled so hard it almost snapped.

Bee took another steadying breath and rubbed her thumb over his, back and forth, soft and slow.

He bumped his foot against hers. Bee wasn't sure if he'd done it on purpose until he tickled her arch with his big toe. She giggled and ran her heel up his calf.

Adam mumbled something that sounded an awful lot like, 'Oh hell,' and then he was rising on one arm, hovering over her, his hand tangled in her hair. 'Is this OK?' His breath ghosted across her lips. 'Do you – do you want—'

'Yes.' She wrapped her hands behind his neck and urged him closer. 'Yes.'

She could feel him smile in the dark.

He was still smiling when he kissed her.

PRESENT

Bee regretted consciousness the moment she achieved it. Memories of Ibiza had plagued her fitful sleep. They'd known, going into it, that the mark fancied Adam. That was why they'd laid their pretend relationship on so thick. They'd wanted to draw him out. She hadn't expected the fake relationship to be real. And neither of them had expected the mark to show his displeasure by trying to kill her. The mark himself hadn't expected Adam to take the bullet instead. It had all been one giant mess that had led to a giant heartache, and Os had only sighed and complained that she'd failed to put a tracker on their target.

She rolled on to her back and winced, her side shouting out a complaint. She cracked one eye open. Then she closed it, because what the hell had she just seen?

Stacks of unsteady cardboard boxes towering to the ceiling greeted her. On the side of every box were the letters MRE written in thick black Sharpie.

Bee wiped the drool off her chin and turned her head. Malika slept next to her in the full-sized bed. There was the barest of spaces between the mattress they shared and the wall of plastic shelving units filled with paper and personal hygiene products.

'Woah.'

'Yeah,' Malika said, voice groggy. 'Seems like Linda is a bit of a prepper.'

Bee rubbed her eyes and left her hands there. How much pressure would it take to push her eyeballs into her skull?

Her empty stomach turned at the memory of the Mammoth and her shoe. Groaning, she pulled the covers over her head and decided to live underneath them for the rest of time.

'Bee,' Malika yawned. 'Don't rouse me with your angst.'

Bee burrowed deeper under the blankets. 'I'm not angsting. I'm just never leaving this room. Why would I? It's got all the toilet paper I could ever need.'

'Mmhmm.' Malika tugged the blanket off Bee until it clung to the tip of her nose. 'It's gonna be OK. We're getting Oliver back today. No matter what.'

She tilted her head back on the pillow and stared at the bars of light across the ceiling. She wanted to trust Malika, wanted to trust in herself, in the plan that she'd made and now only needed to check off the steps of. A to-do list of survival.

But most of all, she wanted to trust Adam.

She still loved him. Damn it all, she still loved him.

Bee blinked rapidly up at the light. 'You, uh, you know where the bathroom is?'

'Down the hall two doors.'

She tossed off the covers and eased herself out of bed. Someone – she assumed Malika and Linda – had dressed her in a pair of elastic-waisted grey slacks and an old nurse's scrub top decorated in various Snoopies. 'Ah, fashion,' she said.

Her side throbbed in protest, but she kept moving anyway. 'Why don't you see what Cardova arranged for us?'

'No problem,' Malika said. 'Hey, Bee?'

She waited, holding the doorknob.

'I love you.'

'I love you too.'

THIRTY-TWO

The sun was stuck behind Liliana's Art Deco mansion, keeping the Miami heat at bay while they walked to her massive wrought-iron doors. The handful of ibuprofen Bee had dry swallowed in Linda's house that morning was fading fast. Her side throbbed with every step she took, but she walked through it anyway, a smile on her face.

It wouldn't do her any favors to look weak.

Adam used the pewter handle to knock. The door creaked open, and Liliana appeared in the small space, grinning from ear to ear. The door swung wide to reveal Liliana's father, Martin Delgado, standing beside her.

'You made it.' He shook Adam's hand, kissed Bee's cheek and nodded at Malika. 'Big day.'

'Yes, sir.' Bee breezed inside. 'Waiting for our arrivals and then we can get this done.'

Adam shut the door. 'You ready for this, old man?'

'He's like a kid at Christmas right now, are you kidding?' Liliana said. 'I told him I'd better get a couple Chanels out of this. Also, Bee, babe, what are you wearing?'

Bee looked down at her borrowed jeans and plain white T-shirt. 'You shoulda seen the Snoopy gear I had earlier.'

'It's, you know, mom jeans. You're a mom so it is what it is. Maybe we can brush your hair before you leave though.'

Tires kicked up gravel in the carport. Malika peeked behind the curtains. 'They're here. This is it. Right?'

'Yeah.' She rolled back her shoulders and exhaled. 'This is it. You ready?'

Adam barely nodded, his mouth small, and opened the door for her.

Cassie, Banks and Mr White unloaded from a black BMW Gran Coupé and found their way inside the house. Charlie exited from the passenger side and waited at the hood, watching her with a frown.

When Liliana shut the door behind her newly arrived guests, Charlie meandered to Bee with his eyes on her waist.

She dropped her chin to her chest and tugged the hem of her shirt down. He touched her hand to still her.

Bee let him lift her shirt.

Charlie blew out an angry breath. He raised his face to the sky and cracked a wicked grin. 'You killed those bastards, didn't you, Gage?'

Adam's non-answer was answer enough.

He inhaled deep, his eyes bright, and took her face in his shaking hands. 'I'm so sorry, Bee.' He pressed a lingering kiss on her forehead. 'So, so sorry.'

She wrapped her arms around him. Charlie made a noise of surprise but responded quickly, his arms around her shoulders, his lips on the crown of her head. Bee nestled her face against his chest and held her breath until she could hear his heartbeat.

'Thank you for coming.'

'Anything for you, Beebee.'

Bee smiled. 'We need to talk, Charlie. Our friend is waiting inside.'

He nodded against her hair, his attention on the house behind her. 'Yeah. You and me and Delgado, huh?'

She had a plan. A way to get out of this, to get the money, to get free. But she needed to get all these men on the same page first. No easy feat when Charlie was one of the men involved. 'Yeah. You and me and Delgado.'

He kissed her forehead again. 'I love you, Bee.'

She closed her eyes to keep the tears where they were supposed to be and pressed her nose against his cheek. 'I know, Charlie.' She sniffled. 'I know.'

Adam drove to the parking garage. Charlie, Cassie and Malika were in the back. Bee was in the passenger seat, mumbling directions to Adam. Being Sunday, the Cardello Industries office building was near deserted.

Charlie rolled down his window and told the security guard to put the garage on lockdown. 'Don't let anyone in,' he said. 'Not until you see me leave.'

They drove up to the fourth level. One more and they would've been on the roof. It was mostly empty, save for a sparse smattering of Toyotas and Hondas, and a brown delivery truck parked near the entrance. Alvarez was already waiting for them, wearing grey slacks and a cream shirt. Oliver waited in front of him, a different gaming system than the one Cassie had bought him in his hands. He waved when he saw them pull up, and Bee breathed so deep in relief her head spun.

Only Martin Delgado stood at Alvarez's side. His right-hand man, and their best hope to get out of this alive.

Even though they'd agreed to do this without extra bodies, she was still relieved to see he'd kept up his end of the bargain. For this at least.

Adam parked a few spots away, next to a mid-level sedan, and Bee wiped off her new borrowed outfit. A black blouse over a black tank, black trousers and sensible shoes. Liliana had dressed her for a funeral.

It certainly felt like one.

Cassie sniffed loudly and rubbed her wet eyes. 'Do we have to do this? Really?'

'Come on,' Charlie said instead of answering. 'Your uncle is waiting.'

He'd agreed to do exactly as Bee said. If he followed through with that promise, it'd be an absolute miracle, but Bee believed that all things were possible if you planned hard enough.

Charlie was the first one out the door, leading the way for the rest of them to follow like baby ducks, Adam bringing up the rear.

'Mom! Dad!' Oliver shouted. 'Malika!'

'Go on then,' Alvarez said, not unfriendly.

'Hi, baby!' Bee hurried to him, the pain in her side a distant memory. She gathered him up in her arms and kissed the top of his head.

Charlie adjusted his suit jacket, reached in to scratch at his side then held out his hand for Alvarez to shake.

Alvarez did, then he brought Charlie into an embrace.

They clapped each other on the back, very manly, and held each other at arm's length.

Charlie had the decency to look sheepish. He opened his mouth, closed it again, and Alvarez squeezed his shoulder.

'I'm glad we have the opportunity to put this behind us,' he said.

'Mom,' Oliver said, 'I missed you!'

'I missed you too.' She squeezed him as tight as she could and set him back down on his own two feet. 'Malika's gonna take you into the elevator, OK?'

It took every ounce of willpower to hand him to his nanny. She'd only just gotten him back. But it wasn't safe here, and all that mattered was Oliver's safety.

Malika winked when she took Oliver's hand. 'Come on, little badass – the elevator's this way.'

'OK. Bye, Dad!'

'Bye, Olly.' He ruffled Oliver's hair. 'Love you, buddy.'

'Love you too, Dad. Hey, Malika, can I press the buttons on the elevator?'

'Dude, you can press all the buttons you want.'

Alvarez held his arms open wide. 'Come here, Cassandra. Your aunt has been so worried about you.'

Cassie moved into her uncle's arms like a prisoner approaching the noose. She hung her head on his shoulder and sobbed.

'Please don't make me leave him,' she begged. 'Please, Uncle. I love him.'

Alvarez shot Charlie a look over Cassie's dark head.

'Cassie, Cassie baby,' Charlie cooed. 'We've talked about this. This is what's best for you. Your uncle wants you to go to college.'

Bee pressed her palm to her forehead. She'd forgotten how young this girl was.

Cassie broke away from her uncle. 'I don't want to go to college. I want you, Charlie. Please don't do this to me. Don't throw me away. I'll be better. I'll be whatever you want.'

She grabbed on to Charlie's hands and kissed his knuckles. 'I love you. I love you. Please. Please.'

Alvarez ground his teeth. 'Cassandra. Martin is going to take you home.'

Cassie cried, folding in on herself.

'I'll follow you.' Charlie looked to Alvarez for permission. 'We can talk about it. You and me and your aunt. Yeah?'

Alvarez nodded, his eyes narrowed. 'She rides with Delgado. You hear me, Cassandra? I will let you work through your feelings, but you are not to leave Martin's side.'

She bobbed her head up and down, a floppy-eared puppy being offered a treat, and smiled through her tears. 'Thank you, Uncle.'

Delgado dug keys out of his pocket and tossed them to Charlie. 'The grey Honda over there is ours.' He pointed at the car they'd parked next to. 'You can use it. I'll have one of the boys pick it up later.'

Charlie jingled the keys in his fingers then clutched them to his palm. He turned and caught Bee's eye. His pupils were dilated, sweat beading beneath his thick hairline.

Nausea rolled over her at the sight of him. 'Goodbye, Charlie.'

He did his best to smile at her, lips turning up at the corners, and ducked his head.

'See you around, Beebee.'

Martin and Cassandra climbed into a silver BMW sedan. They drove off before Charlie even had a chance to buckle his seatbelt.

Alvarez sighed and took what looked like a small calculator out of his pocket.

'Well, now that that's done.' He pressed his thumb against the device.

Charlie's car caught fire.

The dashboard ignited with barely a noise. A sudden rush of flames filled the vehicle.

Heat and smoke poured into the garage. The smell of burning metal stung her nose.

Bee waved a hand in front of her face.

'You think it'll spread to the car I parked?' Adam asked. 'Didn't know there was gonna be fireworks or I woulda taken precautions.'

'Nah.' Alvarez stashed the device back in his pocket. 'It's a nifty little trick. Just enough fuel to burn the vehicle. Shouldn't attract outside attention until the workers come in the morning.' He showed off his movie-star-perfect teeth. 'Things are easier without witnesses.'

She took a second to discreetly survey the garage. The delivery truck near the entrance was gone, and there were at least two security cameras pointed in their direction.

'Wouldn't you agree, Adam?' Alvarez pulled out a matte black Heckler & Koch P30L and handed it to her bodyguard.

Adam took it with one hand; let it dangle by his side. And then he looked at her with such an expression on his face that she stepped back in fear.

A shadow of rage changed the color of his eyes to something she didn't recognize. His jaw was tight, his mouth a snarl, and yet his posture was still so relaxed.

This is what it's like, Bee realized. *This is what it's like to be on the other side of Adam's violence.*

Her lips trembled around the 'No' she gasped. 'Don't let this be happening. No.' She dug her fingers into her hair and yanked. 'Don't do this, Adam. Don't do this.'

One eyebrow twitched, one shoulder raised infinitesimally, and he drew back the hammer on the pistol.

Bee covered her mouth and nose and cried, hysterical. 'How can you do this?' Her cry echoed in her palms. 'How can you do this? I love you, Adam. I love you!'

Her legs went limp beneath her. She sank down, and her knees scraped the concrete. Her whole body shivered uncontrollably, tears flooding down her cheeks. 'I love you, Adam.' She held on to the concrete beneath her with both hands. 'I've loved you for years and years and years and I–I didn't want to. I tried to pretend, but it was real for me, Adam. Everything with you was real for me.'

She inhaled, and it felt like there wasn't any air left in the garage; that the fire that burned Charlie's car from the inside out had found its way to her lungs. 'But this whole time . . . were you lying? What about on the ship, Adam? Were you lying then?'

Bee could see him past her wet lashes. A blur of calm hatred.

'Yeah,' he said and raised his gun. 'None of it's been real, Bee. That's what we do.'

'And Oliver?' She hiccupped. 'My Oliver?'

'You brought me my niece,' Alvarez said. 'Therefore, Ms Bee, I can assure you, no harm will come to your son.'

In the end, that was all she wanted.

'Just do it,' she bawled, sitting up high on her knees to give him her heart. 'Just pull the trigger. Do it, Adam. Please! Just kill me!'

He pulled the trigger.

The gunshot boomed.

Bee saw blood spread across her black blouse, and then her eyes rolled back in her head.

Adam watched Bee bleed out in front of him.

'Here.' He gave Alvarez back the gun. 'That worked out easier than I thought.'

Alvarez smiled. 'You call that easy? How much of a beating did you take earning her trust?'

'Eh.' He shrugged. 'Had worse.'

'It is a pity,' Alvarez said, looking at Bee. Her dirty hair covered her face. She was still, lifeless, in the puddle of blood that surrounded her. 'She was a pretty little thing.'

Adam shrugged again. 'Bit mouthy for me.'

'You got the information, I'm assuming.'

He pulled out a small piece of paper from his pocket. On it was a local address in Charlie's handwriting.

Alvarez nodded, impressed, and plucked the paper from Adam's hand. 'Good work, Gage.'

He stuck the barrel of the gun against Adam's side and pulled the trigger.

Adam didn't have time to think, to fight back, to shout in pain. He fell hard on to the concrete, unable to even brace himself.

The last thing he saw was Bee's blue eyes.

THIRTY-THREE

Malika checked her watch when Adam handed over the piece of paper, her mouth moving along with every second that ticked away.

One. Two. Three. Four.

The gun went off.

Five. Six.

Adam went down.

Seven. Eight. Nine.

The service doors by the elevator swung open, FBI agents in full tactical gear swarming out. Swat team members from the top floor of the garage swung in on harnesses. Cop cars raced on to the floor with sirens blaring.

Malika grinned and touched her comm.

'You guys doing OK?'

'Yeah,' Mr White said in her ear. 'We'll meet you at the rendezvous point.'

Alvarez held up his hands in surrender, slowly spinning around to see every law enforcement officer that had him surrounded.

The agent in charge – a tall, thin, balding man with a too-pointy nose – held up his badge. 'Theo Alvarez? You're under arrest.'

Alvarez smiled and shook his head. 'I think there's been some sort of mistake here, Agent . . .?'

'Meyer,' the agent said, pocketing his badge and pulling out cuffs. 'And there's no mistake. We watched you murder a man in cold blood.'

'Only after he murdered my dear friend here,' Alvarez said even as Meyer handcuffed his hands behind his back. 'This is not what you think.'

'Oh no?' Meyer pulled a thick envelope out of Alvarez's suit pocket. He opened it up and ran his thumb over the edge of the bundle of cash stored inside.

Alvarez furrowed his brow. 'That – that's not mine. How did it get there?'

'This your car?' one of the agents asked Alvarez, messing around with the handle of a black Mercedes Maybach.

Alvarez frowned in response.

The trunk popped open, revealing an extensive stash of powdery white bricks and several plastic grocery bags filled to the brim with green ones.

Agent Meyer whistled. 'So, you get the cash and the drugs, huh?'

'No.' Alvarez shook his head. 'That's not mine. I have no idea where that came from. That is not mine!'

An agent pulled the registration out of the glovebox. 'Says Theo Alvarez right here.'

Meyer grimaced. 'That doesn't look good for you, buddy. Sorry to say.'

'No, this isn't happening.' Alvarez smiled again. 'It's not happening. How is this happening? This is not going to hold up in court,' Alvarez assured everyone around him. 'This is planted, phony evidence. And I am not going lightly. Do you hear me?'

Meyer opened the back door to a cop car and pushed him in. 'Yeah, I hear you. That's what doors are for.' He slammed the door shut; smacked the trunk twice. It left the garage with a heavy police escort.

EARLIER THAT DAY

Bee licked her chapped lips and glared half-heartedly at the FBI agent sitting across from her at the coffee shop located in a chain bookstore. They'd been the first ones through the doors when the store opened. Bee had very little time to waste placating promotion-minded agents out for their own personal glory.

'You look terrible,' Agent Meyer said.

He really did look like a ferret who'd learned how to walk on his hind legs and was much too proud of himself over it. Cardova had nailed her description.

'Do you want some ice water?' he asked.

Bee rested against the wooden rail of the high-top chair. Her side throbbed.

'I'm not dehydrated,' she said. 'Well, maybe. I got stabbed yesterday. Look, Agent Meyer, I don't have a lot of time. I've got a plane landing in an hour, and I have to be there to meet the passengers or the whole thing falls apart.'

He ran his thumb along the edges of the dossier detailing many of her past aliases and alleged crimes that sat heavy next to his half-drunk soy mocha latte. 'What whole thing? You've haven't given me squat.'

She leaned forward, ribcage pressing against the edge of the table, and arched both eyebrows as high as the Botox allowed until she was certain she had his full attention. 'I can give you my ex-husband, Charles Cardello, selling drugs to Theo Alvarez. On video. With the cocaine and the cash on the scene.'

His hands stilled on the folder. 'Did you say Theo Alvarez?'

'The one and only.' She steepled her fingers. 'I'll also make sure you have eyewitnesses that can testify to first-degree murder against Alvarez.'

Meyer sat back, forward, back again. He rubbed his palms on his navy slacks. 'You – you know where Alvarez . . . you can get him with the drugs and the cash?'

'Yep.'

'How?'

'Do you really need to know how, Agent Meyer? Because I'm much more comfortable sharing the where and the when.'

Meyer stared at her, unblinking. 'What do you want in return?'

Bee didn't even have to think. 'A chance to start over.'

While Bee was placating ferret-looking FBI agents, Malika and Adam gathered around Martin in a small semi-circle. His daughter's home still blocked the brunt of the sun's rays, casting a long shadow over them.

He popped the trunk to a black Mercedes Maybach.

'Yeah,' said Adam, peering inside. 'That's a shit ton of cocaine.'

'Is it enough?' Malika waved her hand over the evidence. 'I don't know a lot about, like . . . Is this a good amount?'

Martin closed the trunk. 'It'll work.'

She nodded; crossed her arms. 'Cool. Cool.'

'The cash was a good addition too.' Adam adjusted the sleeves of his borrowed suit. 'Alvarez's?'

'Of course.'

Malika grinned. 'Hoisted by his own petard, am I right?'

Adam looked at her, unsmiling but amused, and jerked his chin in Martin's direction. 'You sure you're up for this?'

'The men'll fall in line,' he said. 'The ones that don't will die.'

Malika nodded again. 'Cool. Cool. Well. I'm off to make arrangements at the garage. I'm taking White with me. We have, like, so many cars to park. And I've gotta pick up the truck. Um, you guys don't, like . . . do any of the drugs while I'm gone, OK?'

Adam stuck his hands in his pockets and smiled. 'I mean, no promises.'

Charlie was the first one out the door of their borrowed vehicle, leading the way for the rest of them to follow like baby ducks, Adam bringing up the rear.

'Mom! Dad!' Oliver shouted. 'Malika!'

'Go on then,' Alvarez said, not unfriendly.

'Hi, baby!' Bee hurried to him, the pain in her side a distant memory. She gathered him up in her arms and kissed the top of his head.

Charlie adjusted his suit jacket, reached in with his left hand to pull out an envelope folded in half then held out his right hand for Alvarez to shake.

Alvarez did, then he brought Charlie into an embrace. Charlie slid the envelope into Alvarez's pocket.

When Alvarez agreed to let Charlie follow behind Cassie, Delgado dug keys out of his pocket and tossed them to Charlie. 'The grey Honda over there is ours.' He pointed at the car they'd parked next to. 'You can use it. I'll have one of the boys pick it up later.'

Charlie jingled the keys in his fingers then clutched them to his palm. He turned and caught Bee's eye. His pupils were dilated, sweat beading beneath his thick hairline.

'Goodbye, Charlie.'

He did his best to smile at her, lips turning up at the corners, and ducked his head.

'See you around, Beebee.'

Martin and Cassandra climbed into a silver BMW sedan. They drove off before Charlie even had a chance to buckle his seatbelt.

The window tinting on Liliana's car was so black it offered some cover to the Honda it was blocking. Charlie scooted to the passenger seat, cracked open the door and eased on to the concrete.

He crawled on all fours to hide behind a piling.

Alvarez sighed and took what looked like a small calculator out of his pocket.

'Well, now that that's done.' He pressed his thumb against the device.

Charlie's car caught fire.

But Charlie was halfway across the garage, hunched down and hiding behind every sedan strategically placed by Malika and White until the brown delivery truck came into view.

Malika peered around the side, wearing a maroon suit jacket with an American flag pinned to the lapel. She waved him forward when the coast was clear. She had a tablet in her hands, the live feed of the garage displayed on the screen, and she was busy deleting any video evidence of Charlie surviving.

Charlie panted and climbed into the passenger's seat.

'Hey, Mr C,' White greeted from behind the wheel, a friendly smile on his face, like Charlie hadn't just risked life and limb. 'You ready?'

'Yeah, let's get the hell out of here.'

Oliver popped up from the back and said, 'Hi, Dad!'

Charlie startled. 'Oh, Olly.' He chuckled through his rapid breathing. 'Hey, buddy. Stay down, OK?'

'OK, but this time I refuse to have Hogarth's butt in my face.'

'Uh,' Charlie said. 'What?'

The delivery truck made its way down the spiraling floors of the garage.

Charlie waved at the security guard as they drove past.

He waved back and raised the metal gates for the cop cars waiting to go in.

PRESENT

Meyer turned to the two bodies on the floor and said, 'Nice work.'

Bee rolled on to her back and groaned. 'Ow.'

'Ow?' Adam winced. 'I think I cracked a rib. It grinds when I breathe.'

She opened one eye. They were shoulder to shoulder but lying in opposite directions. 'Need I remind you that I was stabbed yesterday? Also, I skinned my knees real good there.' She raised her head to look at the wounds then decided against it. 'Ow.'

Adam glared. 'Grinds. When. I. Breathe.'

'Yeah, yeah,' she teased. 'Big baby.'

She touched her side and hissed through clenched teeth. 'I think I popped a stitch.'

'Yeah, yeah,' Adam said. 'Big baby.'

She pulled up her shirt, so the blood pack that had splattered and the bullet that had struck her vest were visible. Sure enough, two stitches had come loose, and her side was bleeding again.

'Yeah,' Meyer said, 'I thought there was more blood than in the pack we gave you.'

'Yeah, you thought, huh?' Bee tried to sit up on her elbows but gave up and collapsed on to the concrete.

He loomed over her in what he thought must have been an intimidating position. But really he looked adorable – absolutely like a cuddly little ferret in a tie.

She smiled up at him.

'I need to speak to Cardello.'

Her smile faltered. 'I'm – I'm right here, dude.'

'No.' His expression remained cutely stern. '*Charles* Cardello. The deal was both him and Alvarez, and yet he's nowhere to be found.'

She full-on frowned. 'He's not here?'

'No.' Meyer wasn't doing a good job sounding patient. 'No, he is not. Where is he?'

Bee covered her heart with both hands. 'I swear, I have no idea.'

'He isn't here, Mrs Cardello.'

She had a perfect view of his nostrils.

They could be cleaner.

'I thought he was here,' Bee said. 'If he's not here, then he's screwed me over just as much as he's screwed you over. There's a reason he's my ex, you know?'

Meyer's ferret face scrunched up tight. 'I don't believe you.'

'Look, asshole' – Adam sat up on his elbows – 'if she says she doesn't know where he is, she doesn't know where he is. Now, we just got shot at very close range doing you a favor, so if you could give us a minute, that'd be great.'

'Yeah!' said Bee. 'You go find him, huh, how about that? That's what the F in FBI is for anyway!'

'Yeah,' Adam agreed, lying back down. 'Ferret-looking motherfucker.'

Bee said, 'Asshole.'

And Adam repeated it. 'Asshole!'

Meyer licked his lips. 'Are you both concussed?'

Bee tried to stop, but the giggle escaped, bubbling out of her on its own. She snorted and clamped her hand over her mouth, mortified and still laughing.

Adam chuckled softly, growing louder with each new breath.

Meyer threw his arms up and walked away. 'The F is for federal!' he called out, his voice echoing. 'Federal!'

Bee swallowed the last of her laughter, a bright smile still on her face, her side still aching with every inhale.

She held up her fist.

Adam tapped it with his knuckles.

And then he took hold of it, brought it to his mouth and kissed the back of her hand.

She caressed the side of his face. His stubble scratched her palm. She traced his cheekbone, careful to dodge the bruises and scratches that marred his skin.

They'd done it. They'd really done it. And he was still here, with her.

It was real.

And that mattered.

He pushed her hair out of her eyes, let his fingers linger behind her ear.

His face was happy, his eyes light, and her cheeks warmed at the way he was looking at her. Like she was a piece of art displayed on his wall. The most priceless thing he'd ever seen, even covered in blood with hair that desperately needed a good shampoo.

Adam kissed her wrist. 'You think you can stand up?'

'If I say no, will you carry me?'

'All right, on the count of three,' Adam grunted. 'Three.'

She got up and let out a creak like an old screen door. 'Let's never get shot again.'

'Yeah, that sucked. Hey. Come here.'

He opened his arms and enveloped her in them, their foreheads touching, their noses brushing.

Bee breathed him in. 'Is it really over?'

'Yeah.' He held her tighter. 'Yeah, it's really over.'

A black, four-door SUV pulled up in front of them. Malika, wearing a sharp maroon pantsuit, an FBI badge dangling from a chain around her neck, stepped out.

'You two, get in the car,' she ordered. 'You need to be debriefed. By the chief.'

'Director,' Adam said.

Malika opened the car door. 'That's what I said. Chief director in charge of debriefing. Just – just get in the damn car.'

'Yes, ma'am,' said Bee. It took great restraint not to bring both of them into a hug. Or one of those group huddles at sporting events where they put their hands in and shouted something in unison. 'You got any of those FBI hoodies or something? I'm covered in fake blood. And real blood.'

'You are so high maintenance.' Malika shut the back door on them and headed for the driver's side. 'And no, I didn't have time to fetch you official hoodies. So you will be bloody, and you will be quiet about it.'

Bee chewed on her lip to mute her laughter. She picked up Adam's hand and set it on her lap. He flipped his palm around, and her hand got lost in his.

'By the way,' Malika looked at them in the rearview mirror. 'Excellent performances, guys. Really. Bra to the vo.'

Bee grimaced. 'I oversold it, didn't I?'

'No way. It was Oscar worthy,' Malika said. 'Super nuanced.'

'OK.' Bee laid her head on Adam's shoulder. 'Thanks for your support.'

He kissed her hair then rested his cheek on the top of her head, and she closed her eyes.

THIRTY-FOUR

Adam shifted next to her, releasing her hand to wrap his arm around her back. He pulled her close to his side – because who cared about seatbelt-related safety? – and pressed his lips above her ear.

'Hey, listen,' he whispered.

She listened.

'After. When all this is over.'

'Yeah?'

He reached for her left hand, his lips moving softly across her temple. 'We're gonna need new names. New aliases.'

'Yeah,' Bee agreed, not sure what he was getting at. 'Malika can do that stuff, no problem.'

'Yeah, yeah, I know. I was, um, I was thinking.'

She said, 'Uh-oh.'

He grinned against her cheek and gave her ring finger a squeeze. 'I was thinking maybe our aliases can have the same last name.'

A smile split her face, so big she couldn't see anything but her own lashes. She tilted her head back to look him in the eye, but he ducked down and kissed her shoulder.

'Adam Gage, is your alias proposing to my alias?'

'I just thought it'd be easier, you know. For what comes next.' He ran his thumb across her palm, and the spot below her belly button tightened. 'If we look like two people who are married. What with the kids and all.'

She whipped her head even further back. 'Kids?'

'Yeah.' He nodded at Malika. 'And Oliver. The four of us.'

'The four of us,' Bee repeated, wiping at her eyes.

His mouth moved over silent words, panic covering his face. 'Bee, if you don't, I—'

She grabbed on to the back of his neck and yanked him to her, landing a messy, happy kiss on him.

'Sounds like a good plan.' She smiled against his lips.

'Well, I have my moments.' He rested his forehead against hers.

'Not much of a thinker, just the punch-up artist, but I have my moments.'

She giggled. 'I'm the mouthy one, remember?'

'Yeah.' He kept one hand clutching hers; curled the other around the back of her head. He kissed her eye. The bridge of her nose. Her other eye. 'I remember.'

Bee could feel the words on her tongue. They wanted out, to be said, and she licked her lips to chase away the feel of them.

But they clung tight.

Malika put the car in park. 'OK, you can stop being gross now. We're here.'

Impossibly tall palm trees lined the road into the cemetery, leaving it looking more like an old Hollywood movie set and less like a place to lay the dead to rest. Adam took her hand to help her out of the car and didn't let go.

The grounds had closed for the night. The wrought-iron gates underneath the archway entrance were shut, but the heavy lock that held them together lay broken on the ground.

'Guess they made it.' Adam pushed the gate open and led the way inside.

The tropical breeze hummed over the headstones. Statues of angels raised their hands to the heavens underneath dogwood trees. And the only lights were the stars in the sky and moving beams at the other end of the cemetery.

Charlie, Oliver, Mr White and Banks waited for them at the foot of a grave marked only with a cross and a bouquet of red roses. Hogarth was busying himself desecrating gravestones.

Mr White tossed Adam a shovel.

Adam grunted and took off his jacket.

'I'll take it,' Bee said.

Charlie took off his jacket. She rolled her eyes.

'Oh my gosh, give it to me,' Malika said. 'Come on, come on. I'll hold all the jackets if it means I don't have to dig.'

Mr White and Banks took her up on the offer.

'It's only summer in Miami,' she said. 'Why wouldn't you be wearing three-piece suits?'

Adam was the first to break ground. The other three men joined in at their own corners.

'Uh, hey.' Oliver tugged on Bee's bloody shirt. 'Are we gonna see a dead body? Because I think I've had enough of zombies for one lifetime.'

'Hmm. I don't— Charlie!'

He stuck his shovel in the ground and wiped his forehead with the back of his dirty hand. 'No, buddy, no body. There's a,' he panted, 'there's a coffin.'

'OK,' Oliver said. 'Still kinda gross.'

Malika nodded and hid her face behind the jackets. 'Oh no, bad idea.' She gagged and dropped them on the ground. 'Dude sweat. Yuck.'

Bee wasn't sure how long it took the four of them to reach the bottom of the six-foot hole, only that her feet were sore from standing by the time Mr White let out a loud whoop. She hugged Adam's stained jacket tight to her chest and peered into the grave.

On top of the coffin were a dozen white-and-green boxes that read 'Recycled Printer Paper' on the tops and sides.

Bee's jaw shook open. Her legs trembled, and she teetered on the edge of the grave.

'It's all – it's all here, Charlie?' Her eyes burned, her pulse racing in her ears. 'It's all here?'

His smile didn't reach his eyes. 'Yeah. It's all here.'

Bee bent down and held on to her knees for dear life. 'I'm gonna puke,' she told the dirt. 'I'm definitely gonna puke.'

Mr White threw his arms around Charlie and lifted him off his feet. 'You beautiful son of a bitch!'

Malika laughed, hysterical, a hyena in the pride lands. Hogarth howled at the sound. And then they were all laughing, hugging, clapping each other on the back and shaking hands.

The six of them pulled out the heavy boxes in an assembly line until they were stacked in a neat pyramid by the cross.

'Thirty-seven and a half million.' Banks observed the boxes with his hands splayed on his Hermès belt. 'Split six ways that's six and a quarter a piece.'

Bee took off the lid to the topmost box and started counting. Each box contained a little over three million in hundreds.

'I never want this to end!'

Banks stood at her side and started divvying up the second box. 'Not a bad payday, huh?'

Soon they were all pitching in, counting out money, talking about plans.

Oliver picked up a stack of bills. 'I'm going to buy Nintendo. The whole thing. Imma buy it.'

Bee ruffled his hair and smiled at his father. 'Who was the dead guy anyway, Charlie?'

Charlie shrugged then pushed his sloppy sleeves back above his elbows. 'He got buried the day we were hiding the money. Wanted a site where the dirt was supposed to be unsettled.'

Banks brushed up against her arm. She ignored it, glanced at Adam across from her and smiled at Charlie again.

'I'm impressed,' she admitted. 'I never would've thought of this.'

He ducked his head and kept working. 'Been more trouble than it's worth.'

'Yeah,' Bee said. She reached over their son to pinch his arm. 'Probably.'

Charlie dropped his voice low. 'You should take my share. You and Oliver.'

'What?' Bee glanced around the group; Malika and Mr White had taken over repacking the boxes. 'Charlie, you're the reason we have this in the first place.'

He shrugged. 'I shouldn't have done it.'

'No, you shouldn't have.' She rubbed the spot she'd pinched, then wrapped her arm around his back for a side hug. 'But it's over now. And you earned your share. Just don't do anything like this again, yeah?'

He smiled, shy, still not able to look at her. 'You sure?'

'Yeah.' She squeezed him again and let go. 'I'm sure.'

Oliver ran over to Adam, waving his fistful of cash in the air. 'Pizza for dinner forever!'

Adam tried to snatch the money from Oliver. But he clutched it to his chest and laughed maniacally, running behind Mr White for cover.

Bee bit her lip and giggled.

Charlie said, 'He's good. With Olly, I mean.'

'Yeah. Yeah, he is.'

'And you. You love him, yeah?'

Her cheeks warmed. She stared at her borrowed shoes. 'Yeah. Yeah, I do.'

Charlie nodded. 'Good. I'm glad you guys'll be safe.'

'Charlie' – she turned to him – 'you're talking like you're not coming with us.'

He showed his palms at his side. 'I'm not.'

She smiled, confused, half a laugh in her throat. 'You have to. You have to come with us, Charlie. I mean, at least, you can't stay here. You know that, right?'

He twitched his eyebrows up in the facial equivalent of a shrug. 'I'm not leaving Cassie.'

Bee reeled back on her heels. 'So we get set up and Cassie says that she's going to study abroad. Her uncle doesn't have to know that she's meeting you wherever her new school is.'

'I'm not leaving my business, Bee.'

She raked her fingers through her hair. 'You have to, Charlie. That's the whole thing. Banks is going to take over. We talked about this. We're dead, as far as Alvarez knows. All of us. And if you're not dead, and he sees that you're running things, he's going to put two and two together and realize I'm not dead either. He's in jail, and I know Martin thinks he'll get everyone who doesn't fall in line, but he won't. That's not how these cartels work. Some will still be loyal to the man behind bars.

'If you don't come with us, the whole thing falls apart. Not to mention I promised the feds Alvarez *and* you.'

'I know, I know.'

'If you stay, they're gonna be knocking on your door, Charlie. You can't do this! It's not – it's not the plan.'

He rubbed her biceps; squeezed them softly. 'It's OK, Bee,' he said, his voice quiet. Meant only for her. 'I'm gonna take care of myself. You don't need to worry about me. You've got Adam and Oliver, and you guys are gonna be long gone before Alvarez or the feds realize anything is amiss. I got this here. I can handle Banks. Maybe he'll be the face of the business, and I'll be the man behind the curtain.

'You don't need to worry about me anymore. These are my choices. And I'll live with the consequences.'

She clapped both hands over her mouth and nose, and groaned out an exhale. 'Fine! Fine. We're even?'

He kissed her forehead. 'We're even.'

Banks approached them with one hand in his jacket, not unlike Napoleon, if Napoleon wore too-tight pants and Gucci loafers. 'You guys are all set. My boys will fill the grave back in.'

Charlie squeezed her arms one more time before he let go. 'I'll be seeing you, Bee.'

She frowned when he walked away.

'You should get going,' Banks said. 'Don't know how long it'll be until the feds find you guys.'

'Yeah.' She tucked her hair behind her ears, left her hands pressing on the back of her head. 'Listen, thanks. Thanks for everything. You earned your share.'

He smiled, false and easy. 'Yeah,' he said. 'You too.'

He held out a hand, and Bee carefully studied it before reaching out and finding it as smooth and clammy as ever.

'Good luck in all your future endeavors.'

'Yeah, um.' She forced the confusion off her face. Apparently, his declaration of love had been rather temporary. 'You too.'

Malika walked by carrying her two boxes, only her eyes visible over the top. 'Come on – let's go! I got things to buy!'

Charlie sank to his knees on the grass and wrapped his arms around Oliver. 'I love you, buddy. Be good for your mom.'

'I can't make any promises.'

He stood up and shook Adam's hand. The two didn't exchange words, but the handshake, Bee could tell, was a very manly way of passing the torch.

She rolled her eyes.

Bee picked up her two boxes and saw stars. 'Maybe you can carry three,' she huffed at Mr White. 'And then Adam can carry three. And then everyone wins.'

Mr White passed her carrying his two boxes. 'I'm sorry, I can't hear you – all this money is in the way.'

'Adam!' Bee heaved. She set the boxes at her feet. 'Oliver! Mama needs help!'

They pulled up to a private hangar. Cardello company contractors busied themselves getting the white-and-navy Boeing Business Jet ready for take-off.

Malika pointed her chin at it through the windshield. 'You can fly this thing?'

Mr White grinned and tipped an imaginary hat. 'I can fly anything.'

'Let's get unloaded then.' Adam slid out of the driver's seat and popped the trunk. 'We handle our own luggage.'

It didn't take long until they were comfortably seated inside the jet. The tan leather couches on either side of the plane each had their own coffee table and set of end tables; each could turn into full-sized beds. They were separated from the back of the plane – the main seating area – by a plastic partition made to look like glass, an opening wide enough for only a single-file line. Each of the dozen chairs in the main sitting area had its own TV and could be fully reclined.

And best of all, it came with its own stewardess, dressed like she'd bought a Pan Am costume that morning, her brunette hair pinned under a small blue hat.

Malika looked around. 'Is this – is this the "Toxic" music video? Is Britney Spears gonna show up? Am I dreaming?'

The stewardess brought them all a glass of champagne. Except for Oliver, who got a mug of apple juice.

He sighed in dejection.

Hogarth licked his chin.

'Yeah, could be worse, huh, boy?' Oliver asked. 'You didn't even get water.'

'Courtesy of Mr Banks,' the woman said. 'Congratulations.'

She shimmied to the back of the plane.

Mr White clinked his drink against Bee's and Malika's. 'Cheers, ladies.'

'Can you drink before take-off?' Adam asked. 'I don't want a tipsy pilot.'

'Are you kidding? I'd need half a dozen of these to slow me down.'

Adam looked at Bee. She glared at their transporter, who was in the middle of draining a large gulp. 'Can we at least do a proper toast? Before you fly us all to our doom?'

Mr White spat the drink back in his glass.

'Yuck,' Bee said. 'OK. A toast then.'

The five of them raised their glasses, and Bee realized that they were all looking at her for the toast in question. 'Right.' She cleared her throat and looked Malika in the eye, then Adam, Oliver, and Mr White. 'May they never see us coming.'

Malika tapped her glass against Bee's with a grin. Then she leaned over her seat and cheersed Adam. 'Good work.'

Half his mouth turned up in a grin. 'You too,' he said and met Bee's eyes when their glasses touched. 'Good work all around.'

Bee was smiling when she drank her champagne.

'This apple juice tastes funny,' Oliver said. 'You think she gave me some champagne by accident?'

Bee licked her lips. She wanted to say something, but all the words were gone.

She tried to look for Adam.

Everything was dark.

THIRTY-FIVE

The first thing Bee noticed when the light came back was how dry her mouth was.

The second was that her arms were bound behind her back.

'What fresh hell is this?' she slurred. She tried to pull her arms apart, tried to stretch to see if maybe this was sleep-paralysis related, but frayed rope dug into her wrists.

Malika grunted to her right. 'I'd say we were drugged.'

Bee rested her head on something soft and stared at the recessed lighting on the ceiling. She needed to focus. What was happening?

They were on a plane.

And the plane was in motion.

Why were they on a plane?

Oh right. The money.

The money. Where was the money?

She shook her head and willed her thoughts to form an orderly line.

Her hands were tied, but nothing was holding her down except for the pounding exhaustion in her head. She slid her eyes off the lighting and towards Malika; found her to be bound in the same way. Mr White was nowhere to be seen. Adam was stuck at the end, awake, staring straight ahead. Bee followed his line of sight.

Across the plane, Banks was reclining on the second couch, Hogarth, her fat dog, curled in his lap. He held a brushed silver Desert Eagle .50 loose on the armrest. His other arm was wrapped tight around the shoulders of a dozing Oliver.

Her son was curled into Banks's side, his dark head tucked under the man's chin.

'Hello, Bee,' he said. 'How's that Cardello ketamine treating you?'

She heaved a throaty exhale. 'You drugged my son? Seriously, Banks? You gave Oliver ketamine?'

'Not a lot.' Banks raked his fingers through Oliver's curls. 'He'll be fine. It's a good nap at least.'

Bee squeezed her eyes shut and prayed this was a dream. She was going to open her eyes and wake up on a plane out of the country with the only drug in her system a doctor-prescribed Xanax that Linda had so thoughtfully given her.

But when she opened them this time, she saw a dozen men sitting in the tan leather seats behind the glass partition.

Hogarth jumped to the ground with a sneeze and a wag of his tail.

Banks pressed a kiss to Oliver's temple then eased her drugged son off his arm to lie on the couch cushions with a gentle shushing.

Bile bit at the back of her throat.

'You see,' he said and trailed his knuckle over Oliver's cheekbone, 'I can plan too, Bee.'

Banks approached and all traces of the false, easy smile she'd grown accustomed to were gone. In its place was something wild, wicked, the mask peeled away. He kicked the coffee table away from them; the muffled scratch of the legs sliding across the carpet tickled her ears.

He hunkered down in front of her, eye to eye, nose to nose. 'I planned all this. It was my idea for Charlie to steal that money. But he's such an idiot, it's easy to make him think it was his idea. Of course, you know that, don't you, babe?'

His orange Tic Tac breath wrinkled her nose.

'So, he steals the money, and I go' – he walked his index and middle fingers over her knee – 'and run off to Alvarez, like, "Can you believe this guy? This guy we both trusted? Taking your money and your niece like that? I'll tell you how to get him back. You go after his family, and he'll give you the money. He'll even surrender himself. And I'll handle it from there." Of course, I had to cover my tracks. Couldn't let Charlie figure out it was me. Couldn't let you figure out it was me. But Artie was easy enough to twist. Too easy actually. I did us all a favor turning him.'

The cogs in her brain ticked into motion. 'You did this? You – you're the reason all this happened?'

He set his cold palm on her knee, his thumb tracing a circle inside her thigh. 'Yeah. I did this.'

Confusion contorted her face. 'You said you think about me all the time. That no other woman you've met compares to me.'

'And you said, "Thank you."'

Well. That was true. That she remembered.

'But you'd set in motion for me to die ahead of telling me how much you thought about me so why – why lie? I don't get it.'

'I didn't lie.' Banks squeezed her leg and stood up. 'Alvarez was never gonna kill you. We'd agreed to that. Charlie, sure, but not you. And then I'd have the money and the business and you, all wrapped up in a cute little bow. Like it was always supposed to be.'

Her stomach flipped upside down. 'Where's Charlie? What did you do to Charlie?'

'Don't worry about that. I took care of him. He's not gonna mess up your life ever again.' He used the barrel of the gun to lift her chin up. 'Don't you see, Bee? It was always supposed to be me. I could've given you everything he did. I could've given you even more.'

She jerked her head away, pinched her lips tight and willed herself not to cry.

He chuckled. 'But then, you surprised me. Like you always do. And you went to Alvarez with what he thought was his ace in the hole at your side.' He pointed his elbow in the vicinity of Adam. 'He thought he could use Gage and cut me out. He thought he could cut me out of our deal, out of the business that's rightfully mine. Charlie was an idiot. I made that business what it is.' He tapped his heart with the Desert Eagle barrel. 'I moved us into legitimacy. And Alvarez decided he could take it from me?

'But then you surprised him too, didn't you? And so I had to make a new plan.' He paced before his captive audience. 'I go along with your charade until I have all the money in one place. Then I get rid of all the obstacles on my own time, in my own way.'

'Well,' Malika said. 'Shit.'

Banks smiled at her. 'Yeah, you got that right, girl whose purpose I don't understand.'

'Harsh.'

'I don't know,' said Adam. 'Seems like a lot of serpentine shit for the fuckhead who cries on scenic helicopter rides.'

'Oh please!' Banks glowered. 'That was an act!'

'Whatever you gotta say to yourself, jerkoff.'

Banks held his gun up in the air, finger on the trigger, and Bee ripped out her own arm hair.

Tears filled her eyes and she shouted, 'I don't understand!'

This man had put her son in danger. This man had put her life in danger. This man had done something unthinkable, unspeakable to Charlie.

He lowered his gun and glanced back at her.

She blinked to let her cheeks get wet. 'Why are you doing this to me if you care about me?'

'Hey, hey.' He eased down to his knees in front of her. 'It doesn't have to be like this. Don't you see? You made me do this to you.' Again he touched the silver barrel against his heart. 'I didn't want to. I love you.'

Her lashes fluttered but never touched. 'Really?' She puckered her trembling lips. 'You love me?'

'Are you kidding me?' He scratched his temple with the gun. 'I spent ten years not thinking of anybody else but you. Ten years of screwing around with blonde bimbos, trying to pretend they were as good as the real thing. But they weren't. None of 'em could even come close. But now . . . now I got the money, Bee. I schemed and I planned. I lied. Aren't you impressed?'

She swallowed down the bile rising in her throat. 'I definitely didn't see it coming.'

'Me neither,' Malika agreed.

Adam said, 'Nope.'

Oliver whimpered on the couch but didn't wake.

Banks smiled. His eyes were wide, but there was no light in them. 'So of course I love you. Don't you see? I did all this for you. We can be together now, like I always pictured it. Me and you. And Charlie's money. And Oliver too of course.' Banks cupped her chin. 'What do you say?'

Bee closed her eyes like his touch was too much to bear. 'Are you really proposing to me while you have me tied up?'

'Yeah, not cool, dude.' Malika tsked. 'Not a good look.'

'You're right, you're right.' Banks put his gun down next to his knee and reached around Bee to untie her, covering her face with his chest, nuzzling his cheek against the top of her hair.

She side-eyed Malika, who did her best to muffle her snicker.

Banks grabbed his gun and helped her to her feet. 'I love you, Bee. I always have.'

She touched the hollow of her throat with her fingertips, bent one knee in front of the other and twirled her hair with her free hand. 'All of this?' She gazed at him in full timidity. 'You did it all for me?'

'Of course. Of course I did.'

She moved to fill the space between them; traced his jaw with her knuckles. 'How wonderful,' she whispered against his lips before pressing her own on them.

His tongue, flat and cold, made her shiver for all the wrong reasons.

But he held on tight, his left hand clutching her waist, his right holding the gun. She moved her right hand from his face to his left shoulder, down his left bicep, tickling his left forearm, running her fingers over the ones that touched her side. He didn't notice her free hand until the gun was already in her grasp.

Banks pulled away with a slobbery pop. 'Whatcha gonna do with that?'

Bee pulled the trigger.

The Desert Eagle clicked in her hand.

She drew back the hammer, pulled again.

And again, nothing.

Bee stepped away from Banks, the gun between them like a shield, her breath hitching in her chest. She drew back the slide to discharge the misfire, but there was no bullet.

She dropped open the magazine only to find it empty.

'Yeah,' Banks said. 'I'm not an idiot. I'm not gonna wave a loaded gun around on a plane, and I'm certainly not going to kill you. I love you, remember?'

He tilted his head. 'Wait, did you just try to kill me?'

Bee picked up speed to the cockpit. 'You're out of your mind!'

'I am not out of my mind, Bee,' Banks said. 'And I'm not a monster. I was never gonna hurt you. You're a mother! I love you! What? I would murder a woman I've known for years and her innocent son just because she rejected me! I was planning on leaving the lot of you in the middle of the Mexican desert!'

'Oh, that's so much better, thank you so much! You are a saint!'

The suits in the back of the plane roused at her shouting. She flung open the cockpit door only to catch sight of Mr White.

Her mouth fell all the way open. 'You! How? *Why?*' He hadn't been drugged with the rest of them, which could only mean one thing: collusion with the enemy.

'Hey,' he said with a grimace. 'Sorry about this. But I'm gonna have to ask you to sit down and buckle up.'

'Oh are you now, you worthless traitor?'

'Worthless?' Mr White huffed. 'Rude.'

Adam swore. He pulled his arms, and the rope behind him came loose. 'Where's Howard?'

Malika blinked at him.

'Howard!'

'Right, right.' She shook her head to clear it. 'In my bag.'

Her duffle bag lay not far from her, under a nearby end table.

The first suit came in from between the partitions.

Adam swept his leg out and knocked him off his feet. Then he sprang up and jabbed a pencil-sized razor into the suit's neck.

The man choked on his own spurting blood.

'This is Martin's jacket,' he said by way of explanation as to why he'd had a hidden razor up his sleeve.

Malika shrugged and kicked her bag to him.

The suits could only fit through the partition one at a Joey Triggerman, a true genius, decided to pull out his oversized gun, a massive Smith & Wesson 460 XVR Magnum.

'Are you nuts?' another suit demanded. 'We're in a plane! Not hunting wooly mammoths!'

Bee stumbled away from the cockpit and the turncoat, straight into Banks's chest. He grabbed a fistful of her hair and yanked, the back of her head hitting his shoulder.

She reached for his hands; tried to pry his fingers off her head.

'You can end all this right now,' he whispered, his lips gliding across the shell of her ear. 'Come with me and we'll be happy. I can make you happy, Bee.'

'You bastard!' she screamed, scratching her thumbnails over his eyelids. 'My hair!'

Hogarth growled and lunged, biting Banks on his thigh.

He cried out and let go of her long enough to kick her dog in his round tummy. Hogarth yipped in pain, skidding across the aisle.

'Fucking bitch!' Banks wrapped his arms around her from behind and lifted her in the air, and she realized it felt vaguely familiar.

She grabbed hold of his forearms and dug her heels into his shins. He cried out in surprise, in pain, and let go of her.

But she didn't let go of him. She tucked her chin to her chest and fell forward.

Banks fell over her and landed flat on his face.

She rolled away and sprang to her feet. Adam was digging around in Malika's duffle bag as a suit with an average-sized pistol stormed through the partition.

'Adam!'

He yanked the taser free and engaged it directly against the suit's face, holding it above him like Arthur freeing Excalibur from the stone. The suit went down hard. Adam tossed the taser in her direction. It slid across the floor, and she raced to stop it before it got lost under a seat. He snatched Oliver off the couch and plopped him down by Malika then pulled out Bee's Colt 1911 and his own Beretta M9. And then he was on his feet, firing with both hands, driving bullets into the suits' guts. He didn't miss.

One after another they went down. The gunshots were deafening as they launched the bullets that tore into the bodies of the men closest to the divider.

Joey Triggerman pulled his Magnum back out.

Adam grabbed a dead man and tossed him on top of Malika and Oliver.

'Oh. My. God!' Malika cried from underneath the corpse. 'Oh my God, it smells so bad. Oh my God. Oh my God.'

Joey shot his massive bullet. The crack of the gun was earsplitting. And the aim off – high and to the left.

The suction created by the bullet hole pulled in the nearest decorative pillow.

He fired again. His bullet sailed over Bee and tore into Mr White's arm, blood splatter covering the windshield. The traitor screamed in pain.

The plane nose-dived. Alarms screeched in warning. Everyone, dead or alive, floated, weightless.

'Oh, this would be so much cooler if a dead guy's tongue wasn't in my face!' Malika cried.

Mr White struggled to get the plane righted, whimpering with every movement.

Bee's shoulders pushed into the roof of the plane.

Adam grabbed on to floating dead guys to propel himself towards Joey. The Colt was empty, but it was heavy, and it cracked Joey's skull with ease.

The plane leveled out.

Everyone, dead or alive, fell hard to the floor.

'Adam!' She launched the taser across the plane.

He caught it with one hand and loomed over the remaining three goons. 'Who's next?'

Goon #1 launched himself at Adam's knees, bringing the bodyguard down. But the taser quickly freed him.

Banks came to. He righted himself, cracking his neck, a broken doll forcing the pieces back together. He wiped the blood off his smiling lips. 'This isn't over yet.'

Bee squared her shoulders. 'We'll see about that.'

He closed the distance between them in a hurry. But not fast enough.

She ducked in time for his arms to close in above her.

Then Bee sprang up, the top of her head banging into his jaw with a furious snap.

Banks stumbled backward, holding on to his face. Bee kicked him in the kneecap and watched him go down.

Adam and the last goon were facing off in the back of the plane.

She scrambled for the discarded Desert Eagle. Jumped on Banks's waist. One hand clutched his neck; the other brought the heavy pistol down on his head. Once, twice. Over and over, as hard as she could, numbers and time and death and life losing all meaning.

This man had put her son in danger. Had put her in danger. Had done something unspeakable, unthinkable to her son's father. And she'd be damned if she let anyone ever love her like that again.

'Fuck.' Tears filled her eyes until she couldn't see the dead man between her thighs. She fell off him, clutched a hand over her mouth, and swallowed down the screams and the vomit that were trying to force their way out.

But Adam was there. Hauling her up to her feet, enveloping her in his arms. He was cut up and bleeding, his red hands staining her ruined clothes. 'It's OK.' He kissed her hair. 'Oh God, Bee.' He wiped his damp cheek against hers and sniffled the manliest of sniffles. 'It's OK. I've got you. Shit, Bee. I've got you.'

Her knees buckled, but he held tight.

'Bee!' Malika pushed the corpse off her and Oliver, the boy still sleeping soundly on the carpet, Hogarth, uninjured, sitting by his feet. 'Holy guacamole, you killed the big bad!'

She laughed through her tears because there was nothing else she could do.

'At least Oliver's still asleep,' Malika said. 'I doubt he'll remember any of this.'

Adam helped Bee to the floor. 'I just gotta wrap one thing up, OK?' He kissed her brow and strode to the cockpit.

Adam cocked the Beretta and pressed the barrel against Mr White's temple. 'You gonna explain yourself?'

Mr White sniffed. 'It hurts, man. Just let me land this thing, or we all die.'

'Why did you do this?' Bee asked. 'Why did you betray us?'

'Adam and I have worked together for years. I know him, and I knew – I knew he wouldn't be able to double-cross you. I knew I'd get the short end of the stick. So yeah, I called an old friend from Alvarez's crew and had him pick up the kid from the church. They were never gonna hurt him, and I thought at least I'd get the finder's fee. But then you went and screwed that up too, so I talked to your boy Banks. We came to an agreement. And now I'm the one bleeding out, and you've got all the money and a sea of corpses, so just let me land this stupid plane and we can call it even and I can get to a freaking Mexican hospital.' White groaned. 'Man, maybe you should just kill me and get it over with.'

'Don't be so dramatic,' said Malika. 'Mexico has universal healthcare.'

Adam glanced at her, the gun still aimed to kill. 'What do you say, Bee?'

Her heart twisted. Was he really offering to kill his longtime partner for her? Why did that make her want to coo out loud? Wow was she gonna have to light a lot more candles at a lot more churches to atone for all this. 'We'll take his share, split it three ways. He can live if he lands us safely.'

Adam tucked the gun away. 'You heard the boss.'

Malika stood on shaking legs. 'You know,' she said, 'there are a lot of dead guys in this plane. Like, too many dead guys. What are we supposed to do with all these dead guys?'

Adam said, 'Let's worry about that when we've landed,' and sat next to Bee.

'Good.' Bee pulled Adam into an embrace and pressed her forehead to his. 'Thank you for being on my team.'

He kissed her, soft and open, and Bee forgot where they were until Mr White told them to buckle up for the landing.

THIRTY-SIX

Mr White landed the plane in a strip of barren land.

There *were* an awful lot of dead guys on the plane.

Bee guided a sleepy Oliver down the jet's steps and set him up underneath a nearby tree. Mr White hobbled off, and Bee – very generously if she did say so – let him go. She tied Hogarth's leash to a low-hanging branch by her son – eyes shut again – and joined the rest of the team. Adam pillaged the suits for weapons. Malika and Bee dumped every personal item they'd brought with them for their new lives out of their luggage – save for Malika's laptop, the gaming system Oliver had gotten from Cassie and his set of Percy Jackson books – and transferred Alvarez's cash from the boxes into the duffle bags.

Then they lit the whole thing on fire and stood by Oliver to watch it burn.

'Look at us!' Malika held Adam's hand and wrapped her arm around Bee's shoulders. 'Duffle bags of gangster cash at our feet. A private jet filled with anonymous corpses burning brightly before us.' She sighed. 'One big happy murder family.'

'Yeah, this is much bigger than I thought it would be,' Bee said. 'It's going to draw attention.'

'Yeah, we should definitely not be standing here,' Malika agreed. 'Come on – before we get caught. Again.'

'On your feet, Olly.' Adam dragged the boy into a standing position.

He yawned. 'All right, all right. I was just getting comfortable.'

They walked for a few minutes in silence, each person dragging a duffle bag filled with gangster cash behind them. Hogarth peed on an ant hill.

Oliver said, 'I had the weirdest dream that Uncle Banks was a vampire.'

They boarded the nearest bus in separate groups to avoid attracting attention: Malika and Oliver and Hogarth, with Adam and Bee following behind. But it was pointless. At that time of night, no one but the bus driver was in need of transit.

The bus stopped twice. At the third stop, the signs all written in Spanish, Adam rose to his feet and the others followed.

Bee shook the driver's hand and left $100 in his palm with a wink.

He nodded, grinning.

Everyone spoke the language of a bribe, no matter where they were born.

The fleabagiest of fleabag hotels had two connecting rooms available and a hostess who didn't care to ask questions. Of course, the rooms were on the second floor. And also of course, there was no elevator.

Malika carried a sleeping Oliver in her arms, groaning with every step. 'He needs to go on a diet,' she said. 'Or, I don't know, never get drugged again so he can walk up his own stairs. Listen, I got the news report on the bus. Charlie's in the hospital. Feds found him in the cemetery, shot in the back three times. He's critical but stable.'

Bee blinked rapidly, surprising herself. 'Oh,' she said. 'Oh. Good.' And surprising herself again, she meant it. 'If only he'd listened to me, Alvarez would've gone to jail thinking Charlie was dead.'

'You did what you could,' Malika said. 'And more than he deserved.' She opened her door with an actual metal key and said, 'I'm gonna put him down in my room.'

Bee froze. 'Are – are you sure?'

'Yeah.' She didn't smile, but she sure looked like she wanted to. 'Could use the company.' She laid him down on the bed furthest from the door.

Bee took his sneakers off and kissed his forehead. 'I love you, buddy.'

He said, 'Mmm puff mmm,' and yanked the covers over his head.

Hogarth tried to jump up on the bed with his boy but, after three failed attempts, sat on his butt and looked up at her, tongue lolling out and panting. She rolled her eyes and took pity on him, hoisting him up on to the mattress. 'You keep our boy warm, yeah?'

He spun around and plopped on Oliver's feet, hiding his face in his paw.

'Good night, Malika.'

Malika toed her shoe off and tossed it underhand at Bee's calf. 'Goodnight, boss.'

Bee unlocked the door to the adjoining room, unsurprised to find Adam had already opened the door on the other side. She closed it with a click and found herself very much alone with the man who'd saved her life.

She could still see the man who'd opened her kidnapper's car door buried underneath all his bumps and bruises. And if she looked real close, she could see the man who'd kissed her when they'd danced under the stars in Ibiza.

Bee moved with more confidence than she felt to the bathroom – fake it till you make it and all that – and ran the shower. Adam hovered outside the doorway, unsure, and she offered him a smile.

And then she took his jacket off.

Realization dawned over his face, along with something else, something that made her cheeks burn and her hands shake. She focused all her attention on unbuttoning each of his shirt buttons, careful not to rush.

She was going to enjoy this even if it killed her.

Adam didn't say anything. He stood still, watched her undress him and only made a noise of relief when he was under the warm water.

Bee bit her smiling lips and tried not to stare. She peeled her bloody shirt over her head and dropped her pants to the floor.

Adam pulled back the shower curtain and let her in.

The water was warm, and the shower was small. Bee closed her eyes and tipped her head back under the spray. Adam was in there with her. He was right there. Her elbow brushed against his chest when she fanned her hair under the water.

She heard a click and cracked an eye open.

He squeezed a dollop of hotel shampoo into the palm of his hand. It shook, ever so slightly, in his fingertips.

Bee dropped her arms, her shoulders relaxing underneath the shower head.

'Turn around.' His voice, low and quiet, trembled when he spoke. He cleared his throat. 'I'll, uh, I'll wash your hair. If you want.'

Poor thing was nervous. Well. She supposed she could go easy on him.

Bee turned. The water hit her chest, rolled down her stomach.

Adam worked the soap into a lather in his hands then massaged her scalp. Her eyes slid closed.

He worked her hair between his hands, worked his fingers through the knots.

Then dropped a kiss on her shoulder.

She sighed.

He rinsed her hair under the water, shampoo bubbles running down her back, pooling around her feet then swirling the drain. His fingers ghosted over her neck, glided over the small of her back. Adam wrapped his arms around her stomach and held her against his chest; kissed her other shoulder.

She grinned. 'It's your turn.' Bee plucked the hotel soap off the indent in the wall, left his embrace and faced him. With her teeth, she opened the wrapper. Adam watched her mouth. Bee tossed the trash on the floor and lathered the white bar in her hands.

Soapy hands caressed his pecs, and wow, were they ever so nice. She ran her hands down one arm, cleaned the blood off his hand and repeated the action with the other. The clear water turned to rust by the time it reached their feet.

'Turn,' Bee squeaked. She swallowed. 'Turn around.'

Now it was his turn to grin. Bee cleaned his back, careful of the dark, angry bruise on his ribcage.

'You want me to wash your hair?' She giggled. 'I'm not sure we have your brand.'

Adam spun round so fast she squealed. His hand on her cheek guided her back against the cold, yellowing tile. His lips found hers. Soft and careful, unimposing. Asking for permission.

Bee gave the permission with a groan that deepened the kiss, arms around his broad shoulders, holding him to her.

His palms slid down her back. With a gentleness that never ceased to surprise her, he grabbed her rear and lifted her to his hips.

'Adam! Your rib!'

'Yeah,' he ground out. 'Yeah, this was a bad idea.'

He flipped the water off and yanked back the shower curtain, the metal rings scratching over the rod. 'It's fine,' he panted. 'I'm fine. It's fine.'

Bee laughed.

He stumbled out of the bathroom and set her gently on the bed. She giggled. Adam crawled over her, forearms on either side of her head, chest to chest but keeping his weight off her.

She smiled so bright her eyes crinkled. His thumbs were on her cheeks, pushing her wet hair off her face. His breath fanned out across her nose, and honestly, it could be better, but she was so happy it didn't matter.

Nothing mattered except that this was real. He was real, and he was with her. Her son and Malika were safe in the next room.

She was safe in Adam's arms.

'You think Ibiza needs bookstores?' she asked.

Adam's face lit up with happiness. 'What's their view on extradition?'

She giggled again. 'I have no idea. We'll have to ask Malika.'

'You want me to go get her?' Adam sat high up on his elbows. 'You wanna call a meeting?'

'Shut up!' She grabbed his face with both hands and pulled him to her. Skin to skin, still wet from the shower, the motel's sheets beneath scratchy and uncomfortable, she'd never been happier.

His kiss this time was open and languid, luxurious. A kiss that could last as long as they wanted.

He pulled back to press his forehead to hers.

Bee blinked her eyes open. She loved the color of his eyes. Had she ever told him that? How lame would that be right now? Her hands had a mind of their own, roaming from the back of his head to his neck, along the ridges of his shoulder blades. In the dim lamplight, the scar under his collarbone looked like a shadow. She lifted her head to press a kiss to the wound that had saved her life.

Adam hissed in a breath.

She kissed along his collarbone, up the column of his neck. On his pulse point she sucked – then licked away the mark she left.

Bee lay flat against the bed and pressed one hand to his cheek; ran the pad of her index finger over his bottom lip. 'You never told me about this one.'

'Eh, this one?' He touched the half-moon scar in the center of his bottom lip with a knuckle. 'Yeah. Got into a fight with a guy wearing a ring.'

'Is that all? I was thinking there would be more to the story.'

'He was trying to make off with the Van Gogh self-portrait I'd recovered.'

Bee gasped.

'It's gone now, Bee. Long sold.'

'Hmm.' She traced the scar over and over again. 'To whom?'

His mouth moved under her fingers when he smiled. 'That's my girl.'

Then he kissed her, and all thoughts of what she would steal next were chased away.

THIRTY-SEVEN

The adjoining room door was flung open, and Oliver launched himself on to the foot of the bed that Bee and Adam had curled themselves up in.

'Good morning!' he shouted, bouncing up and down. 'Actually, it's the afternoon. I feel really well rested. Like, I slept super awesome good. How about you guys? Guys? Are you awake?' He jumped. 'Hello!'

Adam buried his face between her shoulder blades.

'Stop jumping,' she yawned. 'We're up, we're up.'

He jumped one more time and landed on his butt. 'That's fine. I'll play my game right here. Do you want to watch?' The device in his hands chirped merrily. 'I'm the best at this game.'

'Not really,' Adam said.

Oliver stuck his tongue out at him.

'Good. You're up.' Malika stood in the doorway with one hand holding on to the frame and the other dramatically pressed against her forehead. 'It's gonna take me a few days to make IDs good enough for us to dig our way out of the hole we currently find ourselves in. I'm probably gonna have to ask for favors. Talk to this guy I hate on the dark web. I hate him so much, guys. But.' She sighed. 'You gotta do whatcha gotta do.'

She slouched into the room and grabbed the motel's memo pad and pen. 'So. Who do you want to be?'